Embers of Desire

Kimberly Kogut

Embers of Desire
By Kimberly Kogut

Published by **Kogut Blackbloom Press**
Where forbidden love takes root.

ISBN: 979-8-218-76558-3 (paperback)

First edition: 2026
Printed in the United States of America

For the love that blooms in shadow,
sharp with thorns and heavy with consequence.
May you always choose it anyway.

1

Jubilee traced the delicate veins of a fern, her fingertips brushing the cool, damp earth. The ancient woods, her sanctuary, sang with the hum of life. Sunlight dappled through the emerald canopy, painting shifting patterns on her elegant, moss green gown, adorned with embroidered dewdrop flowers. Her long, brown hair, a waterfall of silken strands kissed by the sun, cascaded down her back. Her emerald eyes, usually sparkling with gentle curiosity, held a hint of unease today. A whisper of something foreign, something dark, had been carried on the wind, disturbing the harmonious rhythm of the forest.

A twig snapped. Jubilee froze, her hand instinctively going to the small, wove pouch at her waist. It wasn't the familiar rustle of a badger, nor the playful scamper of a squirrel. This was... heavier. Intentional. Her senses, honed by centuries of living in harmony with nature, screamed danger.

Then he emerged.

He moved with a predator's grace, silent as the shadows that clung to him. Tall, undeniably, with an athletic build that spoke of power held in check. His clothes, long and flowing, were a tapestry of silver and black, intricate patterns weaving a tale of mystery. But it was his hair that first truly captivated her - a cascade of molten silver, tumbling to his shoulders, so striking against the deep greens of her world. And his eyes. Violet. A shade she had never witnessed, deep and mesmerizing, yet holding an almost tangible aura of ancient pain. They were fixed on her, an intensity that made the air crackle with an unbidden tension.

Slash. The name rippled through her mind, not a thought, but a primal recognition. The shadow Fae. Ancient enemies, their presence in these sacred woods a violation. Yet, as their gazes locked, the animosity she *should* feel was eclipsed by a raw, undeniable current that arced between them, sparking like flint on steel.

"You are far from your shadowed lands," Jubilee's voice, usually as soft s a forest breeze, carried a surprising steel. She stood her ground, her chin tilted defiantly, through her heart hammered a frantic rhythm against her ribs.

A slow, dangerous smile curved his lips, a flash of white against his tanned skin. " And you, little sunbeam, are far from the safety of your gilded grove." His voice was a low growl, rough as gravel and smooth as silk, sending a shiver - not wholly of fear - down her spine. The "sunbeam" grated, yet a perverse part of her found the audacity intoxicating.

He took a step closer, then another, closing the distance between them with unnerving swiftness. Jubilee's hand tightened on her pouch, but she didn't retreat. This was her domain. She was rooted here, as deeply as the ancient oaks.

"What business do you have in the heart of the Emerald Woods, shadow walker?" Her emerald eyes, usually pools of gentle light, now glinted like a sharpened jade.

His violet gaze, burning with an almost feral intensity, swept over her, lingering on the curves of her body beneath the soft fabric of her dress. A spark ignited within her, a heat the spread through her veins despite herself. He didn't answer her question directly. Instead, he stopped mere feet from her, close enough for her to catch the subtle scent of ozone and something uniquely male that clung to him.

"Trouble brews," he murmured, his voice dropping to near whisper, yet it resonated deep within her, a strange, compelling vibration. "Boundaries blur. Alliances shift."

Jubilee's brow furrowed "Your people are the very embodiment of trouble here."

A short, humourless laugh escaped him. "And yours, sweet fae, live in a delusion of untouched purity." His eyes, however, help no malice, only that raw, searching intensity. "We seek answers. And I suspect… so do you."

A silent challenge hung in the air, a dare. His words, through veiled, hinted at something larger than their ancient quarrel. A shiver of unease traced its way up her spine. She had felt it too, that disquiet, that sense of an encroaching darkness. Could it be... shared?

He reached out a hand, slow and deliberate. Jubilee tensed, ready to strike, but she held her ground. His long, elegant fingers, adorned with a single, dark ring, stopped just inches from her face. She could feel the warmth radiating from his skin. The air around them thrummed, thick with unspoken urges.

"Your essence... it calls to me," he said, his voice a low thrum that reverberated in her very bones. His violet eyes, so close now, seemed to pull her into their depths, a vortex of hidden magic and untol stories. She found herself unable to look away. His gaze dropped to her lips, and a jolt, electric and insistent, shot through her. Her own breath hitched.

This was wrong. Their races were enemies. Their histories interwoven with conflict and blood. Yet, standing before him, feeling the simmering heat and undeniable pull, a forbidden curiosity blossomed within her. She wanted to know what secrets those violet eyes held, what mysteries lay beneath the facade of the dangerous shadow Fae.

He shifted, his body unnervingly close, and she could feel the subtle brush of his arm against hers. The contact was brief, yet it sent a searing heat through her, a rush of sensation that made her cheeks flush. An involuntary gasp escaped her lips.

"You tremble, little sunbeam," he observed, a hint of something dark and knowing in his tone. A smirk, slow and utterly captivating, playing on his lips. "Do I intimidate you so?"

Jubilee, recovering her composure, met his challenging gaze with a fire of her own. "I do not tremble before shadows, sir. I simply analyze them." It was a lie. She was trembling. Not from fear, but from the sheer, overwhelming proximity of him, the intoxicating scent of him, the burning intensity of his gaze.

He chuckled, a low, guttural sound that vibrated through her. "Analysis, is it? Perhaps then, you'd are to analyze me closer." His hand, which had been suspended in the air, slowly, delicately, reached out to a strand of her brown hair that escaped its braid. His fingers, surprisingly gentle, brushed against her cheek as he tucked the errant strand behind her ear.

The touch was feather light, yet it ignited wildfire within her. Her skin tingled where he touched, a searing warmth spreading through her veins. Her breath caught in her throat. His thumb, lingering for a fraction of a second, just grazed the delicate curve of her jawline. A shiver, deep and involuntary, coursed through her.

His eyes, still locked on hers, darkened, a flicker of something primal igniting within their violet depths.

The air thickened, charged with undeniable, potent energy. The forest, her calm sanctuary, seemed to hold its breath. This wasn't just attraction; it was an eddying current, pulling them inexorably closer. A dangerous, forbidden dance had just begun.

2

Jubilee reeled, the feather light touch of his thumb against her jaw sending a shockwave through her entire being. The air vibrated, thick with unspoken desire, and The ancient trees seemed to lean in, observing. Her carefully constructed composure shattered, revealing the raw exposed nerves beneath. This was not the measured analysis she'd proclaimed. This was something wild, elemental, and utterly terrifying in its intensity.

His thumb, still grazing her skin, slowly withdrew. The loss of contact, brief as it was, left a phantom ache, a yearning she instantly chastised herself for. His violet eyes, now pools of burning intensity, devoured her, seeing beyond the brave front, straight to the tumultuous churn within her. He knew. He saw the effect he had on her, a slow, triumphant awareness flickered in his gaze.

The silence stretched, taut as a bowstring, pregnant with unasked questions and forbidden urges. Every instinct Jubilee possessed screamed for her to flee, to break this dangerous trance. This was Slash, a shadow fae, her ancestral enemy. Yet, her feet felt rooted to the earth, trapped by his mesmerizing presence, by the intoxicating, dangerous promise in his eyes.

"You feel it, don't you little sunbeam?" His voice, a low rumble, seemed to vibrate directly in her chest. "This... connection. Stronger than any ancient feud."

The audacity of him! To name the unspeakable, to acknowledge the raw, undeniable pull that defied logic and centuries of conflict. A crimson flush spread across Jubilee's cheeks. She couldn't deny it, not to him, not to herself, not with her heart hammering a desperate rhythm against her ribs. But to acknowledge it would be to surrender a perilous current.

"I feel... an anomaly," she countered, her voice breathy, barely a whisper. " A disturbance in the natural order." It was a desperate attempt to regain control, to douse the flames licking at the edges of her self-command.

A wry smile touched his lips, a flash of white against his tanned skin that pulled at something deep inside her. "Anomaly, little sunbeam? Or destiny?" His gaze dropped, lingering on her lips once more, and a jolt, sharper than before, shot through her. He was so close. One step, one lean, and their mouths would meet. The though, unbidden and potent, was both terrifying and utterly compelling.

Her breath hitched. This was too much. The scent of ozone and male musk, the heat radiating from his body, the searing intensity of his violet eyes - it was an assault on her senses, threatening to unravel centuries of discipline. She had to break free. Now.

With a sudden, almost desperate surge of will, Jubilee tore her gaze from his. She couldn't look at him, not for another second. The fragile peace of her ancient woods was shattering, not by his shadow, but by the devastating light he ignited within her.

"Stay away from me," she whispered, her voice trembling, though she tried to infuse it with defiance. It sounded weak, ever to her own ears.

He chuckled, a sound that held no malice, only a deep, knowing amusement. "Do you honestly believe, sweet faeling, that you can command that?"

Jubilee didn't answer. She couldn't. The humiliation of her own body's betraying reaction, coupled with the sheer danger of his presence, spurred her into action. She turned, a whirlwind of moss green fabric, and fled.

She didn't look back. Her feet pounded across the mossy floor, dodging ancient roots, leaping over streams. The ancient woods, her sanctuary, now felt like a labyrinth, each familiar tree witness to her shameful retreat. The cool, damp air did little to quell the inferno raging beneath her skin. Every breath was a gasp, every heartbeat, a drumbeat resonating with his touch, his scent, his eyes.

She ran until her lungs burned, until the comforting green blur of her forest swallowed her whole, until the sounds of his presence faded into the harmonious hum of nature. She ran until she was sure he couldn't follow, until the memory of his raw, captivating intensity was merely a haunting echo.

But even then, deep within the heart of her sacred woods, Jubilee couldn’t escape the truth. The forbidden dance had indeed begun, and she, the stoic forest guardian, was irrevocably caught in its dangerous rhythm. And the most terrifying thought of all? A part of her, a newly awakened rebellious part, ardently wanted to dance again.

3

Jubilee collapsed onto a bed of soft, springy moss, her chest heaving. The glade was her private solace, a hidden haven nestled deeper within the woods, where ancient, gnarled oaks formed a natural cathedral, their leaves filtering the sunlight into dappled patterns on the forest floor. Here, the air was always cooler, the silence profound, broken only by the gentle murmur of a nearby hidden spring. She buried her face in her hands, trying to scrub away the lingering sensation of his touch, the phantom scent of ozone and shadowed earth that still clung to her.

Her mind was a tempest. "Anomaly," she'd called him. It was a pathetic lie, a transparent shield against the devastating truth. He was no anomaly. He was a force of nature, a rouge wave threatening to capsize her meticulously ordered existence. And the worse part? A part of her thrilled at the thought of being utterly, gloriously undone. She hated him for making her feel this, for cracking open a part of her she hadn't known existed. She hated herself for wanting it.

A twig snapped.

Jubilee's head shot up, her emerald eyes wide, instantly alert. It couldn't be. She was too deep. This glade was known only to her, its entrance obscured by ancient magic only she could perceive. It was her sanctuary, utterly inviolable.

But there he stood, framed by the emerald light of the glade's entrance, as if he simply stepped out of the air itself. Slash. His silver hair was slightly mussed, his black leather tunic clinging to his broad shoulders, highlighting the lean power of his frame. His violet eyes, darker now than before, were fixed on her, a predatory gleam within their depths. He wasn't even breathing heavily, as if the grueling journey through the enchanted woods had been no more than a leisurely stroll.

A cold dread trickled down Jubilee's spine, eclipsing the lingering heat of their previous encounter. He hadn't just followed her. He had found her. He had penetrated her illusion.

"How... how did you find me?" she managed, her voice a reedy whisper, raw from her desperate flight.

A slow, utterly infuriating smile spread across his lips, revealing a flash of white even teeth. "You radiate, little sunbeam. A beacon in the gloom. And your scent... it drew me like a moth to a flame." His gaze dropped, lingering on her still flushed cheeks, then to her pounding chest, visible beneath the lace of her gown. "Besides, did you truly believe a few trees could hide you from me?"

He began to walk slowly towards her, each deliberate step radiating a quiet power. Jubilee scrambled backward on her hands and knees, until her back was pressed against the rough bark of the ancient oak. Her breath hitched. She was trapped.

"I told you to stay away," she whispered, trying to imbue her voice with some authority, some of her usual composure. It was a futile effort. She felt like a cornered animal.

Slash knelt before her, his large hand brushing aside a strand of moss on the ground, his movements graceful, fluid. The scent of him, that intoxicating mix of ozone and shadow, filled her lungs, cutting through the clean forest air. He was so close she could feel the subtle heat radiating from his body.

His violet eyes locked with hers, intense and unblinking. "And I told you, sweet fae, that you cannot command me." he paused, his gaze softening almost imperceptibly, a hint of something deeper, more complex, surfacing in their depths. "You ran." it wasn't a question, but an observation laced with knowing amusement.

"I needed... to think."

He chuckled, a low, rich sound that vibrated through the earth beneath her. "Did you, now? Or did you just need to try and outrun what you feel?" His hand reached out, not to touch her but to gently pluck a single green leaf that had fallen onto her hair. His fingers were long, dark, so close to her temple. "This connection, Jubilee," he murmured, his voice dropping to a seductive whisper that curled around her like tendrils of smoke, "it's stronger than your fear. Stronger than your ancient prejudice. And it's just begun."

4

The words hung in the air, a potent spell weaving itself around them. Jubilee's breath hitched, trapped in her lungs. His proximity was a suffocating cloak, his pronouncement a chilling prophecy. Stronger than her fear? Stronger than her prejudice? The audacity! The terrible, undeniable truth of it. She wanted to argue, to deny, to lash out at the arrogant male who dared to strip bare her every protective facade. But the words were stuck, choked by the rising tide of sensation.

His fingers, still poised agonizingly close to her temple, seemed to hum with an unseen energy. She could feel the ghost of his touch, the warmth radiating from his skin. Her gaze was locked with his violet depths, drowning in them. There was no escape. Not from him. Not from herself.

Just as the exquisite tension became unbearable, a sharp, piercing whistle rent the tranquil air of the glade. It was a familiar sound, one that sent a jolt of ice through her veins, a stark contrast to burning heat Slash had ignited.

Both Slash and Jubilee froze, their heads snapping towards the source. From the dense foliage at the glade's eastern edge, a small, lithe figure emerged, clad in moss green tunic and trousers, a quiver of arrows slung across his back, and a finely crafted longbow held loosely one hand. His golden hair, braided with forest blooms, caught the dappled sunlight, and his bright, inquisitive blue eyes scanned the glade.

Eldrin.

Jubilee's stomach plummeted. Of all the fae, why him? Eldrin was her closest friend, her confidante, and fiercely protective. He was also a staunch traditionalist, harboring a deep, ingrained distrust of anything outside the forest's ancient ways, especially shadow fae.

Eldrin's eyes, initially alight with the joy of finding her, widened fractionally as they landed on Slash. The casual stance of his immediately stiffened, and his hand instinctively tightened around the grip. A low growl rumbled in his chest, guttural and unexpected, like a territorial beast.

"Jubilee? What... what is THIS?" Eldrin's voice was laced with disbelief, then outright hostility. He didn't wait for an answer, his gaze fixed on Slash, who had slowly risen to his full height, his powerful frame now radiating a silent, dangerous warning.

Slash's seductive intensity had vanished, replaced by an impassive, almost bored expression. Yet, the coiled tension in his muscles, the subtle shift in the angle of his shoulders, spoke volumes. He was a predator, poised.

"Eldrin, wait!" Jubilee scrambled to her feet, desperate to de-escalate the situation. "It's not what it looks like." A pathetic lie, even to her own ears. It looked exactly like one of the ancient forest fae and a shadow fae locked in a dangerously intimate encounter.

Eldrin ignored her, his eyes narrowed to slits. "You reek of the gloom. A shadow spawn in our sacred glade. How did you breach the wards?" His query was aimed at Slash, but his anger was a palpable force, directed at them both.

Slash merely tilted his head, a faint, mocking smile playing on his lips. "Wards? My dear fae, your wards are like spun sugar to me."

"Silence, creature!" Eldrin snarled, pulling an arrow from his quiver with practiced ease, knocking it to his bowstring in one fluid motion. The sharp click echoed ominously. The point, tipped with ancient, potent magic, gleamed menacingly. "Leave this place or face the consequences."

Jubilee felt a cold dread settle in her heart. Eldrin, for all his gentle nature, was lethal when provoked, especially when he perceived a threat to their lands, or to her. And Slash... Slash had a way of provoking everyone.

Slash's violet eyes flickered to her, a brief, unreadable gleam within them. Then, he turned his full attention back to Eldrin, his smirk widening. "A small, angry bee, is that what you are, little fae? All sting and no substance?" His voice was calm, dripping with condescension.

Eldrin's face contorted with fury. "You dare insult me? You dare threaten our sovereign land?!" With a guttural yell, he drew the bowstring taut, aiming directly at Slash's heart. "This is your last warning. Depart, now!"

The glade, moments ago alive with forbidden desire, was now crackling with imminent violence. Jubilee's heart hammered against her ribs, torn between the two, males, the two worlds colliding in a devastating, inevitable conflict.

5

The ancient magic hummed on the arrow's tip, a chilling promise of oblivion. Eldrin's arm quivering with righteous fury, released the string. The twang reverberated through the glade, a sharp, deadly punctuation mark to the simmering tension. Time seemed to warp, stretching the moment into an eternity. Jubilee watched, her breath catching in her throat, the world narrowing to the silver gleam of the arrow and the impassive, almost bored expression on Slash's face.

He didn't flinch. He didn't visibly react. Not a muscle twitched. Then, with a speed that defied the laws of physics, a blur of shadow detached from his form, intercepting the projectile with a barely audible *whump*. The arrow, still carrying the vast momentum of Eldrin's rage and enchanted power, disintegrated into a shower of shimmering dust, absorbed entirely by the strange, inky mist. The shadow reabsorbed itself into Slash, leaving him utterly untouched, unbroken.

Eldrin gasped, his jaw dropping in disbelief. His powerful, magically imbued arrows had never failed to strike their mark, never been rendered so utterly useless. The air vibrated with the aftermath, an eerie silence descending upon the glade, broken only by the rapid thumping of Jubilee's heart.

Slash merely tilted his head, the mocking smile returning to his lips, more pronounced now, almost triumphant. "Is that all your little stinger has, little bee? A puff of smoke?" His voice, though still calm, was laced with an undeniable undercurrent of dangerous power. The glade itself seemed to shiver, responding to the raw, untamed energy emanating from him.

Eldrin, momentarily stunned, quickly recovered, his face contorting with a renewed, almost desperate anger. His hands moved, drawing another arrow, then another, nocking them with furious speed. "You...you demon! What sorcery is this?"

"Sorcery? Perhaps," Slash murmured, his violet eyes gleaming, fixed on Eldrin. "Or perhaps, merely understanding what truly matters." He took a slow, deliberate step forward, the earth beneath his boots seeming to darken, the vibrant green of the glade momentarily dimming around him.

Jubilee, caught between them, felt a sudden, primal dread. This was no longer just a standoff. This was something far more ancient, far more terrifying. She knew the legends of the shadow fae, of their uncanny ability to manipulate the very essence of darkness, to absorb and nullify light and energy. Eldrin's pure, forest magic, while potent, was no match for this.

"Eldrin, stop!" she cried again, her voice cracking with desperation. "You can't fight him! You don't understand!"

Her plea seemed to pierce the veil of Eldrin's fury for just a split second. His blue eyes flickered to her, concern warring with his ingrained prejudice. "Jubilee, stand back! This creature is a blight, a corruption! He must be driven from our lands!"

"And what if i don't wish to be driven?" Slash's voice was a low purr, a dangerous challenge. He too another step, his shadow lengthening, reaching for Eldrin like a predatory tendril. "What if I find this glade... rather appealing?" His gaze flickered to Jubilee, a brief, possessive glint in his violet depths that sent a shiver down her spine.

"You will not defile this place!" Eldrin roared, releasing both arrows in quick succession. They flew true, imbued with the full force of his desperate, righteous magic.

Again, the shadow detached from Slash, a rippling, inky shield. The arrows hit, not with the sound of impact, but with a silent, consuming emptiness. They simply ceased to exist, swallowed whole, leaving not even a wisp of dust.

Eldrin staggered back, his bow arm dropping, not in surrender, but in utter, horrified impotence. The formidable protector of the forest, the skilled hunter, was utterly outmatched. His face was pale, his eyes wide with a dawning fear he had never known before.

Slash merely chuckled, a low, chilling pronouncement of dominance. Eldrin, though visibly shaken, was not yet broken. A flicker of something primal, not courage, but sheer, unadulterated desperation - ignited his eyes. He advanced, slowly, inexorably, towards the stunned fae. "Now, little bee," he purred his voice dropping to a silken whisper that seemed to caress the vibrating leaves, "perhaps it is time for you to understand your place."

6

Slash's words hung in the air, a chilling pronouncement of dominance. Eldrin, though visibly shaken, was not yet broken. A flicker of something primal - not courage, but sheer, unadulterated desperation - ignited in his eyes. He glanced wildly around the glade, his gaze sweeping over the ancient trees, the sun-dappled moss, the very earth that had been his sanctuary, his home. This place was sacred, and this... this creature, this*darkness*, tainted it just by breathing

His hand, trembling slightly, reached for the small pouch at his belt. It was a last resort, a desperate gamble. Inside lay a tiny, intricately carved acorn, imbued with generations of forest fae protective magic, meant to ward off the most potent of curses, the deepest of shadows. It wasn't a weapon in the traditional sense, but a tether to the very lifeblood of the forest itself.

"You will not desecrate this glade!" Eldrin's voice, though hoarse, was laced with unwavering conviction that defied his trembling form. With a grunt, he pulled out the acorn, clutching it tightly, his knuckles white.

Slash paused, his advance faltering for the barest fraction of a second. His violet eyes, sharp and intelligent, narrowed on the small, unassuming object. An almost imperceptible shift rippled through the air around him, a momentary disturbance in the predatory calm he exuded.

"Oh?" Slash's voice was softer, laced with an almost mocking curiosity. "And what pathetic little trinket do you intend to brandish now, forest fairy? A child's toy?"

Jubilee, still caught in the agonizing middle, watched Eldrin with a fresh wave of dread. She knew the acorn; it was a potent symbol of their deepest, oldest magic. But it was defensive, meant to create barriers, not attack. Against Slash, it would be a desperate, futile gesture, an invitation for further humiliation.

"Eldrin, no!" she pleaded again, a tear tracing a path down her cheek. "It's useless!"

But Eldrin was beyond reason. His fear had transmuted into a desperate, almost suicidal defiance. He closed his eyes, focusing all his remaining will, all his love for this glade, this forest, into the small acorn. A faint, emerald green light began to pulse from the carving, growing steadily brighter, radiating warmth and the scent of damp earth and growing things. The very plants around them seemed to respond, leaves unfurling, tiny blossoms stretching towards the glow.

Slash watched, a flicker of something unreadable in his gaze. Not fear, not precisely, but a recognition of a force he had not anticipated. The air around him, previously heavy and still, began to stir, a faint, almost imperceptible counter current of chilly darkness pushing back against the encroaching light.

With a guttural cry, Eldrin hurled the acorn. It spun through the air, leaving a shimmering trail of green light, arcing directly towards Slash. It wasn't thrown with force, but with intent – an elemental challenge, spirit against shadow.

The acorn struck Slash's chest squarely, not with a thud, but with a sudden, silent *implosion* of light. For a slpit second, the glade was bathed in a blinding emerald flash that seemed to consume all other color, all shadow. A wave of raw, vibrational energy slammed into Jubilee, knocking the breath from her lungs.

When the light faded, a collective gasp escaped the trees themselves. Slash was still standing. But he was different. The brilliant green light pulsed weakly around him, like an ensnaring web.
His perfect, unblemished skin was now covered in faint, intricate patterns of emerald light, as if veins of glowing moss had rooted beneath his flesh. It wasn't a wound, but an inscription, a brand. And for the first time, an expression of something other than amusement or casual power crossed his features. It

was a grimace, tight with something akin to discomfort, even irritation.

He raised a hand, touching the glowing patterns on his chest. The lines of light pulsed angrily under his touch, refusing to dissipate entirely. The energy was contained, absorbed, but not extinguished. Eldrin's desperate gamble had changed nothing, yet changed everything.

A lot growl rumbled in Slash's chest, a sound deeper and more primal than any Jubilee had heard from him. His violet eyes, usually so calm and calculating, not burned with a cold, almost infernal fire. The air around him didn't just darken; it seemed to *thicken* with a palpable malevolence.

"Foolish little bug," he hissed, his voice no longer a purr, but a venomous rasp. The vibrant green of the glade began to wilt at the edges of his expanding shadow, a slow, horrifying blight spreading across the moss. "You have made a grave error."

7

The glade, once vibrant and alive, pulsed with an encroaching, unnatural darkness. The air grew heavy, damp and cold, as if the very life force was being siphoned away. Jubilee watched in horror as the verdant moss beneath Slash's bare feet began to turn sickly brown, the delicate ferns curling and crispening as if touched by frost. Eldrin, though still transfixed by the sight of his magic clinging to Slash, unknowingly stumbled back a step, driven by an instinctual repulsion.

Slash's eyes, burning with that cold, infernal fire, locked on to Eldrin. The emerald patterns on his skin pulsed erratically, a testament to the uninvited life growing beneath his shadow. His lips, usually curved in a languid smirk, were pulled back in a snarl, revealing teeth that seemed sharper, whiter in the deepening gloom.

"You have *marked* me, little fae," Slash's voice tore through the air, no longer a rasp but a guttural growl that vibrated through Jubilee's bones. "You have dared to defile my purity with your pathetic, clinging light."

A thick, oily black tendril, like a prehensile shadow, erupted from Slash's outstretched hand. It moved with terrifying speed, a silent, viscous whip that struck Eldrin before he could even register the threat. It coiled around his arm, impossibly tight, instantly drawing a grasp of pain from him. The tendril wasn't merely gripping; it felt as though it was *draining* him, a cold, hungry drain that pulled at his very essence.

Eldrin cried out, his face contorting in agony as he struggled against the unseen force. The vibrant green glow that had pulsed from him moments before, a reflection of his connection to the forest, began to flicker and dim. His usually nimble fingers, still clutching his now useless bow, went slack.

"Slash, no!" Jubilee screamed, her voice as raw, desperate plea. She launched herself forward, propelled by a sudden, fierce protectiveness for her friend. But she was too slow.

Another tendril, even thicker than the first, erupted from Slash, wrapping around Eldrin's other arm. Eldrin gasped, his eyes wide with terror as the shadow constricted, crushing his bones, threatening to tear his limbs from their sockets. He thrashed, a terrified animal caught in a snare, but the shadowy bonds were unyielding. His cries grew weaker, his body convulsing as the oppressive gloom emanating from him.

Slash took a slow deliberate step towards Eldrin, pulling him closer to his dark form. The emerald patters on Slash's skin seemed to glow brighter, almost mockingly, a stark contrast to the oppressive gloom emanating from him.

"You wished to tether me to your pathetic world?" Slash hissed, his face inches from Eldrin's contorted features. His voice was a cruel whisper of victory. "Know that your world, your precious glade, will now pay the price for your folly."

As he spoke, the very air Eldrin seemed to congeal, solidifying into a suffocating, inky blackness. Eldrin's cries became choked gasps, and then nothing at all he snagged, lifeless, withing the shadow's grasp. The vibrant green light that had been his life force was entirely winked out completely, leaving him utterly devoid of color, of warmth. He was a husk, a statue carved from despair.

Jubilee, her heart seizing in her chest, watched in utter horror as Eldrin's skin, once fair and healthy, began to turn sickly gery. The faint glow of his life force was entirely extinguished, replaced by a chillin pallor. He wasn't dead, not quite, but he was suspended in a state far worse, a living emptiness. Just as swiftly as they appeared, the tendrils retracted, drawing the oppressive darkness back into Slash. Eldrin collapsed to the ground, a crumpled, lifeless shadow of his former self.

Slash stood over Eldrin's prone form, his chest heaving with a dark satisfaction. The cold glow of the emerald patterns on his skin seemed to intensify, pulsing with a victorious, violent energy. He looked at Jubilee, his violet eyes still burning with that chilling infernal fire, and a slow, dark smile stretched his lips. It was a smile of pure, unadulterated power, a declaration of intent that left no room for doubt.

"Now, little princess," he purred, his voice regaining its dangerous, silky quality, "shall we begin again?"

8

The glade reeked of death. The air, heavy with the stench of decaying life and raw power, press down on Jubilee, crushing the last vestiges of hope. Eldrin, Her vibrant, spirited friend, lay a great, lifeless husk, a grotesque monument to Slash's terrifying capabilities. His words, "shall we begin again?", hung in the poisoned air, a cruel invitation to a dance she never wished to join.

A cold, Primal Scream tore through jubilee's throat, though no sound escaped her lips. It was a scream of pure, unadulterated agony, a soundless rupture deep within her soul. The loss of Eldrin, the brutal, casual cruelty of slash, ignited a fury she didn't know she possessed. It was a fire that burned away fear, burned away hesitation, leaving only a white hot resolve. She would not let this stand. She would not let him get away with this.

Her hands instinctively clenched into fists, the smooth, ancient work of the glade's protective trees vibrating faintly beneath her fingertips. A shimmering, emerald green light, faint at first, began to pulse from her palms. It was not gentle, nurturing light of healing, but a fierce, crackling energy, untamed and deadly. The air around her shimmered, warping the glazed distorted gloom into shimmering waves of green and black.

Slash, his dark smile still etched on his face, watched her, his violent eyes narrowing slightly in surprise. The emerald patterns on his skin, a remnant of Eldrin's defiant magic, pulsed erratically, mirroring the nascent power now surging through Jubilee.

"Oh?" He purred, his voice losing some of its silky edge, a hint of genuine interest replacing his smug satisfaction. "And what is this, little fae? A final, desperate spark of defiance?"

Jubilee didn't answer. Her eyes, usually the soft warm green uh ancient Moss, now blazed with a fierce, emerald fire. Every atom of her being hummed with an unleashed current, a raw conduit of the forests ancient, protective magic. She had always been a keeper, a steward, never a weapon. But now, faced with such a monstrous darkness, her very essence rebelled.

The ground beneath her feet began to grow restless. Roots, sickest Python coils, erupted from the earth, tearing through the suffocating gloom with surprising speed. They snaked toward slash, not with the gentle embrace of growing life, but with the ruthless intent of a coiled Viper. Sharp thorns, hardened by centuries of slimmer, bristled from their segmented forms.

Slash's dark amusement vanished. He sidestepped the first route, then the second, his movements fluid and unnervingly graceful. But more came, a relentless tide of living wood, rising from the scarred earth. The glade, which had been dying under his shadow, now convulsed with vengeful life, responding to Jubilee's desperate call.

"Impressive," Slash conceited, his voice deepening, a hint of danger now mingling with his earlier arrogance. He extended a hand, and a curtain of inky blackness erupted from his palm, attempting to smother the encroaching tendrils. But this was not Eldrin's magic he faced. This was Jubilee's

The tendrils of ancient roots pulsed with a vibrant green light as they met slashes encroaching darkness. Sparks flew, not of fire, but of opposing magic, a silent scream of elemental conflicts. The air crackled, charged with the kinetic energy, making the hairs on jubilees arms stand on end. The glade itself groaned, caught between the destructive embrace of shadow and the vengeful surge of life.

Jubilee pushed harder, her entire body trembling with the effort her focus narrowed, all her pain, all her fury, channeled into the single, desperate act. She saw slashes calm facade begin to crack, a flicker of genuine irritation crossing his features as the relentless assault of living would refuse to yield.

One root, thicker and faster than the others, broke through slashes shadow barrier. It whipped toward him, tipped with thorns, aiming directly for his exposed chest. His eyes widened, a rare flash of alarm in their purple deaths. He twisted, dodging just in time, but the root grazed his arm, leaving his shallow, bleeding gouge.

A dark curse slipped from his lips, low and guttural. The emerald patterns on his skin flared, almost glowing with an unholy light, as if angered as a wound. He looked at the thin line of blood on his arm, then at jubilee, his face a mask of pure, unadulterated fury.

"You dare?" He hissed, his voice now a dangerous snarl, utterly devoid of his previous charm and mockery. "You actually dare to wound me, little fae?"

The ground swelled, in a massive, gnarled root, like an ancient fist, burst from the earth directly beneath slash, aiming to propel him upwards. He reacted instantly, a blur of shadow, leaping backwards just as the root erupted, leaving a gaping maw in the earth. But the continuous, unrelenting assault was beginning to chip away at his composure, his effortless dominance.

Jubilee felt a surge of grim satisfaction. She was reaching into the deepest reservoirs of her power, drawing on the very heart of the glade. Her body screamed in protest, but she ignored it, fueled by the image of Eldrin's lifeless face. She would make him pay period she would make him feel the wrath of the forest. The dance had begun again, as he had so eagerly predicted, but this time, it was to her tune.

9

"You dare?" Slashes snarl rips through the glade, slicing through the emerald light as effectively as a physical blow. The air, already thick with opposing magics, suddenly went cold, the suffocating chill seeping into Jubilee's bones, momentarily eclipsing the burning pain in her overtaxed muscles. His violet eyes, moments before widened and surprise, now blaze it with a fury that made the glade's gloom seem inviting. The emerald patterns on his skin pulsed like angry wounds, a sickening inverse of the vibrant life source surging from Jubilee.

The wounded arm, still seeping a thin dark line of Archer, was held up, silent, damning accusation slash didn't bother to press the hand to it, was the pain was beneath him, merely an inconvenience. His gaze, fixed on jubilee, was a physical weight, pressing her down, threatening to crack the fragile shield of her defiance.

"Foolish creature," he hissed, his voice dropping to a low, melodic rumble that was more menacing than any shout. "You presume to understand power? You presume to command the very air I breathe?"

As he spoke, the tendrils of shadow erupting from him became thicker, more vicious, no longer merely countering the roots but actively consuming them. The ancient wood, pulsing with jubilees borrowed life, shrieked a silent death as slashes darkness devoured its essence. The shimmering emerald light that had enveloped jubilee began to flicker, dimming under the onslaught of unfathomable gloom.

His hands, still extended, began to draw inward, as if pulling the very light from the glade. The air grew heavy, impossible to breathe, filled with the dust of annihilated magic. Jubilee gasped, desperate, horse sound, as the vibrant green around her was choked, swallowed by an encroaching knight. The ground beneath her, movements before alive and churning, went still, rigid, as if frozen in a sudden, unnatural winter.

Slash took a slow, deliberate step forward, then another, his movements and predatory glide. His dark robes seemed to drink in the remaining light, making him appear even larger, more monolithic, than before. The subtle nuances of his captivating face were erased by the versioning shadow, leaving only the burning intensity of his gaze, twin amethyst stars in the gathering abyss.

"You believe you are special, little fae?" He purred, his voice laced with venomous amusement. "That a few paltry vines can wound me? That burst from borrowed forest magic can truly challenge what I am?"

He raised the hand, not toward her, but towards the sky. The glade groaned in protest, a deeper, mournful sound than before. The few remaining rays of moonlight struggled to pierce the oppressive canopy, where instantly left out, snuffed out, as if a giant unseen hand had pinched them away. The world plunged into absolute darkness, broken only by the searing Violet and slashes eyes and the faint, struggling emerald glow that still clung to Jubilee's heart.

The emerald patterns on his skin, a defiant mark of Eldrin's magic
Then, from the depths of that unfathomable dark, shadows began to collapse, tangibly forming around slash. They weren't merely reflections of his power; there were extensions of his being, living, hungry things. They writhed and stretched, taking on grotesque formless shapes like a nightmare made manifest. What they swirled around him, a storm of pure, concentrated nullity, radiating a cold that went beyond physical temperature, a sole deep chill that threatened to stop Jubilee's heart.

The emerald patterns on his skin, a defiant mark of Eldrin's magic, shimmered violently, as if struggling against their host, but they were overwhelmed, drowned by the sheer magnitude of the darkness Slash was now unleashing. He was abandoning all pretense, all restraint. This was not a warning; this was an annihilation.

"Let me show you, "he whispered, his voice resonating from every point in the glade, from the churning shadows, from the very air that choked her. "Let me show you what true power feels like, little fae. Let me remind you of your place."

A tendril of shadow, thicker and faster than anything Jubilee had conjured, lashed out from the swirling mass around Slash. It wasn't aimed to wound, but to bind. It wrapped around her extended arm, the connection instantaneous, chilling and utterly debilitating. The emerald light that burned so fiercely within her flickered, the died, extinguished by the predatory grasp of his magic.

Jubilee cried out, a sound that was immediately swallowed by the encroaching shadows. The remaining roots, her last desperate defense, withered and crumbled into dust. Her legs buckled as the tendril tightened, like a viper coiling around its prey. Another tendril lashed out, then another, binding her to the spot, trapping her within the unholy darkness, powerless against the overwhelming tide.

She struggled, a primal instinct against the encroaching oblivion, but it was futile. Slash's power was absolute, a suffocating, inescapable presence. He hadn't just countered her; he had consumed her, reduced her defiance to nothing. The glade, which had briefly swelled with vengeful life, now lay utterly subjugated, its spirit broken.

Slash maintained his stance, not moving, merely letting his dark essence flow, seep, and conquer. He allowed the power to wash over her, to drown her, to impress upon her the futility of her fight. The air around her vibrated with raw, untamed power, a dark symphony of dominance.

He took another step, then another, until he was directly before her, his breath, cold as grave dust, ghosting across her face. The tendrils held her immobile, her body screaming under the strain. Her eyes, wide with terror and something akin to awe, met his. The furious violet had softened, replaced by a deep unsettling satisfaction.

"There," he murmured, his voice a silken caress, yet laced with the unyielding iron of his triumph. "Now you understand. Now we can truly begin."

10

The inky blackness that enveloped them seemed to press in on Jubilee, a suffocating blanket woven from Slash's terrifying power. Her body, still bound tightly by the shadowy tendrils, screamed in silent agony, but a strange calm settled over her. The raw terror that had coursed through her moments before now mingled with a desperate, burgeoning curiosity. Humanity, she thought, and then realized the irony. Could an ethereal fae truly appeal to the humanity of a shadow fae, a being whose very essence seemed antithetical to light and warmth? Yet, something in his eyes, even in their terrifying violet depths, hinted at a complexity that transcended mere villainy.

"Begin what, Slash?" her voice was a ragged whisper, a threadbare sound against the oppressive silence. The struggle was over, at least for now. Her rebellion had been crushed, her power extinguished. All that remained was surrender, or perhaps, a different kind of fight – one fought with words, with understanding.

His satisfaction, so palpable a moment ago, seemed to waver, replaced by a subtle shift she couldn't quite decipher. His gaze, fixed on hers, was unblinking, unreadable. "A new age, little fae," he purred, the silken quality of his voice returning, through now laced with an undeniable undercurrent of something she recognized as... loneliness? No, that couldn't be right. An entity of such power, such dominance, could not be lonely. Could it?

"An age built on... subjugation?" she countered, a spark of her defiance rekindling despite her bonds. "On destruction? What purpose does this serve? What do you gain by this, by...by ending him?" Her gaze flickered to Eldrin's still form, a pang of fresh grief piercing her.

A ripple, almost imperceptible, went through his shadow-laden form. The violet in his eyes flickered, as if momentary hesitation had seized him. "Purpose?" he scoffed, though the sound lacked its earlier venom. "Survival, perhaps. A return to balance. Your kind... your people, have grown complacent. Entrenched. You cling to ideals of purity and tradition while the very land starves for different currents."

He leaned closer, his dark hair brushing her sweat-dampened cheek, the chill emanating from him like a physical entity. "You saw what happened, little fae. He attacked. He sought to destroy. I merely... reacted. Like any being, I defend what is mine." His voice dropped to a near-whisper, a seductive rasp that sent shivers down her spine, unrelated to the cold. "And I defend what I claim."

Jubilee swallowed, the dryness in her throat making speech difficult. "But...why me? Why the glade? What do you want with us? With this... this place?"

His gaze intensified, piercing, as if he sought to peer into her very soul. "This glade... is a nexus. A confluence of power. And you, Jubilee of the Eternal Forest, are intrinsically linked to it. You are the eye of the storm, the keeper of secrets this glade has harbored for centuries. Your magic... when unleashed, it resonates with an ancient song I thought was lost."

A tendril of shadow, surprisingly gentle, brushed her bound arm, tracing the line of her skin. It wasn't the searing cold of earlier, but a curious, almost exploratory touch. "And your fear, little fae, is as intoxicating as your defiance. It holds a vibrancy, a vitality that I have not encountered in... a very long time."

Her mind reeled. He wasn't just a force of destruction; he was an entity seeking something, drawn by something. Something within her, within the glade. She pushed past the terror, searching for an understanding that might offer a path, any path, forward. "You speak of balance... but this is annihilation. You extinguished life, Slash. You drained it."

"Extinguished one life," he corrected, his voice flat, devoid of emotion now. "To show another the true cost of ignorance. Eldrin was a zealot, blind to anything beyond his narrow beliefs. He would have dragged you down with him, little light. He already was."

His thumb, surprisingly warm despite the cold of his touch, traced the curve of her jawline. "I saw what happened. Your heart... it yearned for something more. Something beyond the boundaries of your forest. Something dangerous. And I...I answered that call, didn't I, Jubilee?"

11

Jubilee's breath hitched at his touch, the sudden warmth spreading and warring with the lingering chill he exuded. Was it true? Had her subconscious, in its rawest, most unguarded state, truly called out for something this dark, this forbidden? The idea was both terrifying and perversely thrilling. Her gaze locked with his, searching for the answers he seemed to hold, the unread chapters of a destiny she never knew was being written.

He leaned in closer, his voice a low, rough murmur that vibrated through her very bones. "this glade Jubilee, has been a prison. A beautiful gilded cage, yes, but a cage nonetheless. It protects, but it also starves. It holds ancient magic, potent and pure, but it restricts its flow, limiting its true potential. your people, in their earnest desire to preserve, have unwittingly stymied its growth, its evolution." He swept a hand through the air, and for a fleeting moment, the oppressive darkness seemed to pulse, to breath with an ancient rhythm.

"Evolution?" she whispered, the tremor in her voice betraying her shock. "What are you talking about?"

"The balance, little fae. It's not static. It shifts; it breathes. It requires death for life, shadow for light, decay for renewal. Your ancestors, in their wisdom, knew this. They embraced it. But over time, fear crept in and with fear, rigidity. They walled off sections of their magic, fearing its wildness, its untamed power. And this glade, this nexus, became the heart of that suppression." His violet eyes, so often cold and penetrating, now held a strange, almost manic gleam. "I am merely... releasing it."

A tendril of shadow, thicker this time, slowly uncoiled from her bonds, and snaked around her wrist, caressing the delicate skin. It felt less like a restraint and more like an intimate tether. "and that you, Jubilee are the key. Your unique affinity for this ancient magic, your raw, untamed power that you barely understand,,, it's what draws me. It's what draws me. It's what this glade needs. You felt it, didn't you? That pull? That hunger for something more than what your traditions offered?"

It was true. A nascent hunger had always hummed beneath her skin, a craving for knowledge and power beyond the familiar rhythms of her people. She had dismissed it as curiosity, as a youthful wanderlust, but now under his unnerving gaze, she wondered if it was something far deeper.

"What... what do you want me to do?" she asked, her voice barely audible. The question hung in the air, heavy with unspoken implications.

His smile was slow, predatory, and achingly beautiful. "I want you to shed the shackles, Jubilee. To embrace the raw power that is your birthright. To understand that true strength lies not in purity, but in harmony between light and shadow. You and I... we can unlock the potential of this glade, of this world, beyond anything your complacent kinsfolk could even dream."

He let his fingers trail from her jaw down her throat, his touch light, almost reverent, yet utterly possessive. A jolt, like lightning, shot through her, and a soft gasp escaped her lips. "Imagine, Jubilee," he purred, his voice dropping to a seductive whisper, "the two of us. The power of light, unbound from its limitations, interwoven with the power of shadow, no longer constrained by fear. A true rebalancing. A new era, forged by you and I, here in this sacred space." He paused, his gaze dropping to her mouth, his eyes burning with an undeniable desire. "And perhaps... a true connection between us, unlike anything either of our kinds have ever known."

His words, laced with dark promises and intoxicating power, resonated deep withing her, battling with the primal fear that still coiled in her gut. He wasn't just offering power; he was offering a profound, dangerous intimacy, a partnership that transcended their warring histories. A partnership that felt both like utter damnation and an irresistible, terrible salvation.

12

Jubilee's mind reeled, a maelstrom of fear, fascination, and a startling flicker of defiance. His words painted a grand, terrifying vision, but a vision sculpted around his will, not hers. The tingling sensation where his fingers lingered on her throat was less a caress and more a subtle pressure, a reminder of her bound state.

"A true connection?" her voice, through still hushed, was steadier now, a fragile thread woven with nascent anger. "You speak of connection and balance, yet you stand over me, having just drained the life from my friends and shackled me with your... your darkness." She twisted her wrists subtly, testing the shadowy bonds. They held firm, unyielding. "Is this your balance, Slash? My subjugation? My complicity in your plans?"

His smile, previously seductive, tightened at the edges. "Complicity? My dear Jubilee, you misunderstand. This isn't subjugation. It's liberation.

And Eldrin... Eldrin was a zealot. A stubborn, narrow-minded fool who would have rather seen this glade decay than evolve. His sacrifice, though unfortunate, was necessary. A necessary catalyst."

"Necessary?" she scoffed, a bitter laugh escaping her lips. "He was my friend!" the heat of her anger began to shimmer around her, battling with the oppressive chill of his shadows. " and you expect me to simply... accept this? To embrace a 'partnership' with the being who murdered him?"

Slash's eyes narrowed, the violet deepening to an almost black hue. "You speak of murder as if it were a simple act of malice. It was a transfer of energy. A rebalancing, as I said. His life force, though no longer contained within his fragile form, now fuels the very change I speak of. Nothing is truly lost, little fae. Only transformed."

"Transformed into what Slash?" she demanded, the quiet defiance now a palpable force. "Your personal dominion? You talk of unlocking potential, but it sounds more like you want to remake the world in your own image. Tell me," she leaned forward as best she could with her restraints, her emerald eyes blazing with a dangerous intensity, "what exactly is your ultimate goal? Beyond this glade, beyond this 'rebalancing' you speak of. What do you truly seek?"

He release her throat, his hand dropping to clasp her jaw with surprising gentleness, tilting her face up. His thumb stroked her cheekbone, a strangely soothing gesture that only agitated her further. "such fire," he murmured, a low rumble in his chest. "that's what I crave, Jubilee. That untamed spirit. That willingness to defy even in the face of overwhelming power."

"Answer me, Slash," she insisted, her voice tight with suppressed fury. "Why this glade? Why me? What is this 'new era' you envision? Is it a world where shadows consume all light? Where beings like Eldrin are casually extinguished for the sake of your 'balance'?"

His gaze intensified, pinning her, searching her very soul. "The glade is merely a starting point, Jubilee. A nexus of potent, ancient magic that has been stifled for too long. And you... you are the keeper of its heart, whether you knew it or not. Your unique magic, your connection to this sacred space, makes you invaluable to what comes next. As for the new era..." he paused, his gaze sweeping over her face, lingering on her defiant lips. "It is an age where the illusions of absolute good and absolute evil crumble. Where power is understood not as a destructive force, but as a dynamic one, constantly shifting, renewing. It is an age where the light acknowledges its shadow, and the shadow embraces its light. No more stasis, no more complacency. A world where true growth, real evolution, is finally possible."

He leaned in again, his breath ghosting over her lips. "And you, my resistant, beautiful fae, will be as its vanguard. With me." The proposition hung in the oppressive darkness, a sinister temptation, a promise of power and a new world, bought with bloody deeds and shrouded in forbidden intimacy. Jubilee felt a shiver trace down her spine, a profound understanding of the horrifying weight of his ambition, and the terrifying, magnetic pull her exerted over her.

13

A violent shiver raked through Jubilee, but it wasn't from the cold. It was the horrifying recognition of his ambition, a monstrous, seductive thing. The magnetic pull he exerted was almost physical, a hot current drawing her closer even as every cell in her body screamed for escape. He was offering her the world, a new world, but it was a world built on Eldrin's death, a world where she would be his tool, his vanguard.

Her emerald eyes, still blazing with simulated defiance, flickered to the prone form of Eldrin, a dark motionless stain on the living earth. Her heart ached with a grief so profound it threatened to shatter her. But with the grief came a cold, sharp clarity. She couldn't fight him, not openly, not now. Not like this.

A new strategy began to form, born of desperation and the primal need for revenge. It was a bitter pill to swallow, this capitulation, but survival – and justice for Eldrin – demanded it. She would play his game. She would pretend to see his grandiose vision, to accept her role in his twisted 'new era.' But every word, every compliant glance, would be a carefully crafted lie, a stepping stone towards his downfall.

She forced her breathing to even, the rapid pulse in her veins to calm. Her expression softened, the firey defiance dimming, replaced by a subtle, almost mesmerized look. " A dynamic power..." she murmured, her voice barely a whisper, as if grappling with the enormity of his revelation. "An age where light acknowledges its shadow... a shadow embraces its light."

Slash's thumb brushed her lip, his gaze piercing. "You understand, then." There was a hint of possessive triumph in his tone.

Jubilee met his gaze, her own eyes now wide, a flicker of something akin to wonder replacing the anger. "I... I think I'm beginning to," she lied, the words tasting like ash in her mouth. "It's... overwhelming. To think that all this time, the glade, my people, we've been stifling what could be. Holding back true evolution." She let a note of self-reproach tinge her voice. "Eldrin... he was so rigid. So bound by tradition."

Slash's smile deepened, a predatory curve of his lips. "Precisely. He was incapable of seeing beyond the narrow confines of his world. You, however, little fae, possess a spirit that yearns for more. I felt it the moment out paths crossed." He lowered his hand from her jaw, but the shadowy bonds still held her. "This glade... it has merely begun to awaken. With your cooperation, we will unlock its full potential. And your own."

She shivered again, this time with a convincing tremor of anticipation. "My own potential..." she let the words hang in the air, a question, a hint of curiosity. "What would that entail? What would you ask of me?"

His eyes gleamed, a deep violet fire. "Not ask, Jubilee. Guide. Together, we will channel the glade's latent power. We will reshape this sacred space, making it a beacon of this new balance. And you, as the heart of it, will grow beyond anything you could have ever imagined." He leaned closer, his scent, a dangerous mix of ozone and ancient earth, flooding her senses. "You will touch power you never dreamed possible. You will command forces that would make your ancestors tremble."

Her gaze dropped to hi lips, then back to his eyes, a perfectly crafted veil of fascination masking the seething hatred within. "Tell me more, Slash. Show me." Her voice was breathy, laced with a vulnerability she didn't feel. "Show me this new age. Show me the power."

A low chuckle vibrated in his chest. "Oh, I will, my resistant fae. I will show you everything." He finally released her, the shadowy tendrils dissolving as if they were never there. Jubilee rubbed her wrists, a shiver running through her. She was free, for now. Free to move, free to plan. And free to make Slash regret the day he ever underestimated an elven woman's fury. The true dance, she realized, had just begun. And this time, she would lead.

14

A violent shiver raked through Jubilee, but it wasn't from cold. It was the horrifying recognition of his ambition, a monstrous, seductive thing. The magnetic pull he exerted was almost physical, a hot current drawing her closer even as every cell in her body screamed for escape. He was offering her the world, a new world, but it was a world built on Edrin's death, a world where she would be his tool, his vanguard.

Her emerald eyes, still blazing with simulated defiance, flickered to the prone form of Eldrin, a dark motionless stain on the living earth. Her heart ached with a grief so profound it threatened to shatter her. But with the grief came a cold, sharp clarity. She couldn't fight him, not openly, not now. Not like this.

A new strategy began to form, born of desperation and the primal need for revenge. It was a bitter pill to swallow, this feigned capitulation, but survival - and justice for Eldrin - demanded it. She would play his game. She would pretend to see his grandiose vision, to accept her role in his twisted 'new era.' But with every word, every compliant glace, would be a carefully crafted lie, a stepping stone towards his downfall.

She forced her breathing to even, the rapid pulse in her veins to calm. Her expression softened, the fiery defiance dimming, replaced by a subtle, almost mesmerized look. "A dynamic power..." she murmured, her voice barely a whisper, as if grappling with the enormity of his revelation. "An age where light acknowledges its shadow... a shadow embraces its light."

Slash's thumb brushed her lip, his gaze piercing. "You understand, then." There was a hint of possessive triumph in his tone.

Jubilee met his gaze, her own eyes now wide, a flicker of something akin to wonder replacing the anger. "I...I think I'm beginning to," she lied, the words tasting like ash in her mouth. "It's... overwhelming. To think that all this time, the glade, my people, we've been stifling what could be. Holding back true evolution." She let a note of self-reproach tinge her voice. "Eldrin... he was so rigid. So bound by tradition."

Slash's smile deepened, a predatory curve of his lips. "Precisely. He was incapable of seeing beyond the narrow confines of his world. You, however, little fae, possess a spirit that yearns for more. I felt it the moment our paths crossed." He lowered his hand from her jaw, but the shadowy bonds still held her. "This glade... it has merely begun to awaken. With your cooperation, we will unlock its full potential. And your own."

She shivered again, this time with a convincing tremor of anticipation. "My own potential..." She let the words hang in the air, a question, a hint of curiosity. "What would that entail? What would you ask of me?"

His eye gleamed, a deep violet fire. "Not ask, Jubilee. Guide. Together, we will channel the glade's latent power. We will reshape this sacred space, making it a beacon of this new balance. And you, as the heart of it, will grow beyond anything you could have ever imagined." He leaned closer, his scent, a dangerous mix of ozone and ancient earth, flooding her senses. "You will touch power you never dreamed possible. You will command forces that would make your ancestors tremble."

Her gaze dropped to his lips, then back to his eyes, a perfectly crafted veil of fascination masking the seething hatred within. "Tell me more, Slash. Show me." Her voice was breathy, laced with a vulnerability she didn't feel. "Show me this new age. Show me the power."

A low chuckle vibrated in his chest, "Oh, I will, my resistant fae. I will show you everything." He finally released her, the shadowy tendrils dissolving as if they were never there. Jubilee rubbed her wrists, a shiver running through her. She was free, for now. Free to move, free to plan. And free to make Slash regret the day he ever underestimated an elven woman's fury. The true dance she realized, had just begun. And this time, she would lead.

15

The shadow receded, leaving Jubilee standing in the now-muted glade, the oppressive gloom still clinging to the ancient trees. Her wrists, though free, tingled with the phantom pressure of his power. She fought the instinct to recoil, to create distance. No. This was part of the game.

"Come, Jubilee." Slash's voice, a velvety purr, drew her attention. He extended a hand, not to seize her, but in an invitation that felt both intimate and terrifying. "Let us begin."

She hesitated for a beat, just long enough to convey a reluctant curiosity, before placing her hands in his. His skin was surprisingly warm, a stark contradiction to the cool dominion he wielded. A jolt, like a static electricity, arced between them, making the fine hairs on her arms stand on end. She forced a breathy gasp, a performance of awe.

"This glade," he began, his thumb tracing the line of her knuckles, his violet gaze locked on hers. "It pulsates with life, with magic. But it's been... contained. Like a river dammed, its true force diminished. Your people, in their fear of the wild, have tamed it to their own detriment."

Her stomach churned at his casual dismissal of her heritage; of everything she knew. But she kept her gaze wide, a carefully constructed illusion of a mind slowly opening to new possibilities. "Tamed?" she whispered, letting a hint of doubt color her tone.

"Yes. They have channeled its energy into sterile order, into predictability. While others," he gestured vaguely to the surrounding forest, "have drawn from it blindly, draining it without understanding its true source."

Cautiously, she mirrored his action, placing her palm against the tree. She had always felt the glade's magic, a gentle hum of life and growth. But now, as Slash pressed his hand next to hers, something shifted. It wasn't a gentle hum. It was a thrum, a deep, resonant vibration that seemed to emanate not just from the tree, but from deep within the earth itself. It was wilder, more untamed than anything she had ever consciously perceived.

"That," he murmured, his voice a low vibration that seemed to seep into her very bones, "is the glade's true heart. Powerful, raw and waiting to be unleashed." He leaned closer, his breath warm against her temple. "You have always been connected to it, but you haven't truly listened. You haven't truly opened yourself to its deeper song."

He moved his hand, sliding it over hers on the bark, his fingers interlacing with hers. The static charge intensified, blossoming into a warmth that spread through her arm, up to her chest. It was a dizzying sensation, like two currents colliding, intertwining.

"Close your eyes," he commanded softly. "Breathe. Let your barriers fall. Let the glade's power, and ours, flow through you."

She closed her eyes, forcing herself to relax her shoulders, to ease the tension that coiled in her gut. She focused on the pulsing warmth where his hand met hers, on the deep thrum of the ancient oak. And then, she allowed herself to truly feel. Not just the glade's magic, but his. A dark, potent current, not cold or malevolent as she expected, but... vibrant. Alive. It flowed into her, mingling with her own emerald energy, creating a dizzying, intoxicating blend. Her senses heightened. She could hear the faint whisper of sap rising in the tree, the deep groan of its roots anchoring it to the earth. The air itself seemed to vibrate with unseen forces.

"Yes," Slash whispered, a satisfied note in his voice. "You feel it, don't you? The potential. Your potential." He squeezed her hand. "This is but the beginning, little fae. The glade is awake. And so, are you."

A primal hum echoed within her chest, a resonance she didn't fully understand but couldn't deny. It felt dangerous, exhilarating, and utterly, terrifyingly potent. The thought of Eldrin flashed through her mind, a cold splash of reality. This power, this connection... it was nothing short of a corruption. But for now, for Eldrin, she would embrace the darkness, and learn to weild it. The true dance had begun, and she would lead him to his ruin.

16

The vibrations intensified under Jubilee's palm, a wild symphony of power that resonated with something deep within her. Slash's fingers intertwined with hers, his presence an insistent pressure, a dark warmth that coaxed her deeper into the glade's untamed heart. She let herself sway, mimicking the natural flow, allowing the intoxicating current to pull her into the depths. This wasn't merely the glade's energy; it was his, a potent fusion of light and shadow, surging through their joining hands.

"Open your mind, Jubilee," his voice was a low hum, a direct command that bypassed her ears and resonated in her very soul. "Let go of the constraints, the fear, the antiquated notions your people have pressed upon you. Feel the unbound strength that lies dormant, waiting."

She did. Not as an act of surrender, but of infiltration. She focused on the rush, letting it wash over her, cataloging every nuance, every sensation. It was a dizzying rush, pulling her in multiple directions at once, yet somehow anchored by Slash's steady presence beside her. She felt herself expanding, her consciousness stretching beyond her physical form, merging with the very essence of the ancient oak, then beyond, to the entire glade.

Images flickered behind her closed eyelids, shimmering roots plunging deep into the earth, drawing sustenance from unseen wells; ethereal forest spirit, normally hidden, now swirling into view, drawn by the surge of combined energy. She felt the ancient memories of the glade, a timeline of growth and decay, of magic both used and suppressed. And beneath it all, a subtle, dark current, powerful and alluring, that hummed with a promise of limitless potential. It was Slash's influence, weaving though the glade's innate energy, enhancing it, making it more potent, wilder.

"Excellent," Slash murmured, his breath ghosting over her ear, sending shivers down her spine that had nothing to do with fear. "You are a natural. You grasp what others fear to even acknowledge." He tightened his grip on her hand. "Now, bring it forth. Do not hold back. Let the glade respond to your true essence."

He guided her other hand to the bark, pressing it firmly against the rough surface. "Feel the connection. Draw from it. Shape it."

Jubilee breathed deeply, centering herself. This was the moment. The glade's energy, infused with Slash's potent darkness, swirled within her. She visualized it, a vibrant green light, now laced with shimmering violet, pulsing through her veins. With a deep breath, she pushed it outward, focusing on the fallen leaves at the base of the oak.

At first, nothing. Then, a faint shimmer. The leaves, brittle and brown moments before, began to glow with a soft, ethereal green. Tiny emerald tendrils emerged from their decaying form, stretching towards the sunlight. A new fragile life begun to unfurl from the old.

Slash's grip on her hand tightened, a tremor running through him. "Yes! You feel it? The power of creation, of transformation. Not merely growth, but true, raw power." His voice was laced with almost primal satisfaction. "You are not merely a keeper, Jubilee. You are a conduit, a force."

She opened her eyes, startled by the vibrant green glow emanating from the leaves. It was far more potent than any forest magic she had ever consciously wielded. The familiar energy of the glade was now laced with an undeniable, intoxicating darkness, making it sharper, more immediate. This wasn't just life; it was life conjured from the brink of death, imbued with a potent vitality she hadn't thought possible.

Slash, his eyes gleaming with triumphant violet light, leaned in closer. "This is just the beginning, little fae. We will peel back the layer after layer of slumber and unleash the true might of this glade. And through it, your own." His gaze dropped to her lips, a dark promise in their depths. "Our true song has only just begun."

A tremor ran through her, a mix of triumph and dread. The power was intoxicating, yes. But it was tainted with his touch, a dark echo of his influence. She had embraced it, allowed it to flow through her, all for a greater purpose. The dance continued, its steps becoming increasingly intricate, increasingly dangerous. And with every beat of its rhythm, she felt herself changing, adapting, becoming something new. Something she could, and would, use against him.

17

The pulsating energy faded, leaving a faint phantom hum in its wake. Jubilee stared at the emerald touched leaves, a strange blend of awe and revulsion churning within her. The magic she had just channeled was undeniably hers, yet subtly distorted, like a beloved melody played in minor key. It was more potent, yes, but tasted faintly of ashes and forbidden allure.

Slash's face, still close to hers, held a look of profound satisfaction, his violet eyes alight with a dangerous glee. "See? The glade responds to you. But now, it responds to the truest part of you. The part that embraces all that is, not just what is convenient." His thumb brushed her lower lip, a feather light touch that sent another disconcerting shiver through her. "You felt the truth of it, didn't you? The power that was always there, waiting for release."

She pulled back slightly, breaking the magnetic pull of his gaze. "It was... different," she managed, her voice a little breathless. She could still feel the lingering tendrils of his shadow magic interwoven with her own, a dark thread in the tapestry of her forest magic. It was unsettling familiar, intoxicating in its raw strength. The desire to wield it again, to push the boundaries of what was possible, was a whisper at the edge of her consciousness. It was a dark, dangerous whisper, but undeniably alluring.

"different is merely a word for untamed." He corrected, his voice a low purr. He released her hand, but the imprint of his touch lingered, a burning phantom against her skin. "Your people have always sought to tame, to civilize, to control. But true power thrives in the wildness, in the confluence of all energies. Light cannot exist without shadow, little fae. And you, my dear Jubilee, are destined to embrace both."

He turned, gesturing broadly at the glade around them, which seemed to ripple subtly, as if shifting its very nature. "Eldrin, bless his naïve heart, believed in a constrained, stagnant power. He was a caretaker, not a creator. He clung to the past, while the true spirit of this glade yearns for evolution." He walked deeper into the glade, his dark form a stark contrast to the revitalized greenery. "That acorn that marked me... it was a potent symbol of their binding magic. A cage for untold potential."

Jubilee followed, her mind racing. He spoke of evolution, of unbound power. And she had felt it. The jolt of raw creation, the sensation of life being sparked from decay, was a powerful, addictive force. It was unlike anything she had ever experienced, far beyond the gentle nurturing magic her people practiced. It was sharp, immediate, and utterly exhilarating.

She tried to push away the thought, to focus on her resolve, on Eldrin. But the memory of his lifeless form, the quiet horror of it, seemed to blur against the dazzling, dangerous promise Slash offered. Was this power worth the compromise? Could she wield it for her own ends, without succumbing to his darkness?

"This is why you need me," Slash continued, turning to face her, his hands clasped behind his back. "Your inherent connection to the glade was strong, but your spirit was shackled. You were merely an extension of its sup+pressed state. Nopw, you are its true voice, its true power. And with me by your side..." his lips curved into a slow, predatory smile. "We will sing a symphony of power this world has never heard."

His eyes, those fathomless violet pools, held her captive. She felt the pull of their shared moment, the potent cocktail of magic and forbidden intimacy. The lines between right and wrong blurred, and for a terrifying moment, she felt a profound surge of desire to fall into his abyss, to let him guide her into this untamed, exhilarating new existence. It wasn't just physical attraction; it was a deeper, more insidious lure, a promise of untamed potential that resonated with a hidden hunger she hadn't know she possessed.

She squeezed her hands into fists, her nails digging into her palms. "You lie," she whispered, her voice barely a breath. "you manipulate. You destroy."

He chuckled, a low, rich sound that vibrated through the sir. "Perhaps. But tell me, little fae. Did you feel destroyed just now? Or did you feel... alive?"

The question hung in the air, a silent challenge. And the terrifying truth was, she had never felt more alive. The intoxicating rush of raw, unbridled power still thrummed in her veins, promising unimaginable vistas if only she dared to step further into the shadows with him.

18

The glade, once a sanctuary, now felt like a gilded cage. Every rustle of leaves, every scent of revitalized earth, seemed to hum with Slash's presence,with the potent new magic he had awakened within her. The question he posed - "Did you feel destroyed just now? Or did you feel... alive?" - echoed in her mind, a relentlessdrumbeat against her carefully constructed resolve. She had felt alive. Terrifyingly, exhilaratingly alive. And that was the problem.

Her fingers, still curled into fists, trembled. This dark, exhilarating power was a siren song, promising strength shed only dreamed of, a way to transcend the limitations of her past. But at what cost? Eldrin's lifeless form flashed before her eyes, a stark, chilling reminder of the price of Slash's "evolution."

"I...I need to be alone," Jubilee managed, her voice strained, barely audible over the thumping of her own heart. She needed distance, a moment to clear her head, to reaffirm her purpose. She needed to escape the magnetic pull that threatened to unravel her.

Slash's smile didn't falter. "Alone? Here? You are never truly alone, little fae. Not with the glade and certainly not with the magic that now binds is." Yet, he made no move to stop her as she stumbled away from him, towards the edge of the newly invigorated clearing.

Each step was an effort, as if the ground itself, now pulsing with their combined energies, sought to hold her back. The air was thick with it, a tangible presence that clung to her skin, whispering insidious promises. She pushed through a curtain of shimmering vines, her breath ragged. She just needed to be out of his sight, out of the immediate sphere of his oppressive potent charm.

She ran deeper into the forest, not in the panicked flight of before, but with a desperate need for solitude. Every tree, every mossy stone, felt different now, infused with a new, wild vibrancy that was both thrilling and disorienting. Her own magic, once a gentle ebb and flow, now surged, a powerful river threatening to burst its banks. She could feel the pulse of the earth beneath her feet, the whisper of sap in the ancient trees, their life force heightened, almost feverish. This wasn't her glade anymore. It was... more. And less.

She ran until her lungs burned, until the familiar landmarks of her forest home blurred into a intoxicating tapestry of raw energy. Finally, she collapsed against the rough bark of a old pine, burying her face in her hands.

Eldrin. She had remembered Eldrin. His memory was her anchor, her shield against the dangerous allure. She had to avenge him, not embrace the very power that had destroyed him. This was a trap, a seductive lure designed to ensnare her, to turn her into his tool.

A faint shiver ran down her spine, not from cold, but from a familiar, exhilarating hum. It was the magic, yes, the glade's magic, but interwoven with something darker, deeper. She felt its call, a whisper in her very blood, urging her back, back towards its source, back towards him. It was a physical ache, a craving.

She squeezed her eyes shut fighting it, fighting herself. But the forest around her, now vibrant with their mingled essence, seemed to conspire against her. The air grew warmer, infused with an almost tangible desire. She could feel the subtle shifts in the glade's energy, a compelling, magnetic pull drawing her back towards the source of this intoxicating power. It was undeniable. It was primal.

When she opened her eyes, a shiver traced its way down her spine. The forest was no longer a blur. The trees, the ground, the very air itself, seemed to thrum with a palpable longing. And through the leaves, not far, she could already see the subtle, shifting outline of a figure, dark against the burgeoning glade. He needn't have followed. The connection, now forged, would always draw her back. She was no longer just

Jubilee, forest fae. She was a vessel for something new, something dangerous. And she was inextricably drawn to its source.

19

The figure emerging from the deepening twilight, a silhouette of potent masculinity against the glowing heart of the revitalized glad. Slash. As if her restless thoughts had conjured him, he materialized besides her, his presence a warm, heavy cloak she couldn't shake off. There was no surprise in his violet eyes, only a knowing satisfaction.

"Running doesn't change what we are," he murmured, his voice a low hum that resonated withing her, a physical vibration against her very bones. He reached out, his hand brushing a stray strand of chocolate colored hair from her face, his touch a feather-light caress that burned. "It only postpones the inevitable."

Jubilee flinched, pulling back, but the contact had already seared its mark. "This... this isn't what I asked for," she whispered, the words thin and reedy, devoid of their usual strength. The raw power pulsing around them dwarfed her every protest.

"Isnt it?" Slash countered, his smile widening, a slow, predatory unveiling of teeth against the twilight. "You craved more, little one. More than your timid kin offered. More than the stifling traditions of your forest could provide." He gestured around them, at the glade that now throbbed with a life almost obscene in its vibrancy. "This is but a taste. A flicker of what we can unleash, together."

He knelt before her, his gaze intense, pinning her where she sat. "Consider the glade. It was... stagnant. Beautiful, yes, but held captive by your peoples fear of what true power entails. They pruned, they snapped, they tamed. We, Jubilee," he leaned closer, his scent of night blooming jasmine and ancient earth intoxicating, "we unshackle."

His dark eyes held hers, a deep, inescapable well. "Eldrin, bless his traditional heart, was a barrier. A small minded obstacle in the path of evolution. His magic was a shield, yours a burgeoni9ng weapon. Do you understand the difference?" he paused, allowing the weight of his words to settle. "His was meant to protect what was. Yours, little spark, is meant to forge what will be."

Jubilee swallowed, a lump forming in her throat. She wanted to argue, to scream at him, to remind herself of Eldrin's fallen form. But the words caught, trapped by the captivating force of his conviction. He was painting a picture, a dangerous masterpiece that, despite herself, she found herself leaning into.

"You've experienced your full power now," he continued, his voice dropping to a near whisper, intimate and compelling. "This creation, the growth. Imagine that, but amplified. Not just here, in this glade, but across the forests, across the realms themselves. We reshape the world, Jubilee. We don't just watch it decay."

He placed a hand, warm and firm, over her heart, over the thrumming, agitated magic within her. "This feeling," he said, his thumb stroking gently, sending shivers through her. "This wild, untamed vibrancy. Its what you were always meant to feel. Its liberation. Its true existence."

He brought her hand to his lips, his gaze still fixed on hers, and kissed her fingertips, a slow, deliberate movement that sent a jolt straight through her veins. "And you, my stunning fae, are the key. Your light, pure and potent, when mingled with my shadow, creates something utterly new. Something unstoppable. The old ways crumble. The new dawn belongs to us."

His word, meant to seduce, resonated with a terrifying truth she was battling to deny. He wasn't just talking about power, or change: he was hinting at a partnership, an intimacy on a cosmic scale. She felt undeniable pull, the dangerous allure of such a proposition. He wasn't simply dominating her; he was inviting her to reign at his side. The glade pulsed around them, a living testament to his promises, whispering of shared destiny. And against her every instinct, against the ghost of Eldrin, Jubilee felt the insidious, terrifying warmth of acceptance beginning to bloom in her heart.

20

The taste of his lips on her fingertips lingered, a phantom sensation that coursed through her, bypassing re3ason and setting her very blood alight. Jubilee's breath hitched, caught between a gasp of fear and a sigh of burgeoning longing. The glade pulsed around them, no longer a separate entity, but an extension of the tumultuous space between them. Every thrum of magic, every shift of vibrant new growth, echoed his insidious words: "The new dawn belongs to us."

She gazed into his violet eyes, those bottomless pools of shadow and starlight, and saw not just ambition, but a profound belief in their shared destiny. It wasn't the menacing demand of a conqueror, but the intense invitation of a co-conspirator. Her mind screamed for Eldrin, for the pristine, ordered world she had known, but her body hummed with a resonance she couldn't silence. This was new. This was dangerous. And terrifyingly, she craved it.

Her hand, still burning from his touch, instinctively reached out, not to push him away, but to graze the fine definition of his jawline. A tremor ran through him, subtle but present, belying is calm exterior. He leaned into her touch, his eyes never leaving hers, a silent question passing between them.

"Show me," she whispered, her voice rough, barely audible above the insistent symphony of the glade. "Show me this... new dawn."

A slow, triumphant smile bloomed on Slash's face, not predatory this time, but genuinely pleased. He rose, pulling her gently to her feet, their hands clasped. "With pleasure, little spark."

He led her deeper into the transformed glade, past trees whose leaves shimmered with arcane light, past blossoms that pulsed with an unheard rhythm. He didn't rush her instead, he moved with a languid grace that invited her to lose herself in the moment, to shed the last vestiges of her former self. The scent of jasmine and earth grew stronger, wrapping around her like a living embrace.

"close your eyes," he murmured, his breath warm against her ear. "Feel it. Not just what you see, but what lives beneath. The currents. The whispers. The pure, untamed essence of creation."

Jubilee obeyed, her eyelids fluttering shut. Immediately, the glade intensified. She felt incredible surge of life beneath her bare feet, the deep, rhythmic pulse of the ancient oak now intertwined with a fierce, dynamic energy. It was a symphony of power, richer and more complex than anything she had ever experienced. His hand, warm and firm, settled at the small of her back, guiding her.

"Now," Slash's voice was a low thrum against her, "reach out. Not just with your forest magic, but with all of you. Embrace the shadow, little light. Let it flow through you, not as a separate entity, but as an extension of your own magnificent being."

She concentrated, pushing past her ingrained instincts, past the fear drilled into her from childhood. She stretched her awareness, letting her consciousness blend with the very fabric of the glade. And as she did, something shifted. Her pure green energy, always so gentle and verdant, begun to entwine with something darker, deeper, a primal force that hummed with a promise of untamed creation.

A gnarled root, ancient and seemingly dormant, began to glow with a combination of emerald and violet light. It pulsed, then unfurled, unfurling with impossible speed into a magnificent bloom, its petals shimmering with an ethereal luminescence. It wasn't a flower of gentle beauty, but one of fierce, vibrant power.

Jubilee gasped, her eyes flying open. Slash was watching her, his expression a mixture of awe and profound satisfaction. And for the first time, she saw it clearly, the potential, the sheer, unimaginable power that lay awakened within her. The glade mirrored her internal landscape, a tapestry of light and shadow, creation and destruction, all woven together by their combined essence. And she realized, with a shocking clarity that both thrilled and terrified her, that her journey of vengeance was no longer the only path. This new world, this new power, this compelling connection with Slash, it was a different kind of destiny, one she felt inexorably drawn to.

21

The shimmering bloom, born of their combined magic, pulsed with an almost sentient energy, mirroring the frantic beat of Jubilee's heart. Her gaze drifted from the impossibly vibrant flower to Slash, who still watching her, his violet eyes alight with a silent, potent understanding. The awe on his face was raw, unmasked, and for a fleeting moment, she saw beyond the dangerous shadow fae, beyond the conqueror, to something intrinsically vulnerable beneath. It was a vulnerability that resonated deep within her, a strange echo to her own unveiled power.

"You feel it, don't you?" he murmured, his voice a low caress, closer now that she realized. Her awareness of him had sharpened, every subtle shift of muscle, every nuance of breath, a heightened sensation in this transformed glade. "The truth of what we are, little spark. What we can be."

He reached out, his hand raising slowly, and this time, she didn't flinch, didn't resist. His thumb brushed along her jawline, tracing the curve of her cheekbone, then slipped into the silken strands of her hair. His touch was both gentle and possessive, sending a shiver not of fear, but of profound awareness, down her spine. His fingers tangled in her chocolate brown locks, pulling her head back just fractionally, exposing the delicate line of her throat.

Her breath hitched again, a silent gasp caught in her chest as his gaze dropped to her lips, then back to her eyes. The air between them crackled with an electricity that threatened to consume the, a burgeoning intimacy that transcended the physical. She felt entirely exposed, every hidden desire fluttering to the surface, laid bare under his intense scrutiny. Yet, instead of shame, there was a strange, intoxicating freedom in this vulnerability.

"Tell me," She whispered, her voice rough, barely her own. "Tell me what this. What 'we' are."

A slow smile curved his lips, a different kind of smile that she had seen before - softer, more genuine, laced with a triumphant tenderness that sent a jolt through her. He leaned in. His dark head inclining, until their foreheads rested together, the warmth of his skin seeping into hers. His scent, a heady mix of ancient earth and something wild, elemental, enveloped her, drawing her deeper into his orbit.

"This, little spark," he breathed, his voice a low rumble against her, "is inevitability. It is the drawing of forces, the completion of a fractured whole. It is two halves of a yearning spirit finally finding their way home." His words, spoken with such conviction, echoed the pulsing magic that now thrummed through her own veins.

He released her hair, his hand sliding down to cup the back of her neck, his thumb caressing the sensitive skin just below her ear. "Your people called it forbidden. They called it darkness. But you feel it, don't you? This... this is not destruction. Not entirely. It is raw, untamed creation."

Jubilee's mind reeled, trying to grasp the enormity of his words, of the sensations that flooded her. Eldrin's face flashed in her mind, a brief, painful flicker, but it was quickly overshadowed by the overwhelming presence of Slash, by the truth of the power that now coursed through her. She had been so certain of her path, of her revenge, but now the path blurred, fractured into a thousand shimmering possibilities.

She closed her eyes again, pressing into his touch, allowing herself to simply 'feel'. The world narrowed to the pulse of their combined magic, the intoxicating scent of him, the firm unwavering grip of his hand. It was terrifying and exhilarating, this surrender.

When she opened her eyes, she found his own already open, gazing into hers with an intensity that promised devotion and dominion in equal measure. He shifted, drawing her nearer, until their bodies were a breath apart, the subtle friction of their clothing a new, exquisite torment.

"Let go, Jubilee," he murmured, his voice a silken ribbon weaving through the thrum of the glade. "Let go of what was. Step into what can be. With me."

And then, his lips were on hers. Not a brutal claim, but a soft, hesitant exploration, as if seeking an answer, an invitation. Her own lips, trembling, parted in silent welcome. The kiss deepened, a slow, sensual unfolding, a merging of light and shadow, of past and future. It was a covenant, a whispered promise, and a breathtaking surrender, all in one intoxicating breath.

22

His lips, warm and impossibly soft, brushed against hers. It began as a tentative question, a delicate tracing of her mouth, as if he sought permission rather than demanded it. Jubilee, her entire being humming with a mixture of awe and intoxicating fear, instinctively responded, her own lips parting slightly, an unspoken invitation. The glade, which a moment ago had been a symphony of pulsing magic, seemed to hole its breath.

Then, the hesitation vanished Slash's kiss deepened, a slow, sensual consumption that started as a tender pressure and bloomed into a passionate claiming. His hand, still cupping the back of her neck, tightening imperceptibly, urging her closer until there was no space left between them. Her hands, as if guided by an ancient instinct, found purchase on his strong shoulders, her fingers digging into the firm muscle beneath his tunic.

A low groan rumbled in his chest, a sound that vibrated through her, setting every nerve ending alight. His tongue, a velvet stroke, traced the seam of her lips, then slipped inside, meeting hers in a dance that was both primal and impossibly intimate. It was a kiss that devoured her doubts, melted her resistance, and consumed her very essence. The taste of him was wild and dark, like damp earth after a long rain, tinged with a sweetness she hadn't expected, a sweetness that promised untold depths.

The magic of the glade, a dormant beast moments ago, roared to life around them. The luminescent flower they had created pulsed brighter, shedding a soft, emerald glow that painted their entwined forms in ethereal light. Roots beneath their feet stirred, a gentle vibration echoing the frantic beat of Jubilee's heart it felt less like a kiss and more like an elemental force, a binding ritual that sealed their fates not just to each other, but the very essence of this transformed world.

Her mind spun, a kaleidoscope of sensation. Eldrin's betrayed face flickered, a fain ghost quickly eclipsed by the overwhelming reality of Slash. This was not the vengeance she had planned, not the outcome she had envisioned. This was something far more terrifying, far more profound. It was a surrender not of will, but of soul, a merging that transcended hatred and history.

Slash's hand left her neck, sliding down her back, drawing her even tighter, against his lean, powerful body until she could feel the hard planes of his chest, the rhythmic thud of his heart against hers. He lifted her, cradling her as if she weighed nothing, never breaking the searing connection of their lips. Her legs instinctively wrapped around his waist, pulling her higher, closer.

When he finally broke the kiss, it was with a soft gasp, leaning his forehead against hers once more. His eyes, now a swirling vortex of deep violet, were half-lidded, heavy with a raw undeniable hunger that mirrored her own. His breath, warm against her lips, feathered past them as he struggled for air.
:Jubilee," he rasped, his voice thick with emotion, a gravelly sound that sent shivers down her spine. "My little spark... my wildfire."

He shifted them, slowly, gently, until they sank to the mossy ground beneath the ancient oak. He laid her down, cushioning her head with his hand, never breaking eye contact. His body settled over hers, his weight a comforting, possessive pressure. He didn't kiss her again, not yet.

Jubilee, still reeling from the electrifying kiss, could only gaze back. Her body hummed with a delicious ache, a yearning that was utterly new and terrifyingly exhilarating. The need for vengeance seemed distant, hollow echo against the vibrant, all-consuming truth of this moment. He had not just kissed her; he had kissed her alive. He had awoken something deep within her, a wildness, a yearning for power, for connection, that she had never know existed.

"This," he whispered, his thumb caressing the soft skin beneath her eye, "is just the beginning." His words, a threat, a destiny, all rolled into one. And as he lowered his head once more, not to her lips, but to the delicate pulse point at her throat, Jubilee knew, with a certainty that transcended logic, that she was irrevocably, deliciously lost. Lost to him, to the darkness, to the intoxicating pull of their shared, forbidden destiny.

23

His lips found the tender hollow of her throat, a soft, inquisitive nibble that sent a jolt through her already electrified body. Jubilee gasped, an involuntary sound that was half pleasure, half shock. He reveled in it, his tongue tracing a slow, deliberate path upwards, tasting her, claiming her. The scent of him; dark earth and something musky and intoxicating filled her senses, drowning out everything else.

Her fingers, still tangled in his hair, tightened, pulling him closer, an unspoken plea for more. He responded with a soft grunt, his weight pressing her further into the mossy earth. The glade magic pulsed around them, no longer a mere backdrop but an active participant, intertwining their auras, amplifying every sensation. The luminescent flower they had conjured earlier seemed to throb with a life of its own, shedding a softer, more intimate low.

He lifted his head, his violet eyes, now almost black with desire, locked onto hers. "Tell me," he rasped, his voice a low rumble against her skin, "what you truly want, Jubilee." It wasn't a demand, but a whispered invitation; a challenge to shed the last vestiges of her self-imposed restraint.

Her breath hitched. The words felt to big, too dangerous to form. What did she want? Not vengeance, not anymore. She wanted this. The raw, untamed connection, this delicious oblivion. She wanted him. The truth was liberating, terrifying.

"You," she whispered, the single word a fragile thread in the charged silence. "I want... more."

A slow, predatory smile curved his lips, a flash of white against his shadowed face. "More, my spark? Oh, we have so much more to explore."

With a soft growl, he shifted, pulling away just enough to allow his hand to glide beneath the hem of her tunic. His fingertips grazed her bare skin, setting off a thousand tiny explosions. Jubilee arched into his touch, a desperate plea for more contact, more sensation. He understood, his movements smooth and deliberate as he pushed the fabric upwards, exposing her midriff, then her ribs, until the soft skin of her breasts was revealed to the cool night air.

His gaze dropped, lingering for a moment on the swell of her chest, before slowly, tantalizingly, his head descended. Her heart pounded a frantic rhythm against her ribs as his lips, warm and impossibly soft, brushed against her skin, leaving a trail of fire in their wake. He nudged her tunic higher, the fabric gathering around her shoulders until she was fully exposed to his hungry gaze.

Jubilee gasped as his mouth closed over her, a hot, wet suction that drew a whimper from her throat. He suckled, teased, and devoured, driving her deeper into a haze of pure sensation. Her fingers gripped his hair, pulling him closer, urging him on. The world outside the glade ceased to exist; there was only him, only this exquisite pleasure, only the merging of two souls, two powers, into something new and undeniable.

"Slash," she breathed, his name a prayer on her lips, a surrender to the inevitable. He lifted his head, his eyes burning with an ancient desire that transcended their current form, an acknowledgment of their destined collision.

"Yes, my wildfire," he murmured, his voice thick with raw emotion. "Feel it. This is what we were meant for."

His hand tangled in the moss beside her, searching. A small, glowing root, pulsing with the combined energy they had awakened, wound itself around his fingers. He lifted it, its soft, emerald light illuminating their entwined bodies, a silent witness to the unwritten secrets soon to be shared. He brought the root to her lips, and she, without hesitation, bit down, letting the magic course through her veins, preparing her for the depths of intimacy that awaited.

24

The taste of the root was earthy and sweet, a concentrated burst of the glade's magic. It hummed through her, not just as energy, but as a sensual current that unraveled the last threads of her self-consciousness. It felt less like sustenance and more like an aphrodisiac, sharpening every nerve ending, making her skin tingle with anticipation.

Slash watched her, his violet eyes molten with hunger, reflecting the emerald glow of the root. He leaned down, his breath warm against her ear. "Open for me, love," he whispered, his voice a low thrum that vibrated through her core.

Her body, already pliant and yearning, readily obeyed. She arched her back, offering herself to him fully, instinctively. One of his hands slid from the moss, tracing a heated path down her side, past her waist, skirting the delicate curve of her hip. His touch was both feather-light and impossibly heavy, each brush of his fingers raising gooseflesh.

When he reached the soft, inner curve of her thigh, Jubilee gasped again, a soft, involuntary cry. He paused, his gaze fixed on her face, seeking permission she no longer had the will to deny. Her eyes fluttered open, dark and dilated with desire, meeting his. She bit her lip, a silent plea for him to continue, to take what she so desperately wanted to give.

A low growl rumbled in his chest, a sound of triumph and raw pleasure. His fingers, long and skilled, dipped lower, finding the warm, sensitive juncture between her thighs. The shock of his touch was electric, a jolt that sent a tremor through her entire body. She bucked against him, a desperate, unthinking movement.

"Easy, my wildfire," he murmured, his thumb circling slowly, tantalizingly. "There's no need to rush. We have all the time in the world." His voice was a seductive balm, calming the frantic beat of her heart even as his touch inflamed her.

He watched her face, fascinated by the play of emotions – the shock, the rising heat, the pure, unadulterated pleasure that blossomed across her features. Her hips rose to meet his hand, a silent invitation, a wordless plea. He responded with a soft chuckle, a sound of pure male satisfaction.

His fingers delved deeper, tracing the slick, sensitive folds, slowly, deliberately exploring her. Jubilee cried out, not in pain, but in a surge of sensation that was almost overwhelming. Her legs fell open wider, inviting him further. Her hands, still tangled in his hair, urged him closer, her nails lightly scraping his scalp.

The glade pulsed around them, the luminescent flower opening wider, its petals unfurling in a silent echo of Jubilee's own awakening. The energy that had once propelled Eldrin's magic, then her own vengeance, now sang a different song—a melody of raw, untamed desire.

He leaned down, his lips brushing against hers, a whisper of a kiss that promised so much more. "You're so beautiful, Jubilee," he breathed against her mouth, his words a heady wine. "So vibrant. So ready."

His fingers found the core of her, the tiny nub that throbbed with unfulfilled longing. He teased it gently, then with increasing pressure, until Jubilee's breath hitched, a half-sob, half-moan. Her body arched off the mossy ground, seeking release, clinging to him as if he were her only anchor in a world that had dissolved into pure sensation.

"Slash," she whimpered, her voice hoarse, her control slipping. "Please..."

He smiled, a dark, knowing curve of his lips. "Please what, my spark?" he challenged, his touch unwavering, relentlessly driving her higher.

"More," she gasped, her voice barely a whisper. "Everything."

He chuckled, a rich, deep sound that sent vibrations through her. Without another word, he shifted, aligning himself, his hard, masculine heat pressing against her. Jubilee felt the brush of his erection against her inner thigh, thick and heavy, and a shiver ran through her, a tremor of pure, unadulterated anticipation. All thoughts of resistance, all vestiges of her past life, vanished, consumed by the burning, delicious reality of him. This was the inevitable. This was everything.

25

He pushed in slowly, inch by agonizing inch, a deliberate torment that made her arch and whimper. The glade itself seemed to hold its breath, the luminescent flower's glow intensifying to an almost blinding brilliance. A sigh escaped her, a deep, guttural sound that was part moan, part surrender. With each fraction of an inch he gained, a new world unfurled within her, a sensation so potent, so utterly consuming, that she felt herself unravel.

Jubilee gasped, her fingers digging into his shoulders, drawing him closer. The fullness of him, the sheer, intoxicating breadth, stretched her, filling her in a way she never knew she craved. It wasn't pain, not truly, but a magnificent, exquisite pressure that promised release. Her body, once so attuned to the gentle rhythms of her forest, now vibrated with this deeper, more primal connection.

"Beautiful," Slash rasped, his voice thick with desire, his eyes locked on hers as he watched her every reaction. His hands, one still at her breast, the other tangling in her hair, held her captive, anchored her to the surging tide of sensation. He paused, allowing her to adjust, to absorb the magnitude of their joining. The air crackled around them, thick with the scent of earth and desire, of new life and ancient power.

Then, with a powerful, deliberate thrust, he plunged deeper, burying himself inside her completely. A raw cry tore from Jubilee's throat, not of distress, but of pure, unadulterated pleasure. Her legs instinctively wrapped around his waist, pulling him impossibly tighter against her. Their bodies locked, melded into one, a perfect fit forged in the heart of the glade's wild magic.

He began to move, a slow, hypnotic rhythm at first, teasing, drawing out the pleasure. Each thrust was a pulse of shared energy, a wave breaking over her. Jubilee met him, her hips rising to match his cadence, desperate for more, for everything. The glade pulsed around them, the roots beneath them thrumming with their combined magic. She felt a profound shift within, a loosening of old constraints, a flowering of untamed sensuality.

With every stroke, his shadows seemed to entwine with her light, not as opposing forces, but as complementary components, weaving a tapestry of pure, undiluted power. She felt the ancient magic of the glade, amplified by their union, swirling around her, through her, and into him. It was a current of life, of creation, unlike anything she had ever known.

Slash's pace quickened, his breaths coming in ragged gasps against her neck. His strength, his raw power, filled her completely, driving her higher and higher. She was no longer just Jubilee, the forest elf; she was a vessel for something far greater, something wild and untamed, born of this impossible connection. Her vision blurred, consumed by the ferocity of their coupling.

"Look at you," he breathed, his voice a low growl of triumph as he buried himself within her once more. "Pure fire. Pure magic."

Jubilee's own magic, once a gentle whisper, now roared to life, mingling with his shadows, creating sparks that danced just beneath her skin. She was on the precipice, trembling on the edge of a perfect, shattering release. Her entire being focused on the powerful thrusts that rocked her world, pushing her closer and closer to that ultimate sensation. She dug her nails deeper into his back, and the glade surged in response, the luminescent flower's petals unfurling violently, showering them with glowing pollen.

With a final, desperate cry, she shattered. A million tiny fragments of light exploded inside her, radiating outwards. Her body convulsed around him, clinging, clenching, lost in the overwhelming ecstasy. A guttural groan tore from Slash's chest as he followed her, his own release potent and profound, spilling into her, mingling their essences in a swirling vortex of energy.

He collapsed onto her, heavy and sated, his breath hitching. The glade hummed, a gentle, satisfied song. Their bodies, slick with sweat and desire, remained intimately joined, connected not just by flesh, but by the very magic that pulsed around them. Jubilee lay beneath him, gasping, her limbs weak, her mind a dizzying whirl of sensation. The world had shifted on its axis. The past was a distant echo, and the future... the future was tangled with his.

26

A sudden, discordant screech ripped through the post-coital hush, jarring Jubilee from the languid bliss. It wasn't the familiar cry of a nocturnal predator, nor the gentle rustle of leaves. This sound was sharp, metallic, alien. Slash's head snapped up, his body tensing above her, the profound contentment in his eyes instantly replaced by a predatory alertness.

"What was that?" Jubilee whispered, her voice still thick with recent pleasure, tinged now with a growing unease. The glade, which moments ago had vibrated with their shared ecstasy, now felt...wrong. The luminescence of the flower flickered erratically, casting strange, dancing shadows.

Slash rolled off her, his movements fluid and swift, pulling her to a sitting position with him. He didn't bother with words, his violet gaze sweeping the periphery of the glade, a low growl rumbling in his chest. "Something has entered."

Before he could elaborate, the screech came again, closer this time, followed by a chorus of agitated chirps and snarls. Twigs snapped, not from the easy passage of forest creatures, but from something heavier, clumsier, yet moving with deliberate speed. The earthy scent of the glade was now overlaid with something acrid, metallic – a smell that made Jubilee's ethereal senses prickle with disgust.

From the shadows beyond the ancient oak, forms began to emerge. They weren't the lithe, graceful creatures of her forest, nor the shadowy, agile beings of Slash's kind. These were hulking, grotesque figures, their skin a mottled, sickly grey, their limbs too thick, too short. Their eyes, visible even in the dimming light, glowed with an unnatural, malevolent red. Their movements were jerky, unnatural, and as they lumbered into the glade, Jubilee saw the implements clamped into their clawed hands – crude, jagged weapons that seemed to tear at the very air.

"What are they?" she breathed, her hand instinctively reaching for Slash's.

"Grolak," he growled, his grip on her hand tightening reassuringly, though his attention remained fixed on the encroaching threat. "Subterranean scavengers. They rarely surface, and never in such numbers. And they don't carry those... for foraging."

The Grolak beasts began to fan out, their guttural snarls echoing through the glade. One, larger than the others, stomped forward, its red eyes fixing on Jubilee and Slash with unnerving focus. It raised its primitive, obsidian axe, a low, rasping challenge emanating from its throat.

"They're after the glade's magic," Jubilee realized, remembering Slash's earlier words about the suppressed power. The sheer audacity of these monstrous creatures, invading her sacred space... but this was no longer just her space. It was theirs.

Slash's form shimmered, tendrils of shadow already beginning to coil around him, subtly enhancing his lean physique. "Our power," he corrected, his voice a dangerous whisper. "And they will not have it."

He pushed her gently behind him, placing himself between her and the largest Grolak. His stance was coiled, ready, and Jubilee felt a surge of reassurance mingled with an exhilarating thrill. Just hours ago, she would have faced this alone, or with Eldrin. Now, she had Slash - a formidable, dangerous partner whose very presence promised carnage for their foes.

"Stay behind me," he commanded, his eyes blazing, a stark contrast to his calm tone.

But Jubilee felt the glade thrumming with renewed purpose beneath her feet, a powerful response to the emerging threat. The luminescent flower, still showering them in glowing pollen, pulsed with defiant energy. The raw, untamed magic she had just shared with Slash, the power that had shattered her and rebuilt her, pulsed within her veins, hot and eager.

"No," she responded, stepping out from behind him, her own hands beginning to glow with an emerald light. Her forest magic, now emboldened, sharpened, and intertwined with the memory of his shadow, felt more potent than ever. "This is our glade. We defend it. Together."

A feral grin spread across Slash's face, a flash of pure, primal satisfaction. He glanced at her, a flicker of something akin to pride in his violet eyes, before turning back to the advancing Grolak.

"As you wish, little Elf," he murmured, the words a dark promise. "Let's show them what happens when shadows and light unite."

With a roar that was more beast than elf, Slash launched himself forward, a torrent of sharp, coiling shadows erupting from his hands, striking the lead Grolak with brutal force. Jubilee, feeling the surge of power within her, unleashed a wave of emerald energy, lashing out at the grotesque creatures from behind him, determined to protect their sacred space, and their incredible, dangerous connection.

27

The glade pulsed, not with shared passion, but with raw, searing power as Jubilee unleashed her fury. Her emerald glow intensified, pushing back the oppressive darkness of the Grolak. Roots, once docile and entwined with the earth, now clawed their way to the surface, lashing out like vengeful serpents. One slammed into a Grolak's chest, lifting it clean off its feet before flinging it into the deeper shadows of the forest. Another erupted beneath a cluster of scavengers, sending them sprawling in every direction.

Slash watched, his eyes wide, a flicker of pain momentarily forgotten in the sheer, blinding spectacle of Jubilee unbound. Her magic was a tidal wave, a hurricane of verdant energy that didn't just repel, it annihilated. The luminescent flower, revitalized by her ferocious surge, flared so brightly it cast long, dancing shadows, momentarily turning the glade into an ethereal, emerald-lit sanctuary.

The Grolak, creatures of instinct and opportunism, were utterly overwhelmed. Their cunning evaporated, replaced by genuine terror. They didn't just retreat; they fled, scrambling over each other in a desperate, panicked rout. Their guttural cries of aggression morphed into whimpers of desperate flight as Jubilee's magic chased them, pushing them far past the glade's sacred borders.

Jubilee stood panting, her chest heaving, the emerald light slowly receding from her form, leaving behind only the lingering shimmer of exhausted power. The glade remained vibrant, pulsating with renewed life, purged of the scavengers' foul presence. She turned, her gaze immediately finding Slash, who was still leaning heavily against the ancient oak. The obsidian wound on his side, though no longer actively draining him, still seeped a dark, viscous fluid.

"Slash!" she gasped, rushing to him, her rage evaporating, replaced by gnawing concern. She knelt, her fingers hovering over the wound, not daring to touch the poisoned blade that remained lodged in his flesh.

He offered her a weak, lopsided smile, one that didn't quite reach his pain-filled eyes. "Impressive, little sprout. Quite the... fireworks display." His voice was raspy, laced with effort. "Didn't realize you had that in you."

"You're hurt," she whispered, her voice thick with unspent emotion. The thought of losing him, after just finding him, after just surrendering to him, was a sharp, unbearable pain. "That obsidian… it's poisoned."

"A minor inconvenience," he dismissed, though his pallor and the tremor in his hands belied his words. "It drains magic. Keeps the victim weak. A favored tactic of my people's enemies." He trailed off, his gaze scanning the now-quiet glade, then lingering on the direction the Grolak had fled. "But they weren't acting alone."

Jubilee frowned, following his gaze. The Grolak were unintelligent scavengers, opportunists drawn to disruption. They weren't known for coordinated attacks, much less carrying weaponized obsidian.

"What do you mean?" she asked, a new unease settling over her.

Slash slowly pushed himself upright, wincing with the movement. "These creatures are just puppets. Scavengers, yes, but easily manipulated. And that blade…" He touched the hilt, a dark scowl deepening on his face. "That's no Grolak craft. That is Elderwood Obsidian. Forged by dark fae who consider even my kind… crude."

A cold dread spread through Jubilee, eclipsing her concern for Slash's wound, if only for a moment. Elderwood. A name whispered in hushed tones in even the most ancient elf tales, a name synonymous with ruthless power and insatiable ambition. If they were involved, if they were manipulating the Grolak, then this was no random skirmish. This was a calculated attack.

"Who would send them?" she breathed, her eyes widening as the implications slammed into her.

Slash met her gaze, his violet eyes simmering with cold fury, tinged with a predatory glint. "Someone who wants this glade. Someone who wants us. And judging by that blade, someone who wants to break me. Which means," he added, his lips curling into a dangerous smile, "they just made a very grave mistake."

The glade, now returned to its gentle luminescence, felt different. No longer merely a sanctuary, but a beacon. A dangerous, alluring prize, now publicly claimed. The Grolak had been a nuisance, but their swift retreat under Jubilee's power had revealed a much larger, and far more formidable, shadow already lurking in the periphery, watching, calculating. Their battle had only just begun.

28

The emerald inferno that erupted from Jubilee wasn't just light; it was life, rage, and an unyielding will. It slammed into the Grolak, not merely repelling them, but searing them, leaving trails of acrid smoke where it touched. They fell back, a scattering tide of grotesque fear, their primitive minds incapable of comprehending such raw, focused power. The glade, which had dimmed with Slash's pain, pulsed anew, reflecting Jubilee's unleashed fury.

Slash, still swaying, watched her, his violet eyes wide, not with pain, but with something akin to awe. He saw the shift in her, the complete absence of doubt, the fierce, protective instinct that burned brighter than any flame. His own shadow magic, though weakened, instinctively responded to her surge, a subtle hum of recognition beneath his skin.

"Jubilee..." His voice was a rasp, a mixture of disbelief and wonder.

But she didn't hear him. Her attention was solely on him, on the dark, spreading stain on his hip, on the malevolent shimmer of the obsidian. The instant she got close enough, pushing past the last lingering Grolak, the glade's magic surged into her hands. It was an intuitive, unbidden response, a desperate need to mend.

She knelt beside him, her fingers brushing against the obsidian blade. It felt cold, ancient, insidious. It was tethered to him, drawing from his very essence. Her magic, the vibrant green that usually pulsed with gentle life, hardened, becoming a sharp, focused beam aimed at the blade. It was a surgical tool crafted of raw energy.

"This isn't just a simple wound," she murmured, her voice tight with concentration. She recognized the nature of the obsidian, its parasitic properties. "It's draining you."

Slash gritted his teeth, a flicker of vulnerability in his gaze. "Elderwood," he managed, his breath ragged. "They learned how to copy... the deeper magic."

Jubilee didn't fully grasp his meaning, but she understood the urgency. Her hands, still glowing with emerald light, pressed against the wound, not on Slash's skin, but around the embedded obsidian. She wasn't trying to pull it out; she was trying to sever its hold, to disrupt its malevolent absorption.

A jolt, sharp and unexpected, shot through her. It wasn't pain, but a sudden, overwhelming influx of information. She felt the ancient, dark magic of the blade, its history, its purpose, its insidious connection to the Elderwood. And then, she felt Slash. Not just his physical wound, but the intricate web of his shadow magic, the raw power that flowed beneath his skin, the fragile balance that the blade was disrupting.

It was as if she could see the swirling colors of his essence, the violet and black intertwining, now marred by a siphoning gray. A new instinct bloomed within her - not just to heal, but to actively counter, to replenish.

Her emerald power didn't just push against the blade; it threaded itself into the very fabric of Slash's shadow, a delicate, complex dance of restoration. She wasn't just sealing a physical cut; she was mending the tear in his being, closing the drain.

A gasp tore from Slash's lips, not of pain, but of profound shock. His muscles, rigid with strain, relaxed incrementally. The oppressive gray around the wound began to recede, replaced by a subtle, deep purple glow emanating from Jubilee's hands.

The luminescent flower in the glade, which had been barely glowing, brightened considerably, mirroring the surge of energy between them. The air itself thrummed, a tangible resonance of light and shadow finding harmony.

Jubilee pushed deeper, abandoning caution, guided by an intuition that transcended anything she'd known. She felt the obsidian shiver, its hold weakening. With a final, agonizing surge of her new, potent magic, she pulsed, severing the last threads of its parasitic grip.

The obsidian blade, now inert and dull, clattered to the ground.

Slash's wound, though still a jagged tear, no longer bled. The rapid, corrosive spread of the dark magic had halted. A faint, silver glow, not emerald, not violet, but something entirely new, rippled across his skin where her hands had been.

He looked at her, his expression a mixture of profound relief and utter bewilderment. His hand, no longer clutching his side, reached out, trembling, and cupped her jaw. His fingers traced the delicate curve of her cheek, his thumb brushing over her lips.

"Jubilee," he whispered, his voice deep, raw with emotion. It was a question, an affirmation, a desperate plea. "What... what was that?"

She met his gaze, her own emerald eyes wide with the realization of what she had done, what she was capable of. A new power, a new understanding had blossomed within her. She had not only healed him, but touched the very essence of his being, fusing with him in a way more profound than physical intimacy.

"I don't know," she breathed, the words barely audible. "But Eldrin... this glade... it taught me."

He pulled her closer, his embrace still hesitant, but filled with an unspoken gratitude that resonated deeper than any words. The danger was not over, she knew, but for this moment, in the heart of their transformed glade, they were whole, and unimaginably more powerful.

29

The fragile peace of the moment shattered, ripped apart by a guttural, terrifying roar that echoed from beyond the glade's shimmering borders. It wasn't the familiar, frantic snarl of a lone Grolak scout. This was a symphony of savagery, a concerted surge of grotesque fury.

Jubilee and Slash sprang apart, their earlier intimacy replaced by an immediate, instinctive readiness for battle. The air, which had thrummed with gentle healing magic moments before, now vibrated with raw malevolence.

"They're back," Slash growled, his hand instinctively going to where the wound had been, finding only smooth skin. The relief was palpable, but fleeting. "And there are more of them."

He was right. As the first wave of Grolak burst through the tree line, they appeared larger, their crude weapons glinting with a disturbing, dark sheen, almost an iridescent black. Their eyes, usually dull with feral hunger, glowed with an unnatural, malicious intelligence. They were not mere scavengers this time.

"They've been... enhanced," Jubilee whispered, a chill tracing her spine. She sensed the insidious essence woven through their forms—a subtle, calculated infusion of shadow magic far more refined than anything the Grolak could conjure on their own. "Elderwood," she breathed, the connection clicking into place.

Slash's jaw tightened. "A pleasure," he sneered, a dangerous glint in his violet eyes. "They always were too cowardly to face me directly." His gaze swept over the approaching horde, assessing their numbers. "There's a puppet master. See if you can sense them."

But before Jubilee could focus, the Grolak charged, a torrent of sharp claws, rusted blades, and guttural cries. They were faster, stronger, and unnervingly organized. The glade, so recently a haven of blossoming life, became a battleground once more.

Slash met the first wave with a surge of renewed shadow energy, tendrils of darkness lashing out, seizing and flinging the creatures aside. But even as they were thrown, they scrambled back up, their enhanced forms remarkably resilient.

Jubilee, no longer hesitant, let her emerald magic flow. She focused on the ground, calling forth roots that erupted from the earth, coiling around the

Grolak's legs, tripping them, ensnaring them. Her light pulsed, not just repelling, but subtly disrupting the dark enhancements that made them so tenacious. Sparking emerald energy flew from her hands, striking the creatures, making them shriek as their unnatural strength momentarily faltered.

"They're not just stronger," Slash grunted, parrying a surprisingly swift strike from a Grolak with a blade forged from darkened wood. "They're less... mindless."

He moved with a deadly grace, a blur of shadow tearing through the enemy ranks. But even his power was being pushed. One Grolak, larger than the others, managed to land a raking blow against his arm, the obsidian-tinged claw leaving a shallow, but instantly darkening, scratch.

Jubilee saw it, and a fresh wave of fury pulsed through her. She unleashed a concentrated burst of emerald light, catching the Grolak mid-swipe, disintegrating it into a cloud of dust and acrid smoke.

"Watch your back!" she cried, a warning that was echoed by a new, more sinister sound. From the shadowed edges of the glade, sleek, dark figures emerged. Not Grolak, but fae. Shadow fae. Their forms were cloaked, their movements silent, their eyes glinting with cold, predatory malice.

They held bows, strung with arrows that crackled with dark energy, and their faces were masked, yet Jubilee sensed the familiar arrogance, the controlled cruelty.

"Ah, there they are," Slash's voice was a low snarl, a hint of dark satisfaction mixed with pure rage. "Always hiding in the shadows."

A volley of dark arrows hissed through the air, aimed directly for Slash. He spun, weaving a shield of shadow that absorbed the projectiles, but the sheer number of them pulled at his replenished energy.

Jubilee, seeing him momentarily engaged, turned her attention to the new threat. Her forest magic resonated defensively, weaving a shield of vibrant green light that deflected the next wave of arrows aimed at her.

"The glade protects!" she declared, her voice ringing with defiance. The ancient oak behind her pulsed, mirroring her power, its very essence rising to meet the challenge. The glowing luminescent flower swayed, radiating a calming yet potent energy that seemed to subtly disorient the advancing Shadow Fae.

"They want *us*," Slash stated, his violet eyes locked on one of the cloaked figures, who seemed to be directing the Grolak. "And they want to conquer this glade. Let's make them regret both."

He launched himself forward, a streak of darkness, straight into the heart of the Shadow Fae formation. Jubilee, now fully attuned to his movements, became his emerald counterpoint. Root-tendrils ensnared, light-blasts disoriented, and the very air around them crackled with the unprecedented fusion of their combined power. The new harmony they had forged, born of intimacy and desperation, was now their most potent weapon. The glade, their shared haven, was under attack, and they would defend it with every fiber of their entwined beings.

30

The glade transformed into a swirling vortex of light and shadow, verdant energy clashing with obsidian power. Slash, a dark blur, tore through the Shadow Fae ranks, his movements swift and brutal. Jubilee, a beacon of emerald light, followed his lead, her magic a fierce shield and a binding snare. Yet, for all their combined might, the sheer number of foes, both Grolak and Shadow Fae, threatened to overwhelm them.

A particularly large Grolak, its eyes burning with enhanced savagery, lunged at Jubilee, a crude, blackened ax lifted high. Before she could erect a full shield, Slash was there, a dark, protective shape between her and the blow. His own shadow tendrils flared, but the Grolak was surprisingly swift, its ax biting into Slash's side.

"Slash!" Jubilee cried, a wave of familiar fear, cold and sharp, striking her. The glade's magic surged through her, an indignant roar against the injustice of its wounds.

Slash barely grunted, a flicker of pain crossing his face before being replaced by a terrifying, cold fury she had only glimpsed until now. He looked at the Grolak, then at the cloaked Shadow Fae still directing the assault, and an almost imperceptible shift occurred within him. The air around him shimmered, growing denser, darker. It wasn't just shadow magic now; it was something profoundly *other*, something ancient and vast.

One of the lead Shadow Fae, clearly a commander, pointed at Slash, shouting an order in their harsh tongue. A surge of amplified Grolak charged, alongside a fresh volley of dark arrows and even a trio of Shadow Fae, their blades drawn, moving with menacing precision.

Slash's eyes, already a deep violet, deepened further, almost black, and pulsed with an inner, incandescent malevolence. A resonant hum filled the glade, emanating from him, vibrating through the very earth. Jubilee felt a primal instinct to recoil, yet a strange, terrifying awe held her rooted.

"Enough," Slash's voice rumbled, no longer human or fae, but something deeper, more elemental. His hand, bathed in an impossibly deep, shifting darkness, reached out. It wasn't a shadow, not exactly. It was a void, a hungry, consuming absence.

Then, he unleashed it.

From his outstretched hand, a torrent of pure, unadulterated darkness erupted. Not a tendril, not a blast, but a sweeping, expanding wave of utter entropy. It washed over the nearest Grolak, and they didn't just vanish; they *unmade*. Their forms dissolved, not into dust or smoke, but into nothingness, leaving behind not even an echo.

The wave surged forward, obliterating the ground, extinguishing light, and consuming sound. The attacking Shadow Fae, caught in its path, shrieked, their cloaks fluttering for a mere heartbeat before they, too, ceased to exist. Jubilee watched, horrified and mesmerized, as the very essence of beings was wiped from existence. The trees shuddered, their ancient magic instinctively recoiling from this ultimate dissolution. Even the air felt thin, robbed of its vibrancy.

The glade, moments ago alive with battle, was plunged into an unnatural, chilling silence. Only the soft pulse of Jubilee's own magic, and the thrumming, now receding, power within Slash, remained. Where the wave had passed, there was only barren, lifeless earth, stripped of all energy, all matter. A perfect, terrifying blankness.

Slash stood amidst the devastation, his chest heaving slightly, the earlier wound on his side gone, his eyes slowly returning to their familiar, albeit intense, violet. He looked at Jubilee, his expression unreadable.

"That," he said, his voice now normal, but laced with a bone-deep weariness, "is why they usually hide."

Jubilee could only stare, her emerald magic flickering uncertainly around her. She had thought she knew the extent of his power. She had been wrong. This was beyond shadow, beyond even forest magic. It was the power to erase, to unmake. And a terrifying, exhilarating shiver ran down her spine. The raw, untamed force she felt within him, the source of this unimaginable power, was something she now knew, on a visceral level, she was connected to. And it shattered her understanding of everything she thought she knew about him, and about them.

31

The silence was absolute, heavier than any sound. Jubilee's breath hitched, caught somewhere between a gasp and a sob. She looked from the barren earth, still smoking with a faint, unholy vapor, to Slash. His eyes, though returned to violet, still held echoes of that terrifying void. The air around him, once thick with destructive power, now felt strangely brittle.

Before she could form a single word, before the enormity of what she'd witnessed could fully settle, Slash swayed. It was a subtle movement at first, barely a tremor, then more pronounced. His broad shoulders slumped, the vibrant intensity in his gaze dimming. A faint sheen of sweat beaded on his brow, catching the last lingering rays of the glade's magic.

"Slash?" she whispered, her voice cracking, the question loaded with a thousand unspoken fears.

He raised a hand, as if to steady himself, but it trembled, then clenched, as if trying to grasp something just beyond his reach. The wound that had been in his side, miraculously gone moments before, now reappeared, a jagged, dark line seeping a slow, black ichor. His skin, usually so vibrant even in its shadow tones, took on an ashen pallor, and a sharp, ragged cough tore from his throat.

Then, with a low groan that pulled at a primal cord within her, he collapsed.

It wasn't a controlled descent, but a sudden, boneless crumple. His dark form buckled, hitting the bare earth with a soft thud. He lay there, unmoving, stretched out on the very ground he had just stripped of life. The powerful, terrifying shadow fae, who had moments ago commanded the forces of annihilation, was now utterly vulnerable, a dark, fragile silhouette against the wounded glade.

Jubilee rushed forward, her bare feet pounding on the cold, desecrated earth. All thought of fear, of awe, of the horrifying power he'd unleashed, vanished. Only instinct remained—the urgent need to reach him, to touch him, to understand. She knelt beside him, her hands hovering, afraid to touch the skin that had just channeled such destruction, yet desperate to confirm he was real, that he was still him.

"Slash!" she cried, her voice rising in panic. She reached out, her fingers trembling as they grazed his cheek. His skin was cold, clammy. The subtle thrum of his shadow magic, always present, was now almost imperceptible, a faint, flickering ember.

His eyelids fluttered, revealing the deepest violet, clouded with pain and exhaustion. He tried to speak, a rasping sound escaping his lips. "Jubilee..."

His voice was a mere whisper, thin and fragile. The invincibility he had projected, the terrifying control, had completely evaporated, leaving behind a raw, alarming vulnerability. She saw the lines of fatigue etched around his eyes, the subtle tremor in his limp hands. He looked utterly drained, as if the immense power he had summoned had not merely eradicated his enemies, but had carved a piece out of himself.

The raw emotion, the lingering tendrils of fear, transformed into a fierce, protective surge within her. He was wounded. He was weak. And despite everything, despite the horror of what he'd done, she found herself consumed by a desperate need to heal him, to protect him. The glade's magic, which had recoiled in terror moments before, now stirred in response to her own fierce resolve, a faint, emerald glow beginning to coalesce around her hands. His power was destructive, but hers... hers was life.

She met his gaze, saw the last vestiges of that ancient void fading, replaced by profound weariness. And in that moment, as he lay broken before her, she knew with absolute certainty that this wasn't just about survival, or destiny, or even desire. It was about connection, stronger and more complex than she could have ever imagined. He, the unmaker, was utterly dependent on her, the life-bringer.

32

The emerald glow around Jubilee's hands intensified, a desperate, intuitive response to the urgent need radiating from Slash. Her fingers moved, tracing the jagged, black line seeping ichor on his side. This was no ordinary wound; it pulsed with a malevolent energy, a slow, insidiousemptiness that seemed to drain his very essence. Her previous healing touch had mended, but this went deeper, attacking the fundamental core of his being. She needed to get him away from here, away from the desecrated ground that still thrummed with the aftershocks of his destructive power.

"We need to move you," she whispered, her voice firm despite the tremor in her hands. He was heavy, impossibly so, a dead weight against the earth. His breathing was shallow, ragged, each breath a struggle. The ashen pallor of his skin filled her with a cold dread.

She tried to slide an arm under his shoulders, to lever him up, but he was like granite, infused with the solid, immovable power he wielded. Even in his weakened state, his physical form held an intrinsic density that defied her strength. It was a stark reminder of the immeasurable power he still held, a power that could annihilate by its mere presence, and yet now threatened to drag him into oblivion.

A low groan escaped his lips. His eyelids fluttered open, his violet eyes unfocused and distant. "Too... heavy..." he rasped, the words barely audible.

"Don't talk," she urged, her brow furrowing with effort. She shifted, trying to get a better leverage, grunting as she strained. The ground beneath them, still scorched and brittle from his entropic blast, crumbled under her knees. She felt the painful scrape of sharp debris against her skin, but ignored it.

The glade, in its wounded state, seemed to whisper to her. The remaining patches of vitality, the twisted roots that clawed at the devastated earth, offered faint pulses of energy. It was a sorrowful, exhausted magic, but it was still magic. Her eyes fell on a cluster of thick, resilient vines clinging to a miraculously untouched part of the ancient oak. An idea, desperate and risky, sparked in her mind.

If she couldn't lift him physically, perhaps she could move him... magically. It wasn't a movement spell she knew. Her magic was for growing, for healing, for defending. But their connection, the potent, dangerous merging of their powers, had transformed her. She had healed him, she had fought with him, she had felt the very essence of his being entwined with hers.

She closed her eyes, reaching out not with her hands, but with her very spirit. She felt the heavy, draining presence of his wound, the rapid ebb of his shadow. Then, she reached deeper, trying to find the core of his being, the anchor of his immense power. It was like trying to grasp smoke, formless yet present.

She focused on the glade, willing it to aid her. The green light intensified around her, now pulsing not just from her hands but radiating from her entire being. She willed the vines of the oak, the very resilient spirit of the forest that remained, to entwine with his essence, to cradle him, to lift him.

Slowly, agonizingly, a faint hum began to emanate from the ground around Slash. The untouched roots beneath him, the tough tendrils of grass that stubbornly clung to life, began to writhe, ever so slightly. A shimmering, green aura enveloped his prone form, a stark contrast to the black ichor seeping from his side.

Her muscles screamed with the effort, her forehead beaded with sweat matching the faint sheen on his. She was pulling him, not with physical strength, but with pure, raw magical will. The glade groaned in protest, its wounded heart still reeling from the chaos. But it responded, nudged by Jubilee's desperate, protective fervor.

Bit by bit, an inch at a time, Slash's body began to float, suspended just above the scorched earth. He hung there, a dark, heavy silhouette cradled by a fragile, emerald glow. It was a terrifying, beautiful sight, the destroyer held aloft by the very life he had ravaged.

"Good," she panted, her voice strained. Her vision blurred at the edges, the strain immense. "Now… we move." She began to guide him, directing the shimmering, vine-like enchantment towards a secluded grotto nestled deeper within the glade, a place of ancient, undisturbed earth where the magic still flowed pure and strong. Every step was a battle against his immense magical weight, against her own dwindling energy, against the very glade's exhaustion. But failure was not an option. He was vulnerable, and she was his only hope.

The journey to the grotto was arduous, a slow, agonizing ballet of magic and sheer determination. Each inch Slash drifted forward, suspended by the emerald currents Jubilee willed into existence, felt like a mile. The glade, though responding to her desperate call, seemed to resist, its wounds echoing her own fatigue. Her arms ached, not from physical exertion, but from the relentless magical strain. Her mind felt like a finely tuned instrument stretched taut, vibrating on the edge of snapping. Yet, with every faint, ragged breath Slash took, with every silent plea from his ashen face, she pushed past the pain, drawing on a wellspring of protective fury she hadn't known she possessed.

Finally, they reached the grotto. It was a haven of moss-covered rocks and ancient, gnarled roots, where a trickle of pure spring water ceaselessly spilled into a crystal-clear pool. Here, the air was thicker, imbued with an undisturbed, potent energy. The scorched earth gave way to soft, cool moss, and the oppressive silence of destruction was replaced by the gentle murmur of unseen life.

With a final, trembling surge of power, Jubilee gently lowered Slash onto a bed of particularly plush, luminous green moss at the edge of the pool. The emerald glow around him dissipated, leaving him starkly vulnerable against the vibrant green. He lay there, utterly still, his breathing shallower, his skin now even more alarmingly pale.

She knelt beside him, her exhaustion momentarily forgotten. Her gaze immediately fell to the wound on his side. Her heart plummeted. It wasn't just seeping; it was actively pulsing, a dark, malevolent heart beating within his flesh. The black ichor was no longer a trickle but a slow, continuous ooze, staining the lush moss beneath him. The wound seemed to writhe, subtly expanding, as if devouring him from within.

"Slash?" she whispered, her voice laced with growing panic. She gently placed a hand on his chest. His skin was cold, clammy. Her previous burst of healing energy, the severing of the blade's parasitic hold, had been enough to stabilize him, to keep him from immediate collapse. But this... this was different. The glade's initial protest to his destructive power, coupled with the Elderwood blade's lingering poison, had left a deeper, more insidious mark than she had realized. It was an attack on his very essence, a corrosive drain on his shadow magic that threatened to snuff him out entirely.

His eyes remained closed. He was slipping away, faster than she could comprehend. Her internal alarm bells screamed. Healing the physical wound, even severing its magical connection, had been reactive. This demanded something more profound, something that would target the very core of his being, that elusive, formless essence she had struggled to grasp even in her earlier attempts to move him.

She spread her hands over the pulsing wound, willing her purest emerald magic to flow. A faint green light began to emanate, bathing his side, but it seemed to be absorbed, swallowed by the encroaching darkness of the wound, doing little to stem the flow of ichor. It was like pouring water into a bottomless pit.

Desperation clawed at her. She heard faint echoes of Eldrin in her mind, a sharp, bitter pang of guilt. Had she healed him too, he might have been able to help now. But Eldrin was gone, and she was all he had. The weight of that responsibility settled heavy on her shoulders.

"No," she murmured, her voice hardening with resolve. "You don't get to die. Not now. Not after all of this."

She closed her eyes, pushing deeper than she ever had before. She didn't just seek to mend his flesh, or even sever the dark threads of the lingering poison. She sought the connection she had felt during their union, the intimate merging of their light and shadow, the fundamental resonance that bound them. Her magic, the purest, brightest emerald, would have to merge directly with his intrinsic shadow, not to fight it, but to bolster it, to mend the very fabric of his being. This wasn't about healing a wound; it was about rejuvenating a dying star, knitting back together the fragmented essence of a god-like being.

It was audacious. It was terrifying. But it was his only chance. And hers.

Jubilee took a shaky breath, then plunged inward, not just into her own magic, but into the memory of their intertwined power. She recalled the intoxicating rush when his shadow had met her light, when the glade itself had bloomed with impossible beauty. She visualized that union, that perfect, dangerous balance, and reached for it now, desperately.

Her emerald light pulsed, not around the wound, but directly into the heart of the darkness seeping from it. It was like tendrils of pure consciousness, probing, seeking the very core of Slash's being, that primal shadow essence that had been corrupted and diminished. The process was agonizing, a tearing sensation within her own magical core as she bypassed all physical defenses, all previous understanding of healing, and sought to merge with something fundamentally alien to her own nature.

A jolt, like lightning, coursed through her. It wasn't Slash's consciousness, not exactly, but a raw, unadulterated echo of his power. It was vast and cold, ancient and boundless. She felt the searing pain of his wound as if it were her own, the gnawing emptiness where his power had been drained. For a moment, she was overwhelmed, a fragile vessel trying to contain a supernova. Her vision swam, and a whimper escaped her lips.

But beneath the pain, there was something else. A flicker of warmth, an ingrained memory of dominance and fierce protectiveness, the very essence of Slash that had both terrified and drawn her. She latched onto that, pouring her own life force into it, nourishing it with her emerald vibrancy.

Slowly, imperceptibly at first, a shift began. The black ichor on the moss beneath Slash's side began to recede, absorbed back into the wound as if drawn by an invisible force. The angry pulsations of the wound lessened, replaced by a faint, rhythmic thrum. Jubilee felt a profound, almost sexual current resonate through her, an ethereal hum born from the merging of their two disparate, yet profoundly connected, energies.

Her emerald magic, no longer merely flowing *into* Slash, began to intertwine *with* his shadow. It was not a battle, but a dance, each seeking the other, bolstering, rebuilding. She felt the chill of his essence, the subtle taste of cosmic dust and ancient power, infusing her own being. And in return, she offered him the warmth of life, the vibrant pulse of the glade's renewal, the unyielding strength of her light.

A breath hitched in Slash's throat, a ragged gasp that was, nonetheless, stronger than any she had heard from him since his collapse. His eyelids fluttered, a sliver of dark violet visible beneath the lashes. A tremor ran through his languid frame.

Then, the glade around them responded. Not with the frantic, terrified magic of earlier, but with a deep, resonant hum. The moss beneath them pulsed with an inner luminescence, brighter than before. The spring water in the grotto shimmered with an almost iridescent glow, reflecting unseen colors. The air grew thick with a potent, heady scent of ozone and freshly turned earth, a primal aroma of creation and immense power.

It wasn't just Slash she was healing; it was the glade. It was herself. Their very essences were becoming inextricably linked, forging a bond far more profound than their first magical union under the ancient oak. This was a merging at a cellular, elemental level, rewriting the rules of their existence.

As the last vestiges of the black ichor vanished and the raw wound transformed into a faint, healing scar, Jubilee felt an intense surge of power ripple through her. It was Slash's power, intermingled with her own, not diminished, but somehow... amplified. Different. His eyelids parted fully, revealing pupils that were not merely violet, but shot through with startling flashes of emerald, like fractured jewels. His gaze, though still clouded with exhaustion, was undeniably his. He looked at her, his lips parting in a silent, almost reverent awe, as if seeing her for the first time, seeing the impossible magic that now bound them. The world shifted on its axis, irreversibly changed.

35

A low growl rumbled deep in the earth, far more guttural and expansive than any Grolak. It vibrated through the moss beneath Jubilee, thrumming against her very bones, a direct counterpoint to the vibrant, healing energy still coursing between her and Slash. The iridescent glow of the grotto flickered erratically, as if struggling against an encroaching darkness. The air, so recently thick with potent creation, now tasted metallic, stinging with an acrid ozone far less pleasant than the last.

Slash's eyes, still shimmering with emerald flecks, snapped fully open. The apathetic exhaustion that had held him captive moments before was replaced by an alertness so sharp it was almost painful. He pushed himself up, a slight tremor in his muscular arm, but the raw power radiating from him, even in his weakened state, was undeniable. The scar on his side, though faint, pulsed with a faint violet light, a testament to Jubilee's profound intervention.

"They return," his voice was still rough, a gravelly whisper, but laced with a lethal certainty that made Jubilee's blood run cold. "And they bring more than just their foul creatures this time."

Before she could form a question, the grotto entrance, previously shrouded in the glade's healing magic, shimmered and then dissolved. A wave of sickly, oppressive gloom poured in, chilling Jubilee to the core. It was a darkness far more ancient and malevolent than Slash's shadow, almost a void that consumed light rather than merely obscuring it.

From this encroaching emptiness, figures emerged. Not the crude Grolak, nor the simple cloaked Shadow Fae from before. These were darker, taller, their forms shifting like living shadows, their eyes burning with a cruel, malevolent light that seemed to mirror the Elderwood's poison. They moved with a predatory grace, weapons materializing from the shadows they embodied — obsidian daggers, bows strung with strands of pure night.

"The High Shade," Slash hissed, leveraging himself upright, his emerald-shot gaze fixed on the lead figure, whose presence commanded the very darkness around them. "They'll stop at nothing to claim this glade. They taste the power we've just awakened."

Jubilee, still reeling from the profound magical merger with Slash, felt a surge of fear, but it was quickly overshadowed by a fierce, protective defiance. This grotto, this glade, had just become a part of her, and even more so, a part of Slash, whom she now found herself inextricably bound to, almost like a piece of her own soul. The echoes of his vast, ancient power still resonated within her, a thrilling, terrifying thrum of understanding.

Before the High Shades could fully materialize, Slash launched forward, a shadow bullet. Despite his recent reanimation, he moved with a speed that defied their expectations, a dark streak coalescing into raw power. He met the approaching darkness with a furious, primal roar, his re-infused shadow magic lashing out in devastating tendrils. The Grolak, caught in the wake of the High Shades, shrieked as they were caught and disintegrated.

Jubilee, for a fraction of a second, wavered. Her healing had been exhausting, and the direct communion with Slash's core essence had left her feeling both exhilarated and strangely hollowed. But seeing him, still weakened yet fighting with such ferocious abandon, ignited a fresh surge of power within her. Her emerald magic flared, a defiant beacon against the encroaching gloom. The roots beneath her feet began to writhe, an emerald light rippling through the grotto's very stone.

"This glade is ours!" she roared, her voice echoing with a newfound authority, a blend of ancient forest magic and the raw, untamed power that now bound her to Slash. She extended her hand, not towards an attacking enemy, but outwards, encompassing the very magic of the grotto, drawing it inward, preparing to unleash it with a fury born of desperate love and unbreakable connection. This was no longer just about survival; it was about protecting what they had forged, what they had become.

36

The tendrils of emerald light coalesced in Jubilee's outstretched hand, forming a shimmering orb that pulsed with untamed power. She felt the ancient magic of the grotto rise to meet her, eager to be unleashed. But before she could launch her attack, a low, guttural snarl rippled through the encroaching darkness, a sound that froze both the High Shades and Jubilee herself. It was not a Grolak's shriek, nor Slash's primal roar. This was the sound of something vast, ancient, and utterly merciless.

The oppressive gloom, momentarily held at bay by Slash's ferocity, seemed to shudder. A section of the grotto's entrance, previously vacated by the advancing High Shades, rippled violently. Then, with a sound like tearing fabric, the shadows there parted, and a creature stepped through.

It was immense, its form vaguely leonine, but crafted from pure, swirling void. Its mane was a cascade of nebulae, its eyes two smoldering coals in the darkness. Obsidian claws, each the size of a sapling, clicked against the grotto floor as it moved. A faint, ethereal glow emanated from it, not of light, but of pure cosmic emptiness. The High Shades, for the first time, recoiled, their predatory confidence replaced by a primal, superstitious dread. Even Slash, in the midst of his furious assault, faltered, his shadow tendrils recoiling slightly from the monstrous arrival.

"A Void Beast," Slash rasped, his voice raw with disbelief and a hint of something akin to fear. "Impossible. They haven't stirred in millennia."

Jubilee stared, her emerald orb flickering. This new entity was magnificent and terrifying, a force of nature that dwarfed even the formidable High Shades. It moved with a slow, deliberate majesty, its attention fixed not on the battle, but on something just beyond the grotto's fragmented entrance, something unseen but clearly its target.

Then, a voice, deep as a subterranean river and resonant as a cosmic hum, echoed through the grotto, not from the Void Beast, but from the darkness behind it. "Indeed, Slash. It seems your little 'awakening' has drawn more than just petty scavengers."

A figure emerged from the swirling shadows, walking with an unnerving stillness that made the Void Beast seem almost... tame. He was tall, impossibly slender, clad in robes the color of a moonless night, edged with what looked like starlight. His face was sharp, aristocratic, framed by hair as white as bleached bone. His eyes, however, were the most arresting feature: twin points of pure, pulsating red, like distant supernovas.

"Malakor," Slash spat, a venomous edge returning to his voice, all hint of fear gone, replaced by incandescent rage. "I should have known you'd slither from your forgotten corners."

Malakor simply smiled, a chilling, humorless baring of teeth. "The glade hums with a power it hasn't known since before the Great Sundering. Such a pity to see it wasted on... sentiment." His gaze, those burning red points, settled on Jubilee, a assessing glint forming in their depths. "And what is this? A forest nymph, playing with shadows? You surprise me, Slash. Such... domesticity."

His words, dripping with disdain, sparked a fresh wave of fury in Jubilee. She had been observing, trying to comprehend this new, terrifying presence. But his mockery, his casual dismissal of her, solidified her resolve. This was no ally. This was a new, far more dangerous enemy.

Malakor slowly raised a hand, and the Void Beast, which had been standing passively, let out another earth-shaking growl before turning its attention to the High Shades, who were scrambling back in terror. The ancient creature of entropy lunged, and the sound of rending shadow filled the grotto.

"Your problems multiply, Slash," Malakor observed, his gaze never leaving Jubilee. "And I merely choose the easier path. This magic... will be ours."

37

"Ours?" Jubilee echoed, her voice cutting through the escalating chaos as the Void Beast continued its brutal work. Her emerald orb pulsed, dangerously bright, her anger now directed squarely at Malakor. "You speak of possession, not partnership. This glade does not belong to you, nor does its magic."

Malakor's crimson eyes flickered from the struggling High Shades to Jubilee, a sardonic smirk playing on his thin lips. "Eloquent for a creature of the forest. And naive. All power belongs to those with the will to claim it. Is that not what you learned, Slash?" His gaze returned to Slash, a dark amusement kindling in his gaze. "Or perhaps you have forgotten your lessons, little brother."

The words struck Jubilee like a physical blow. "Brother?" she whispered, turning to Slash, who stood rigid, his hand clenching and unclenching at his side, his earlier rage replaced by a terrifying, cold stillness. The tendrils of shadow around him seemed to writhe, agitated by Malakor's pronouncement.

Malakor chuckled, a sound like dry leaves skittering across stone. "Oh, dear. He hasn't told you? How very... sentimental." He sighed dramatically. "But then, Slash always was the sentimental one. Always clinging to the vestiges of... 'honor' and 'conscience'." He stepped closer, his movements impossibly fluid, his red eyes burning into Slash. "Tell her, brother. Tell her of our beginnings in the deepest shadows, of our shared purpose before you strayed, before you became... diluted."

Slash remained silent, his jaw clenched, his violet eyes - now fully violet again, though darker than Jubilee had ever seen them - fixed on Malakor with an intensity that promised violence. The glade itself seemed to hold its breath, sensing the profound shift in the dynamics of this chaotic chamber.

"Allow me, then," Malakor continued, savoring the moment. "We are of the same seed, little forest nymph. Born from the deepest shadows of the Elderwood, forged in the crucible of absolute power. We were destined to be the vanguard of a new age, an era of... pure, untamed magic. But my brother... he developed a fondness for the... 'nuance' of the world. He indulged in curiosity, in exploration. He sought 'balance' where there should only be absolute dominion." Malakor's voice hardened, laced with a profound contempt. "He sought to temper shadow with light. A weakness, I always said."

Jubilee's mind reeled. Slash, a twin? And one who spoke of him with such disdain, as if his very nature, the nature she was learning to love, was a flaw. It explained the shared power, the inherent darkness, but also the startling differences in their methods. Slash sought union; Malakor sought annihilation.

"Malakor," Slash finally spoke, his voice low, guttural, a warning that vibrated through the stones of the grotto. "You will go no further."

"Oh, but I will," Malakor purred, his gaze sweeping over Jubilee, then to the glade beyond, which pulsed with the residual light of their combined magic. "I always do. This glade, this potent source of raw, unrefined magic... it is too valuable to be squandered on your quaint notions of 'balance.' Don't you see, brother? We both seek to reshape the world. I simply offer a more... efficient path." His eyes narrowed. "And you, my dear forest nymph," he said, addressing Jubilee, a predatory glint entering his crimson gaze, "you have just awakened a power greater than you know. A power that will either be mine... or destroy you."

The Void Beast finished its gruesome task, its massive head turning slowly towards them, its smoldering eyes fixing on the trio. The tendrils of shadows that now formed its being seemed to undulate, sensing the coming shift in allegiance. The air crackled with a new, terrifying tension. Blood, both literal and metaphorical, was about to be spilled.

38

The air in the grotto thickened, a tangible weight pressing down on Jubilee as Slash's rage, cold and contained moments before, ignited. "You will regret those words," he snarled, a low, dangerous rumble that seemed to vibrate through the very stones. His violet eyes, still tinged with the emerald of Jubilee's healing, flared into twin points of obsidian. The tendrils of shadow that wreathed him intensified, twisting and coiling like angry serpents, no longer agitated, but focused, honed, and terrifying.

Malakor merely laughed, a sound devoid of mirth, a grating rasp that grated on Jubilee's nerves. "Regret? From you, little brother? You who preach balance, yet stand on the brink of another childish tantrum?" He gestured dismissively towards the Void Beast, which had, with unnerving stillness, fixed its smoldering gaze upon them. "And you expect me to believe you've changed? You still cling to that primitive, destructive impulse."

That was the spark. That was the final, critical push. Slash's control, already frayed by Malakor's presence and taunts, snapped. A guttural roar tore from his throat, echoing the primeval fury that had annihilated parts of the glade. He didn't raise a hand, didn't gesture. Instead, shadow simply erupted from him, a violent, chaotic outburst of pure, untamed darkness. It wasn't the precise, controlled magic of his usual attacks, but a raw, unthinking explosion of power, fueled by a lifetime of resentment and Malakor's cutting words.

The shadow surged outward like a tidal wave, blacker than midnight, dense and suffocating. It ripped through the grotto, tearing at the ancient stone walls, dislodging roots, and sending debris scattering. The Void Beast, massive as it was, recoiled, letting out a pained shriek as the wave of destructive energy washed over it, its shadowy form momentarily flickering and shrinking under the onslaught. Even Malakor, for all his bravado, was caught off guard. He threw up a shimmering, ruby-red shield of his own power, but the violent impact of Slash's uncontrolled burst sent him skidding violently backward, smashing into the grotto wall with a resounding crash.

Jubilee, caught in the terrifying vortex of Slash's unrestrained power, gasped. Her own emerald energy flared instinctively, forming a protective cocoon around her, desperately trying to temper the destructive chaos. She felt the fierce, untamed nature of his magic, a terrifying mirror of the force that had transformed her glade, but amplified a thousandfold. The air was thick with the scent of ozone and tormented earth.

Malakor, though clearly shaken, recovered quickly. He pushed off the wall, his crimson eyes blazing with a mixture of surprise and something akin to a perverse delight. "Ah, there it is! The true Slash! The one who embraced chaos and reveled in destruction!" He coughed, a spray of dark ichor spattering the stone. "Still so predictable, brother. Still so... unrefined."

Slash was panting, his shoulders heaving, the wave of shadow slowly receding but leaving a palpable residue of oppressive darkness behind. The emerald flecks in his eyes had retreated, leaving them a stark, deep violet, brimming with raw fury. He advanced on Malakor, heedless of the lingering threat of the Void Beast, his entire being focused on his hated brother.

"You know nothing of me," Slash rasped, his voice still hoarse with exertion. "You never did. You only ever saw what you wanted to see."

Malakor merely smirked, wiping a streak of ichor from his lips. "Oh, I saw enough, little brother. I saw the weakness that led you to this... this travesty of a glade, to this... forest fae." His gaze flickered to Jubilee, a mocking disdain in his eyes. "You seek balance, but you only achieve dilution. You dull your edge, compromise your power. Look at you. You lash out like a frantic beast, without precision, without purpose."

The insult, that last jab at his control and his connection to Jubilee, resonated. Slash snarled, a primal sound that vibrated deep in Jubilee's bones. This was no longer about strategy, but raw, unfiltered animosity. The battle for the glade, for their future, had just become brutally, irrevocably personal.

The Void Beast, seemingly having recovered from the initial shockwave of Slash's uncontrolled power, let out a low, rumbling growl that vibrated through the grotto. Its massive form, previously flickering and shrinking, solidified once more, its smoldering gaze now fixed not on Jubilee, but on Slash. Malakor, still smirking, glanced over his shoulder as the creature began to shift, its shadowy bulk coalescing into a more defined, menacing shape.

"A rather impressive display, I'll grant you," Malakor drawled, his voice tinged with a dangerous amusement, "but ultimately pointless. Your rage only ever serves to expose your vulnerability, little brother." He gestured with a casual flick of his wrist towards the Void Beast. "And now, if you'll excuse me, I have a creature to remind of its purpose."

But the Void Beast, instead of immediately lunging for Slash, pulsed with an almost electrical energy, and with a guttural roar, it erupted in a surge of dark, concentrated shadow, lashing out at Malakor himself. Malakor's eyes widened, his smirk vanishing instantly as he threw up his ruby-red shield just in time. The impact sent him sprawling across the grotto floor again, even harder than before, landing with a sickening thud. The Void Beast, ignoring the fallen

Malakor, now turned its full, malevolent attention to Slash, its multi-faceted eyes burning with an unsettling, primal hunger. It was clear: the creature was not merely Malakor's puppet, but a being with its own twisted agenda, one that now prioritized the powerfully disrupted Slash.

Jubilee, still shielded by her instinctively flared emerald energy, watched in stunned silence as the dynamic shifted. The raw, untamed fury that had surged through Slash moments before had left him momentarily vulnerable, his breathing still ragged, his body trembling slightly from the immense exertion. He stood there, exposed, as the Void Beast lunged, its massive shadowy claws extended, aiming for his chest.

Time seemed to slow. Jubilee didn't think; she reacted. With a surge of renewed emerald magic, born from a desperate, protective instinct, she pulsed her essence outward, a vibrant green energy washing over Slash, strengthening his weakened form. Simultaneously, she lashed out with tendrils of thorny vines, thick and glowing with her ancient forest power, aiming not for the Void Beast's physical form – she knew her magic wouldn't be as effective against its shadowy essence – but for the fissures, the momentary weak points in its form as it attacked.

Slash, invigorated by Jubilee's surge of power, dodged the Beast's primary attack, his shadow magic flaring, more controlled now, more precise. He met the creature's claws with swirling darkness, deflecting the blow, but the sheer force of the Beast's attack still sent him skidding back, closer to Jubilee's protective sphere.

"It's reacting to the raw power," Jubilee gasped, her voice strained as she channeled more of her energy. "It's drawn to you, Slash! To your... untamed state!"

Malakor, now scrambling to his feet, let out a frustrated growl. "Insolent creature! You forget your master!" He snapped his fingers, and a whip of crimson energy materialized in his hand, lashing out at the Void Beast. But the Beast, seemingly immune to his commands in its frenzy, merely roared again, shifting its focus between its two powerful targets.

The grotto became a chaotic maelstrom of conflicting energies. Slash's precise, honed shadows danced with Jubilee's wild, emerald magic, both attempting to deter the relentless onslaught of the Void Beast. Malakor, furious that his creature was defying him, threw himself into the fray, his ruby-red energy clashing not only with the Beast, but occasionally glancing off Slash's defensive maneuvers, adding another layer of volatile unpredictability.

It was a terrifying, beautiful ballet of destruction and defense. Jubilee, working in perfect, unspoken harmony with Slash, found herself weaving her light around his shadow, strengthening his defenses, anticipating his movements. She lashed out with emerald blasts whenever the Void Beast momentarily exposed a weakness, while Slash, still reeling from his previous exertion, focused on deflecting the Beast's more devastating attacks and parrying Malakor's furious, errant blows.

Malakor, caught between his rebellious creature and his hated brother, roared in frustration. "This is madness! The glade's magic will be consumed by this senseless brawling!"

But Slash merely gritted his teeth, his eyes, still tinged with exhaustion, burning with renewed fury. This wasn't a battle for principle, or even for dominance, anymore. This was a brutal struggle for survival, a desperate dance between three immensely powerful entities, each vying for supremacy in a space too small to hold them all. The ground beneath their feet trembled; the grotto itself seemed to groan under the sheer weight of colliding magic. It was clear that this chaotic, three-way battle was only just beginning.

40

A sharp, almost inhuman hiss tore from Malakor's lips, echoing his frustration. As Jubilee and Slash continued their desperate dance with the Void Beast, the grotto threatened to collapse under the sheer force of their conflicting powers. Malakor, having just narrowly dodged a sweeping, shadowy claw from his own rogue creation, glared first at the Beast, then at Slash, a flicker of something akin to cold calculation replacing his earlier fury.

"Enough!" he bellowed, his voice magically amplified, cutting through the cacophony. "This senseless destruction benefits no one! It threatens the very core of this glade's magic, which I intend to claim whole, not shattered!"

The Void Beast, momentarily distracted by the uncharacteristic command from its erstwhile master, paused its relentless assault on Slash, its multi-faceted eyes swiveling towards Malakor. It still pulsed with an untamed hunger, but a sliver of recognition flickered within its depths.

Slash, still reeling from the Beast's last attack, his shadow magic flaring defensively, scoffed. "You think your words hold sway over that thing now? After your 'impressive display' of control?" The sarcasm dripped from his tone, but his exhaustion was evident in the tremor that ran through his arm.

Malakor's gaze narrowed at Slash, then shifted to Jubilee, who was still actively weaving protective emerald energy around them. "Perhaps not control, little brother, but certainly understanding. This creature cares only for raw power, for consumption. And at this rate, it will consume us all, leaving nothing but dust." He extended a hand, not to attack, but in an almost theatrical gesture of truce. "Unless we work together, for now, to subdue it."

Jubilee, her emerald eyes still locked on the menacing Void Beast, felt a chill run down her spine that had nothing to do with fear. An alliance with Malakor? The thought was repugnant, but she saw the logic in it. The Void Beast, fueled by uncontrolled power, was an immediate, existential threat to the glade itself. And Slash, despite his formidable power, was visibly waning. She glanced at him, her silent question mirrored in his own guarded expression.

"You would truly fight alongside me?" Slash finally grunted, disbelieving. "Your own creature?"

"Desperate times, little brother," Malakor sneered, yet his stance was genuine. He positioned himself, his crimson energy already crackling around his hands. "And this glade is too valuable to be annihilated by an unruly pet. My pet." He shot a menacing look at the Void Beast. "Its hunger has overridden its loyalty. We must sate it, or bind it, before it turns on its own master."

Jubilee made the first move. Trusting her instinct more than her judgment, she amplified her emerald magic, not against the Void Beast, but to create a momentary, shimmering barrier between it and her exhausted lover. "What is your plan?" she demanded of Malakor, her voice tight with urgency.

Malakor's eyes flickered with a hint of surprise at her swift decision, but he didn't hesitate. "Its core operates on pure, unrefined shadow. It can be satiated, or overloaded. Slash, you will draw its essence, drain it of its raw power without letting it consume you. Jubilee, you will use your... unique capabilities to stabilize the grotto, to prevent further collapse, and to create fissures in its construct for Slash to exploit." He paused, then finally, begrudgingly, met Slash's gaze. "And I... I will provide the raw power. Pure, dark energy it cannot resist."

He began to channel, and for the first time, Jubilee felt a terrifying kinship between the brothers. Malakor's shadow magic was not the precise, controlled darkness of Slash, but a vast, primordial void, a deep abyss of raw energy that seemed to momentarily overwhelm even the Void Beast, drawing its attention, mesmerizing it with its sheer magnitude. The air in the grotto grew heavy, suffocating.

"It's a risk," Slash rasped, but he moved, positioning himself opposite Malakor, his hands already gathering the diffused shadowy energy from the glade. "A colossal risk."

"One we must take," Jubilee affirmed, already extending her emerald tendrils of magic, reinforcing the grotto's crumbling walls, her focus split between shoring up their defensive and preparing to exploit the creature's vulnerabilities under Malakor's terrifying lure. An unholy alliance was forged, born of desperation, against a common, rampaging enemy.

41

The grotto thrummed with a grotesque harmony of dark magic. Malakor's primordial shadow roared, a hungry, crushing force that momentarily captivated the Void Beast, drawing its multifaceted gaze like a mesmerized predator. Slash, though weakened, responded with instinctual precision, his own shadows weaving and stretching, attempting to siphon off the Beast's unrefined power as Malakor instructed. Jubilee, her emerald light a stark contrast to the oppressive gloom, worked with desperate speed, shoring up the fracturing grotto walls, her magic a delicate web against the monstrous forces tearing it apart.

Malakor's laugh, a low, guttural rumble, echoed through the cavern. "An impressive display, little brother! You almost make a formidable ally." His words, however, held a new edge, a subtle shift in tone that sent a prickle of unease down Jubilee's spine. Instead of focusing solely on the Void Beast, Malakor's crimson eyes darted to Slash, a predatory gleam flickering within their depths.

The Void Beast, momentarily sated by the torrent of raw darkness Malakor provided, began to shrink, its form quivering, losing some of its terrifying mass. But just as Slash extended his shadows to fully exploit the Beast's vulnerability, Malakor's massive burst of energy subtly shifted direction. Not away from the Beast, but towards it, like a feeder line, a direct conduit of power intended to replenish, not drain.

Jubilee gasped. "He's feeding it!" Her voice was raw with realization.

Slash's eyes, usually a calm violet, flared with a savage fury. "Malakor! What do you play at?" His draining shadows faltered, the surge of power from his brother creating a violent feedback loop that threatened to overwhelm his already weakened state.

Malakor merely smiled, a chilling, triumphant baring of teeth. "Did you truly believe I sought to *destroy* my greatest creation, brother? Foolish. I merely needed it brought to heel. And what better way than to let it exhaust itself, then rebuild it with my own essence, infused with the very magic it craves?" His gaze locked onto Jubilee. "And now, little fae, infused with *your* essence."

The Void Beast, rejuvenated by Malakor's deceptive influx, let out a deep, satisfied growl. It expanded, faster than before, its form now tinged with a dark crimson, mirroring Malakor's own power. Its multi-faceted eyes, once clouded with blind hunger, now gleamed with a terrifying, intelligent malevolence. It was no longer just a rampaging beast; it was Malakor's weapon, honed and refocused.

"You disgust me," Slash snarled, his form flickering. The obsidian wound in his side burned, the malicious ichor fighting against Jubilee's earlier healing, fueled by Malakor's rampant darkness. He stumbled, catching himself on a jagged rock.

"Disgusted? Or merely outmaneuvered?" Malakor gloated, stepping back, allowing the now fully re-empowered Void Beast to advance on Slash. "This glade is indeed potent, brother. And its guardian," he nodded towards Jubilee, "a delightful addition. A perfect conduit to tame and refine even my Void Beast. Imagine, my pet, infused with the raw power of the forest, no longer merely destructive, but capable of consuming and corrupting to my will."

Jubilee felt a cold dread seep into her bones. She wasn't just a target; she was an ingredient. Her magic, the newfound connection to the glade, was to be twisted, woven into this abomination. She saw now, with horrifying clarity, Malakor's true intentions. He hadn't sought to destroy the Void Beast, but to transform it, making it even more terrifyingly effective, using Slash's weakening state and her own frantic efforts as leverage.

"Slash!" she cried, rushing to his side, her emerald energy flaring desperately around him. The Void Beast descended, its enhanced form radiating crushing power, its hunger now specifically directed. Malakor merely watched, his eyes gleaming with anticipation, clearly enjoying the grim spectacle of his brothers' downfall and the inevitable claim of Jubilee and the glade as his spoils. The temporary alliance had shattered, revealing a plan far more insidious than mere conquest. They were trapped, caught between a reborn monster and its calculating, formidable master.

42

The words "ingredient" and "abomination" echoed in Jubilee's mind, igniting a fury far hotter than any she had ever known. Malakor's chilling composure, his blatant disregard for life, and the sickening perversion of her beloved glade's magic – it was too much. The terror that had begun to freeze her evaporated, replaced by an incandescent rage.

She stood before Slash, a fragile shield of emerald luminescence against the encroaching darkness of the rejuvenated Void Beast. The air in the grotto crackled with an unbearable tension, a symphony of destructive power and desperate defiance. The Void Beast, now a monstrous silhouette tinged with Malakor's malevolent crimson, lunged. Its multi-faceted eyes, cruel and intelligent, fixed on Slash, a silent promise of obliteration.

But Jubilee, for the first time, felt no fear. Only a singular, focused intent. *No*.

A guttural roar tore from her throat, not a cry of terror, but of primal, untamed power. Her hands, raised instinctively, glowed with an intensity that burned away the oppressive gloom. The emerald energy, usually gentle and nurturing, pulsed with a violent frequency, a raw, elemental force untamed by decorum or tradition. It wasn't just magic now; it was the very essence of the glade, fueled by her grief, her love for Slash, and her absolute, unyielding fury.

From her palms, twin streams of vibrant emerald light erupted, not in delicate tendrils, but in thick, pulsing torrents. They hit the Void Beast full force, a blinding green inferno against its dark mass. The creature howled, a sound of agony and surprise, as the pure, unadulterated forest magic seared its form. Patches of its crimson-tinged shadow began to peel away, dissolving into acrid smoke.

Malakor, who had been watching with a smirk, stumbled back, his eyes widening. "Impossible!" he bellowed, his voice losing its icy composure for the first time. He had assumed Jubilee's power was merely a conduit, easily manipulated. He hadn't anticipated such raw, unbridled retaliation.

Jubilee pressed the attack, her feet rooting to the ground, drawing strength from the very stones beneath her. The grotto walls, still scarred from Slash's earlier outburst, now vibrated with her burgeoning power. Roots burst forth from the earth, not in a gentle embrace, but as hardened, sharpened spears, lashing out at the Void Beast. Vines, thick as a man's arm, coiled and snapped, their thorns glinting with emerald light.

The Void Beast, disoriented and wounded, thrashed wildly, its attacks now erratic and unfocused. Jubilee channeled every ounce of her being, every painful memory, every shattered hope, into the onslaught. She remembered Eldrin's lifeless form, the desecration of her sanctuary, Malakor's cold, calculating cruelty. Each memory fueled the emerald tide, transforming it into a weapon of absolute destruction.

A searing pain lanced through her side as one of the Beast's stray limbs grazed her, but she barely registered it. Her focus was absolute, her anger a blinding emerald fire. She saw the fear flicker in the Void Beast's intelligent eyes, saw Malakor's dawning comprehension of her true, untamed power.

Slash, still weakened but watching her with an almost reverent awe, managed a raspy whisper. "Jubilee..."

He reached for her, his touch a grounding force amidst the maelstrom. She didn't look away from the cowering Beast, but her own power briefly pulsed back towards him, a silent acknowledgment, a shared strength. She wasn't just defending herself; she was defending *them*.

With a final, explosive surge, Jubilee unleashed a concussive wave of emerald energy. It slammed into the Void Beast, lifting its massive form from the ground and sending it hurtling backwards, crashing against the grotto wall with a deafening impact that splintered the ancient rock. Its form shuddered, shrinking violently, the malevolent crimson bleeding from its edges, revealing a form less formidable, more creature, whimpering in pain.

Jubilee stood panting, her body trembling, but her gaze remained fixed on Malakor, who was now staring at her with a chilling new assessment. The smirk was gone, replaced by a calculating, dangerous glint. She had surprised him, undeniably, but the battle was far from over. She had shown her hand, yes, but she had also revealed a power he clearly hadn't accounted for. The game had just changed.

43

Jubilee's ragged breaths filled the sudden, uneasy quiet of the grotto. Her emerald inferno had subsided, leaving behind a lingering hum of raw energy and the acrid scent of scorched shadow. The Void Beast lay whimpering, reduced to a pathetic, shriveled husk against the fractured grotto wall, its earlier menace replaced by a desperate, guttural whine. Malakor, though visibly shaken, was already regaining his composure, his red eyes narrowed on Jubilee with a predatory intensity that sent a chill directly to her bones, bypassing the lingering adrenaline.

"Impressive, little fae," Malakor purred, his voice a low, dangerous rumble that cut through the silence. "Far more... spirited than I anticipated. A true force, indeed." He took a slow step forward, his gaze raking over her, assessing, planning. "Perhaps you aren't merely an ingredient after all. Perhaps you are the catalyst."

Jubilee, still trembling from the exertion, pushed herself upright, drawing what little strength she had left. She would not crack. Not now. Not when she had come so far.

Just as Malakor was about to speak again, a new presence slammed into the grotto. It wasn't a physical crash, but an invisible wave of power that rippled through the air, vibrating the very stones beneath their feet. It was a discordant magic, sharp and metallic, utterly alien to the glade's natural energies.

Malakor's head snapped up, his red eyes widening almost imperceptibly. Slash, still weakened and leaning heavily against the grotto wall, let out a low groan. "No..." he rasped, his voice filled with a fresh wave of dread.

A blinding flash erupted from the grotto's entrance, followed by the clatter of armored boots against rock. Figures began to emerge from the brilliance, cloaked in intricately crafted armor that gleamed with cold, unfeeling light. They were taller than fae, broader, their movements precise and economical. Their faces, what could be seen beneath their visored helmets, were grim and expressionless.

"By the decree of the Celestial Order," a voice boomed, amplified by magic to fill the grotto, "all wild magic, deemed unstable and dangerous, is hereby quarantined and contained. Surrender or face the consequences."

Jubilee stared, bewildered. The Celestial Order? She had only heard whispers of them in ancient texts, a highly advanced, magically-infused civilization that patrolled the boundaries of realms, suppressing what they deemed to be chaotic or excessive magical manifestations. Their appearance here, now, could only mean one thing: the immense surge of power from their battle, especially Slash's entropic burst and her own emerald inferno, had drawn unwanted attention.

Malakor, however, seemed to know exactly who they were. A dangerous, almost gleeful glint flickered in his eyes. "The Watchers," he murmured, a low, predatory laugh rumbling in his chest. "Perfect. The universe truly conspires to make things interesting." He took another step back, melting partially into the shadows, his expression unreadable.

The armored figures, numbering at least a dozen, fanned out, their weapons, long staffs tipped with glowing crystals, trained on the center of the grotto. One, clearly their leader, stepped forward. His armor was etched with intricate celestial patterns, and his voice, though calm, held an undeniable weight of authority. "We sense a massive uncontrolled energy surge. Explain yourselves, wildlings. And cease all hostilities. This area is now under Celestial jurisdiction."

Jubilee felt a fresh wave of despair. Just when she thought they might have a chance against Malakor, a new, unforeseen enemy had arrived, one with the power and authority to suppress *all* magic, regardless of alignment. They were truly trapped now, caught between a malevolent brother, a monstrous and still dangerous creature, and an unyielding, powerful outside force that saw them and their magic as nothing more than a threat to be contained. The glade, their sanctuary, was no longer merely a battleground; it was a cage.

The Celestial leader, their voice devoid of emotion, raised a hand. "By the power vested in the Celestial Order, we declare this region under full magical quarantine. All individuals present are to submit to immediate containment." As he spoke, glowing energy cages materialized from the air, shimmering with an unyielding light, designed to suppress all existing magic within their confines.

One cage shot towards the still-recovering Void Beast, which shrieked, a high-pitched, desperate sound, as the light touched its withered form, binding it tightly. Another, larger cage descended swiftly over Malakor. For a split second, a flicker of genuine shock crossed his sinister features. He tried to melt deeper into the shadows, but the Celestial magic was too fast, too pure. The dazzling bars encased him, and a low snarl of impotent rage rumbled from his throat. The Celestial Order, for all their supposed neutrality, were clearly not taking sides, merely asserting their absolute authority over any "wild" magical manifestation.

"Understood, wildling," the leader stated, his visor turning to Jubilee and then to Slash, who was still slumped against the grotto wall. "Resist, and suffer the consequences."

Jubilee, caught between a growing sense of dread and a bizarre flicker of satisfaction at Malakor's surprise, instinctively drew her remaining essence around her, a faint emerald shimmer. But it was too little, too late. The air crackled around her as a third, smaller cage solidified, ready to descend.

"Wait!" Jubilee cried, her voice hoarse, attempting to sound authoritative. "You don't understand! He..." She gestured wildly towards Malakor, the anger that had fueled her earlier inferno momentarily resurfacing. "He's the threat! He killed Eldrin! He created that... that thing!" Her gaze darted to the now-caged, whimpering Void Beast.

The Celestial leader paused, his head tilting infinitesimally. "Our sensors indicate a vast, destructive power emanating from all three of you," he stated, his voice flat. "Your internal squabbles are of no consequence to the Order. All sources of unstable magic must be pacified."

Slash, pushing himself upright with a monumental effort, a ghostly shadow of his former power, let out a bitter laugh. "Pacified? You blindly stumble in, judging without understanding. You call this 'order'?" He coughed, a ragged sound. "You will regret this."

The Celestial leader ignored him, raising his hand once more. The cage above Jubilee began its inexorable descent. A primal fear seized her. To be contained, her magic stifled, her connection to the glade severed – it was a fate worse than death. She fought against the invisible pressure, but her strength was depleted, her furious surge of power having left her utterly drained.

Suddenly, a massive surge of dark energy erupted from the wall beside Slash. It wasn't the chaotic, destructive entropy from before, but a controlled, precise blast. It slammed into the descending cage above Jubilee, not destroying it, but shunting it violently sideways, sending it crashing into the grotto wall with a shower of fractured light.

All eyes turned to Slash. He stood, wobbling, his eyes burning with renewed violet intensity, a thin tendril of shadow magic still coiling from his outstretched hand. His skin was still ashen, his body clearly at its limit, but an undeniable defiance radiated from him.

"You will not touch her," he rasped, his voice unexpectedly strong, brimming with chilling possessiveness. Then, with a silent, agonizing gasp, he pitched forward, collapsing back into unconsciousness, his last act one of desperate, self-sacrificing protection.

The Celestial guards tensed, their weapons raised. The leader's voice boomed, "That settles it. Maximum containment protocols. Now!"

Jubilee, momentarily stunned by Slash's last act, then spurred by a fierce, protective surge of her own, caught his falling form, lowering him gently. She looked up at the approaching Celestials, her face hardening. The glade roared within her, sensing the encroaching threat to its, and her, very essence. She might be exhausted, but they wouldn't take him. Not after everything. The true battle, it seemed, was just beginning.

Jubilee cradled Slash's unconscious form, his weight heavy and familiar against her. The Celestial guards advanced, their metallic footsteps echoing ominously in the grotto, their faces obscured by polished visors. Their magic-suppressing cages, shimmering with cold, sterile light, were already materializing from the air, each one a promise of oblivion.

"No," Jubilee whispered, her voice barely audible, yet vibrating with a deep, nascent power. It wasn't a plea; it was a declaration. They wouldn't take him. Not after he had risked everything, drained himself to the brink of non-existence, just to protect her. A fierce, protective surge ripped through her, eclipsing the lingering terror.

Her emerald eyes blazed, reflecting the shimmering energy cages, but now, a new light ignited within them – a defiant, untamed inferno. The glade, battered and bruised, mirrored her fury, its remaining life force swirling around her, responding to her raw, unfiltered emotion. She wasn't merely drawing on the glade's magic; she was becoming an extension of it, a conduit for its ancient, desperate will to survive.

A wave of emerald energy, born not of measured control but of pure, incandescent rage and love, erupted from her. It wasn't a delicate stream, nor a calculated burst. It was a violent, tempestuous storm of light and life. The air screamed as her magic collided with the rapidly descending cages.

The first cage, meant for her, shattered with a sound like crystal exploding, its cold light splintering into a million harmless motes. The guards recoiled, their emotionless visors unable to mask their surprise. She didn't stop. Her emerald fury washed over the second cage, this one forming around the Void Beast. It buckled, groaned, and then dissolved into shimmering vapor, freeing the creature, which immediately cowered behind Malakor's still-imprisoned form. Malakor himself, inside his robust cage, flinched, a flash of genuine awe warring with an almost primal fear crossing his face as Jubilee's uncontrolled power pulsed around him.

The Celestial leader, his cold composure finally cracking, barked orders. "Concentrate fire! Suppress her! Now!"

More cages, thicker, reinforced, appeared from nowhere, converging on Jubilee. But she faced them not with fear, but with a primal roar that tore from her throat. Her emerald energy deepened, turning molten, liquid fire. Vines, imbued with potent magic, erupted from the grotto floor, twisting and lashing, forming a living, emerald shield around her and Slash. Roots, thick as ancient tree trunks, burst through the rock, slamming into the Celestial guards with bone-jarring force.

One guard, bolder than the rest, raised a device designed to siphon magic. Before he could activate it, a coil of emerald energy, sharp as a blade, whipped out from Jubilee, severing the device and sending sparks flying. Her movements were fluid, instinctual, powered by a desperate need she hadn't known she possessed. She wasn't just defending herself; she was retaliating, with every fiber of her being.

The grotto groaned under the immense magical pressure, the very air thick with the clash of forces. Jubilee's magic, wild and untamed, was pushing back, not just at the Celestial Order, but at the concept of containment itself. She was a hurricane of light, a force of nature unleashed, fueled by the love for the fallen shadow fae in her arms and the memory of Eldrin, and the glade's ancient desire for freedom. This wasn't strategy; it was pure, unadulterated will, weaponized and aimed. The Celestials, for the first time, were facing something they couldn't simply suppress. They were facing magic that fought back, with a fierce, burning heart.

Even as Jubilee raged, a flicker of cold returned to her core, a familiar dread warring with her incandescent fury. The Celestial forces, though momentarily stunned, were regrouping, their numbers seemingly endless. The air hummed with dozens of potent siphoning devices, coalescing into a shimmering wall of suppression. Her magic, though mighty, was finite, and already she felt the immense strain, the frantic pulse of life within the glade struggling against the cold, sterile encroachment. Just as the wall of suppression began its suffocating advance, an ethereal whisper, cold and sharp as obsidian, brushed against her mind.

* "Jubilee... focus..."

It was Slash's voice, impossibly faint, a mere echo against the roar of her own battling magic, yet potent enough to cut through the chaos. His body, still heavy in her arms, convulsed slightly. His eyes, though still mostly glazed, flickered open, revealing a sliver of the brilliant violet that had captivated her just hours before. The emerald flecks, a remnant of their shared healing, pulsed faintly within their depths.

His arm, which moments before had been limp and lifeless, twitched, then slowly, with immense effort, lifted. His fingers, trembling, brushed against her arm, a surge of icy shadow, like a jolt of pure energy, flowing into her. It wasn't a healing touch, not in the way she had healed him, but a jolt of raw power, a desperate offering.

"Hold... them..." he rasped, his voice barely a breath. The words were a command, a plea, a testament to his unwavering will even on the precipice of oblivion. The effort visibly drained him further, his head lolling back against her shoulder, consciousness threatening to abandon him once more. But in that brief, painful connection, a fragile bridge formed, a conduit for a singular, desperate surge.

From Slash's body, not a torrent, not a wave, but a razor-thin needle of shadow erupted. It was a focused, almost surgical strike, born of instinct and an unbreakable will. It wasn't the devastating, all-consuming chaos he had unleashed earlier; this was precision, a honed weapon aimed at the very heart of the Celestial threat. The needle of shadow, impossibly dense and swift, bypassed the chaotic emerald storm of Jubilee's magic, slicing through the air with an audible hum.

It pierced the shimmering wall of suppression, not with an explosion, but with a chilling, resonant crack. The light of the siphoning devices flickered, then dimmed, as if a vital nerve had been severed. One by one, the dozens of magic-suppressing cages that had been solidifying around them began to waver, their cold light sputtering like dying embers. A low, grinding wail rose from the Celestial ranks as their cohesive magical barrier began to crumble.

The Celestial leader, his voice laced with uncharacteristic alarm, screeched, "What was that?!"

The needle of shadow, having completed its work, dissipated into the air, leaving only a lingering chill. Slash's arm fell limp again, his breathing shallow, yet a profound quiet settled over the grotto, a momentary reprieve from the relentless pressure. Jubilee looked down at him, her heart aching with a mixture of terror and awe. He had reached from the depths of nothingness to protect her, a final, defiant act.

But the silence was fleeting. The Celestials, though shaken, were not defeated. Their initial disarray quickly gave way to renewed resolve, their numbers too vast, their technology too advanced. This time, however, the threat was clearer, more focused. Their siphoning devices, though momentarily disrupted, weren't destroyed. They shuddered back to life, their cold lights flickering with malevolent intent. Jubilee knew this was merely a temporary reprieve, a gasp of air before the next, perhaps final, plunge. Yet, in that shared moment of defiance, a spark of hope ignited, a fierce refusal to surrender. They were in this together, still. With renewed determination, Jubilee tightened her grip on Slash, her eyes scanning their environment for their next move. The fight was far from over.

47

The fragile stillness in the grotto shattered as the Celestial siphoning devices hummed back to full, suffocating power. The air grew heavy, thick with the metallic tang of magic being torn from its source. Jubilee could feel it within her, the subtle draining, the insidious weakening of her own emerald essence as the renewed wall of suppression pressed in. She clutched Slash tighter, his unconscious weight a painful reminder of their precarious situation. His breath was still shallow, his heart a faint flutter against her palm.

"Prepare for full containment!" the Celestial leader barked, his voice echoing with renewed authority. Enforcers, their faces grim under their reflective visors, began to advance again, their arcane cages glowing with an unnerving, icy blue.

Jubilee's mind raced, a whirlwind of desperate plans and fading hope. They were cornered. Surrounded. The grotto, once a haven of raw magic, was now a trap. She braced herself, prepared to unleash whatever meager reserves she had left, to fight until her last breath, if only to buy Slash a few more precious moments.

Then, a low moan escaped Slash's lips, so soft it was almost swallowed by the relentless hum of the siphoning devices. Jubilee's gaze snapped to his face. His eyelids, heavy with exhaustion, fluttered again. This time, they opened more fully, the violet of his eyes glazed with pain but alight with a desperate urgency. The emerald flecks, gifts of her healing, shimmered like distant stars in their depths.

His brow was furrowed, an immense effort visibly twisting his features. He tried to speak, but only a dry, rasping wheeze escaped. His hand, still weakly clutched in hers, twitched, attempting to gain purchase, to exert pressure, to communicate the vital message that clawed at the edges of his fading consciousness.

Jubilee leaned in, her ear practically pressed to his lips. "Slash? What is it? What do you need?" she whispered, her voice laced with an aching tenderness she hadn't known she possessed.

He swallowed hard, a painful, grating sound. His eyes darted past her, towards the encroaching Celestial forces, then back to her face, pleading, demanding understanding. "The... the... stone..." he managed, his voice barely a breath against the din.

Jubilee frowned, perplexed. "The stone? What stone, Slash?" Her mind raced through recent events. Eldrin's acorn? The grotto's magical formations? Nothing seemed to fit the desperate urgency in his eyes.

His breath hitched, and a fresh wave of agony washed over his face. The faint emerald flecks in his eyes Pulsed, then dimmed, as if fighting against the encroaching darkness. "The... the heart... of... the glade..." he rasped, each word a monumental effort. His fingers tightened on hers, a momentary surge of cold shadow, a desperate attempt to imprint the importance of his words into her very being. "It... calls... them..."

He paused, a shiver running through him, a stark admission of his dwindling strength. His eyes, now almost completely violet again, locked onto hers, burning with an incandescent ferocity that belied his physical weakness. "Hidden... below..."

Then, a violent tremor shook his frame. His fingers went limp in hers, his eyes rolled back, and the last flicker of conscious awareness faded. With a guttural groan, Slash succumbed once more to the darkness, his body collapsing fully against hers, a dead weight in her arms.

Jubilee stared at him, reeling. The stone. The heart of the glade. Hidden below. It calls them. The words echoed in her mind, a jumbled puzzle. Calls whom? The Celestials? The High Shades? Malakor? And why? What hidden power lay beneath this ancient grotto that commanded such attention, drawing forth such formidable enemies? A cold dread settled in her stomach, a premonition of something far more ancient and terrifying than she could comprehend. But even as the fear coiled, a spark of resolve ignited. Slash, even in his pain, had tried to give her the key. She would uncover it. She *had* to. The fight was far from over, but now, a new, desperate quest had begun. With the Celestials closing in, she knew she had precious little time to decipher his final, enigmatic message.

The hum of the siphoning devices intensified, a suffocating blanket pressing down on Jubilee. The Celestial enforcers were closer now, their footsteps heavy, their cages poised. Time was a luxury she didn't have, but Slash's words, his desperate urgency, clawed at her. "The stone… the heart of the glade… it calls them… hidden below."

It was too specific, too vital to be the ramblings of a dying fae. He had risked everything, used his last conscious breath to impart this message. He believed she could understand, believed she could act. And in that belief, a flicker of an idea ignited within her.

He was silent now, a heavy burden in her arms, his breathing still shallow, his essence muted. But their connection, forged in passion, battle, and shared magic, ran deeper than consciousness. She had felt his power within her, healed his shadow, merged with his very being. Perhaps, just perhaps, she could reach him, not through words, but through the vibrant, intertwined threads of their souls.

Closing her eyes against the encroaching light of the Celestial cages, Jubilee focused. She took a deep breath, drawing on the last vestiges of the glade's magic that still stubbornly clung to her, a defiant emerald glow against the oppressive grey. She let her mind reach out, not just to the external world, but inward, towards Slash. She visualized the shimmering, invisible tendrils of forest magic that connected her to the grotto, then extended them, seeking out the deeper, darker currents that ran through Slash.

Her consciousness slipped past the veil of his unconsciousness, past the physical pain and exhaustion. She found herself in a vast, cold expanse, the landscape of his mind. It was a place of endless shadow, of ancient, primal power, yet also, surprisingly, of profound stillness. Here and there, faint emerald lights pulsed, the residual echoes of her healing touch.

"Slash?" Her mental voice was a whisper in the echoing void. "Slash, I need to understand. The stone... what is it? What does it call?"

There was no immediate response. The darkness absorbed her call, leaving only the silent hum of the siphoning devices, a distant, muffled thrum, even here. Frustration gnawed at her, but she pushed it down. He was weak. She needed to *give*, not take.

She poured a tendril of her own raw, desperate emerald magic into the void, a beacon, a desperate plea for connection. She envisioned the image of his eyes, burning with urgency, of his hand grasping hers, imprinting the message. She projected her love, her fear, her unwavering belief in his strength.

Suddenly, a ripple. A faint, icy current stirred the shadows. A flicker, barely perceptible, like a distant star winking into existence. It was his presence, a faint spark of his consciousness responding to her desperate reach.

"The... Nexus..." The word formed in her mind, a cold, brittle whisper, not his voice, but the essence of his thought. "Ancient... source... power... corrupts..."

Images flooded her mind, hazy and fractured, yet undeniably potent. A vast, glowing crystalline structure, pulsating with immense energy, deep beneath the glade. Figures, cloaked in robes of deepest shadow, kneeling before it, their hands outstretched, drawing power, but also, subtly, *changing*. Their forms grew gaunt, their eyes hollow. Eldrin's grey skin flashed, then Slash's earlier, fleeting vulnerability, the drain on his power.

"The Celestials... they seek to... contain... the Nexus..." Another flicker of thought, stronger this time, carrying a heavy weight of resignation. "Malakor... he seeks to... control... unleash... its corruption."

Then, a final, searing image: herself, standing alone against the crushing power of the Nexus, the crystalline structure glowing with a malevolent, alluring light. A profound sense of dread, cold and absolute, washed over her.

The connection fractured. She was back in the grotto, clutching Slash, the frigid air biting at her skin. The

Celestial enforcers were almost upon them, their cages poised.

The Nexus. The Heart of the Glade. A source of immense power, corrupting those who touched it, yet drawing everyone to its malevolent allure. The Celestials wanted to contain it, Malakor to control it. And Slash, even in his pain, had risked everything to warn her. He had handed her a burden, a terrifying truth, but also, a weapon. A purpose.

Her gaze hardened, the emerald in her eyes burning with a new, fierce resolve. She knew now. And knowing, she would fight. For Slash. For the glade. For the very heart of magic itself.

The heavy thud of Celestial boots echoed against the grotto floor, a stark countdown to their capture. Jubilee clutched Slash tighter, his unconscious weight a chilling reminder of the impossible odds. Knowing the truth of the Nexus didn't make the immediate threat any less dire. Their siphoning devices hummed louder, drawing closer.

Just as the first Celestial enforcer's shadow fell over them, a deep rumble vibrated through the very rock beneath Jubilee's feet. It wasn't the destructive roar of the Void Beast, nor the chaotic magic of Malakor. This was... ancient. Protective.

The grotto itself seemed to shift, the stone groaning in protest. A section of the rocky wall, previously unremarkable, began to glow with a faint, internal light - not emerald, nor shadow, but a soft, pearlescent shimmer. The luminescence grew, pushing apart the ancient rock as if it were mere dust.

From the newly formed fissure, a figure emerged. Tall and slender, but radiating an undeniable strength, like a living root grown from millenniums of unyielding earth. His skin was the color of polished mahogany, adorned with intricate, glowing patterns that pulsed in sync with the grotto's heartbeat. His eyes, deep pools of liquid amber, instantly locked onto Jubilee, then to Slash. He carried no obvious weapon, yet the Celestials faltered, their confident strides breaking. The very air around him hummed with an untouched, elemental magic, purer and more primal than anything Jubilee had sensed before.

He was a Forest Elemental, not of her kind, but an embodiment of the glade's deepest, most ancient spirit. He was an answer to her despair, a direct response to the glade's cry for help.

"You shall not pass," his voice resonated, deep and guttural, yet surprisingly melodic, like wind chimes crafted from ancient wood. It echoed through the grotto, vibrating in the bones of the Celestials, making their siphoning devices sputter and falter.

The Celestial leader, a gaunt elf with cold, calculating eyes, recovered swiftly. "By the decree of the Celestial Order, all rogue magic is to be contained! Stand aside, ancient one, or face the consequences."

The Elemental tilted his head, his amber eyes burning. "Rogue? This magic is the true heart. You seek to stifle life itself." He extended a hand, his fingers surprisingly delicate, yet radiating raw power. "This glade lives. And it fights."

Without another word, roots, thicker and more resilient than any Jubilee had yet conjured, burst from the ground at the Elemental's silent command. They lashed out, not with the destructive fury Eldrin or even Jubilee herself wielded, but with a precise, almost surgical grace. They bypassed the Celestials shielding the siphoning devices, wrapping directly around the humming mechanisms, squeezing. A high-pitched shriek of tortured metal filled the grotto as one by one, the siphoning cages crumpled, then disintegrated into dust.

The Celestials reeled, their rigid formation broken. Their faces, usually impassive, contorted with shock and confusion. This was not the chaotic, untamed magic they were trained to contain with brute force. This was a deeper, more fundamental power, intertwined with the very fabric of existence.

Jubilee, still cradling Slash, felt a surge of hope so potent it almost brought her to her knees. This was it. This was the glade's response, not just to her, but to Slash's desperate, dying plea. The Elemental turned his gaze back to her, a flicker of acknowledgement in his ancient eyes. He didn't offer comfort or a plan, but his silent presence was enough. He was a sentinel, a protector, awakened when the core of his charge faced ultimate peril.

With the siphoning devices gone, the oppressive pressure on Jubilee's magic lessened. Her emerald glow brightened, revitalized by the Elemental's presence. The glade itself, once dim and fading, pulsed with a renewed, vital energy. The balance was shifting, slowly, irrevocably. The tide was beginning to turn.

The Celestial forces, disoriented and vulnerable, scattered as their siphoning devices turned to dust. This was the moment Malakor had been waiting for. A cruel, knowing smile stretched his thin lips, his red eyes gleaming with renewed menace. "Amateurs," he drawled, his voice cutting through the grotto's stunned silence. "Such predictable, dull tactics."

He exploded into motion, a blur of shadow and malevolence. His target wasn't the re-emerging Elemental, nor the now-glowing Jubilee clutching the unconscious Slash. It was the Celestials, the very beings who had, moments before, attempted to contain him. Malakor moved with a predatory grace, a stark contrast to the Celestial Order's rigid, disciplined fighting style.

His dark magic, a raw, untamed force, lashed out. Tendrils of pure shadow erupted from his fingertips, not to bind or siphon, but to rip and tear. The Celestials, trained in containment and suppression, were ill-equipped for such an aggressive, purely destructive attack. Their gleaming armors, designed to deflect magical surges, seemed to offer little resistance against Malakor's furious onslaught. He didn't seek to merely disable them; he sought to dismantle them.

A Celestial guard, attempting to re-establish their formation, cried out as a razor-sharp shadow tendril severed his arm, his siphoning gauntlet clattering uselessly to the grotto floor. Another shrieked as Malakor's magic wrapped around his head, crushing it with sickening efficiency. The precision of his violence was terrifying, an art form perfected over eons of subjugation.

"You came to control what you cannot comprehend," Malakor sneered, his voice a low growl of satisfaction as he advanced, driving the Celestials further back. "This glade, this power... it is not for your rigid cages. It belongs to those who truly understand its depths." He glanced briefly at Jubilee, a flicker of dark possessiveness in his eyes that made her skin crawl. "And that, my dear brother, is not you." The last words were aimed at the still unconscious Slash, a final, spiteful jab.

The Celestial leader, his gaunt face now etched with fear, desperately barked orders, trying to reorganize his rapidly dwindling forces. "Form ranks! Contain him! Do not let him reach the Nexus!" He pointed a trembling finger deeper into the grotto, toward the very section where the Elemental had emerged. His words struck Jubilee with a chilling certainty: Malakor, in the guise of attacking their common enemy, was merely clearing the path to his true prize. He wasn't interested in the Celestials' defeat; he was interested in their removal as obstacles to his ultimate goal - the Nexus.

The Forest Elemental, who had moments ago saved them from the Celestials, remained a silent, watchful sentinel. His amber eyes, though fixed on the unfolding chaos Malakor wrought, maintained a subtle, protective focus on Jubilee and the still-glowing fissure in the wall. He did not overtly intervene in Malakor's brutal assault on the Celestials, perhaps seeing them as intruders on par with Malakor himself, or perhaps understanding, as Jubilee now did, that Malakor's actions, however violent, were inadvertently serving to reduce a common threat. But the Elemental's calm demeanor did not mean disinterest. Jubilee felt a subtle increase in the magical thrum surrounding him, a gathering of power, a readiness to act should Malakor's deadly dance lead too close to his charge.

The grotto groaned under the combined strains of warring magic, the shouts of the dying Celestials, and Malakor's triumphant cackles. Jubilee felt a surge of nausea. Malakor was powerful, ruthless, and terrifyingly efficient. And he was getting closer to the heart of the glade, to the Nexus, to the very source of all this unbridled power. A new, more profound dread settled upon her. The enemy of her enemy was still an enemy, and a far more dangerous one at that.

Jubilee's nausea hardened into a cold, terrifying resolve. Malakor wasn't just clearing a path; he was clearing *his* path. The Celestials were merely pawns, disposable obstacles on his ruthless chess board. The Nexus. Slash's whispered words echoed in her mind, amplifying the ominous weight of Slash's meaning. The heart of the glade, the source of all she protected and loved. She looked down at Slash, his face pale, his breathing shallow, a stark reminder of the immense cost of this conflict. If Malakor reached the Nexus, there would be no glade, no light, no future. Only his shadow.

Every instinct screamed for her to act. Her gaze flickered to the still-watching Forest Elemental, then to the gaping fissure in the grotto wall, where Slash had revealed the glade's deepest secret. It radiated a potent, untamed energy, vibrating with an ancient power. The Nexus.

"Malakor!" Jubilee's voice, though strained, cut through the din of dying Celestials and his maniacal laughter. Her shout was less a plea and more a challenge, a desperate attempt to draw his attention away from his relentless advance.

Malakor paused mid-stride, a half-formed shadow construct dissolving from his grasp. His red eyes, glittering with malevolent amusement, fixed on her. "Ah, the little forest sprite. Still here? I thought you'd know better than to stand in the path of destiny."

"Destiny?" Jubilee spat, her emerald magic flaring around her hands, a visible manifestation of her fury. "You speak of destiny, yet you bring only destruction! You drain and corrupt, you don't create!"

Malakor laughed, a chilling, humorless sound. "Such pretty words. You'll learn, little one. Power takes what it wants." He took a step towards her, his form shimmering with dark intent. "And I want the Nexus. Along with its... keeper." His gaze lingered pointedly on her, then flickered to the unconscious Slash, as if assessing a forgotten toy.

That was it. The final straw. He wouldn't touch Slash. He wouldn't touch the Nexus.

Without a second's hesitation, Jubilee lifted both hands, channeling every ounce of her remaining energy, every desperate hope, every burning shard of vengeance for Eldrin, into a singular, desperate act. She had planned to protect, to defend, but this was beyond that. This was a preemptive strike, a suicidal gamble.

Instead of directing her magic at Malakor, she flung her arms wide, aiming her power not at the enemy, but at the very ground beneath her. A blinding emerald light erupted from her, tearing through the grotto's floor. The ancient stone groaned and fractured, responding to the raw, untamed magic. Roots, thick and gnarled, imbued with a potent, defiant life, burst from the fissures. They didn't merely grow; they lashed out, intertwining and solidifying into a living, emerald wall that began to rise with terrifying speed between Malakor and the exposed Nexus.

The sudden, unexpected eruption of pure forest magic caught Malakor off guard. His triumphant cackle died on his lips, replaced by a snarl of pure rage. "What have you done, you fool?!" he roared, unleashing a wave of shadow at the rapidly ascending barrier.

But Jubilee's desperate act had drawn not only on her own formidable power, but on the very essence of the glade's fury. The wall Pulsed with incandescent green light, absorbing Malakor's attack, hardening, growing thicker, more impenetrable by the second. She felt the drain, the searing pain as her life force poured into the barrier, but she pushed through it, her teeth gritted, her eyes blazing with an unyielding purpose. The wall rose higher, reaching the grotto's ceiling, effectively sealing off the Nexus from Malakor's predatory grasp.

Before the barrier fully solidified, Jubilee, with a final, agonizing surge of will, reached into the raw, exposed energy of the Nexus. It hummed with immense power, a vast, untamed ocean. She wasn't sure what she would find, or what she could even *do*, but she had to try. She plunged her spiritual essence deep into its heart, desperate for a solution, a last resort, anything to save Slash and their glade. The glade roared in response, her vision blurring with the influx of ancient power, and she felt a terrifying, exhilarating shift within her as the world dissolved around her.

A jolt, sharp and electric, lanced through Slash. Not the pain of his wound, which still throbbed dully, but something far more invasive, more profound. It was a familiar energy, yet amplified to an impossible degree – Jubilee's. And then, woven within it, a raw, untamed hum that vibrated with the very essence of the glade's heart. The Nexus.

His eyes flickered open, or rather, struggled to open. His body felt like a leaden weight, every muscle screaming in protest, but the surge of power, borrowed and infused, spurred him on. The first thing he registered was the blinding emerald light, pulsating violently. It was all-consuming, a vibrant, living wall that now sealed off the very grotto from him, from Malakor. Panic, cold and sharp, pierced through the haze of his weakness. Jubilee. What had she done?

He found her then, through the shimmering emerald barrier, her form silhouetted against an even brighter, searing core of green. She was slumped, half-kneeled, her hands outstretched, deeply, terrifyingly connected to the Nexus itself. He could feel its vast power flowing through her, an untamed river threatening to drown her. His own connection to her, forged in the crucible of their shared magic and passion, was now a conduit to the glade's innermost workings. He gasped, a guttural sound, as fragmented images and sensations assaulted him: the agonizing strain on her, the frantic thrum of the ancient stone, and an overwhelming surge of protective fury for Eldrin.

Malakor's roar ripped through the newly established silence, a sound of pure, unadulterated rage. "Jubilee! You foolish, insipid child! What have you done?!" His shadow magic, frantic and uncontrolled, slammed against the emerald wall, sparking and dissolving harmlessly against its fortified surface. The sound of his frustrated fury was almost comical, had the stakes not been so dire.

Slash tried to move, but his limbs wouldn't obey. He attempted to call out to her, but only a raspy cough escaped his lips. His own power, still weakened, felt insignificant against the maelstrom of energy that Jubilee was now wielding, channeling, *becoming*. The fear that he had momentarily suppressed surged back, cold and primal. She was too deep. Too connected. The Nexus recognized her, claimed her, devoured her.

"Jubilee!" he rasped again, forcing the word out, a desperate plea. He felt the cold shock of the grotto floor against his skin, the dampness of his own blood, but all he cared about was the vibrant, terrifying glow that threatened to consume the woman who now held his heart.

Malakor, having exhausted his initial bursts of impotent rage against the wall, turned his malevolent gaze towards Slash. "Look at you, little brother," he sneered, his voice dripping with venom. "Helpless. And your little pet? She's destroying herself for a lost cause. How pathetic." A twisted smile touched his lips. "But perhaps... perhaps this isn't an entirely useless outcome. If she merges with the Nexus, I can simply extract it from her... or what's left of her."

The words struck Slash like a physical blow. He felt a resurgence of a very different kind of rage, cold and dangerous. Malakor's callous disregard, his willingness to sacrifice Jubilee for his own twisted ambitions, ignited a spark of his own shadow power, a cold, dark flame that had no business being contained. He clenched his fists, struggling against the weakness that held him captive. He had to reach her. He had to.

He could feel Jubilee's conscious mind slipping, dissolving into the ancient power she had called upon. Her presence in their bond was becoming abstract, a raw surge of will rather than coherent thought. But beneath it, a tiny, desperate flicker remained - a spark of the woman who had defied him, healed him, loved him. And he would not let her go. Not for Malakor, not for the Nexus, not for any power in the realms.

With an agonizing groan, Slash dug his fingers into the earth. If his body wouldn't move, his mind would. He sent every ounce of his remaining strength, every thread of his shadow essence, into their shared connection. A silent roar of his own, echoing her desperate call, a promise to pull her back from the brink, no matter the cost. He would drag her back to him, from the very heart of the glade itself.

The shadow surged, a desperate, potent tendril of Slash's will. It wasn't physical, not in the way Malakor's impotent blasts were, but a raw, agonizing pull through the invisible tether that bound him to Jubilee. He poured every drop of his remaining consciousness, every flicker of his dark core, into that connection, pushing past the pain, past the overwhelming emerald light, past the terrifying absorption of the Nexus. *Jubilee!* The silent scream was laced with a tenderness he hadn't known he possessed, a ferocity born of absolute despair. *Come back.*

And deep within the heart of the blinding green, a flicker. A tiny, almost imperceptible tremor within the ancient power. Her conscious mind, on the precipice of melding entirely with the vast, ancient energy, felt the searing intensity of his plea. It was a lifeline, familiar and potent, slicing through the intoxicating oblivion of the Nexus. Eldrin's death, Malakor's sneering face, the Celestial threat—all faded behind the singular, desperate pull of Slash. His presence, a dark, cool anchor in the chaotic storm of raw magic, reminded her of *her*. Her identity. Her purpose. Him.

With a gasping breath, Jubilee's eyes, glazed with emerald fire, snapped open. Her body convulsed, a violent shudder that ripped through her as if she were separating from a living entity. The vibrant light around her flickered, dimmed by several degrees. The guttural sound of a strangled scream tore from her throat, a sound of agony and raw effort. Her hands, still pressed against the pulsating core of the Nexus, began to tremble.

Malakor, who had been advancing towards Slash with predatory slowness, paused. His eyes narrowed, a flicker of genuine surprise crossing his features. "What...?" he murmured, watching the emerald light recede, ebb, and then, with a final, shuddering surge, violently rupture.

With a sound like tearing silk, Jubilee was ripped free. She flew backward, flung from the Nexus's embrace by the sheer force of her own withdrawal. Her form, once glowing, was now terribly pale, almost translucent. Her magic, the emerald fire that had just been consuming the grotto, receded into nothingness, leaving her limp and unresponsive before hitting the hard grotto floor with a sickening thud, a mere foot's reach from Slash.

The impenetrable wall of roots and stone, severing the grotto in two, shimmered and then, as if it had been a mirage, dissolved into glittering emerald dust that settled like fine snow. The air in the grotto, moments before thick with raw power, was now stale, heavy with the aftermath of spent magic.

Slash, spurred by an adrenaline-fueled terror unlike any he had ever known, clawed his way towards her. He ignored the screaming pain in his own body, the throbbing wound, the weakness that threatened to consume him. He reached her, his trembling hand touching her cheek. It was cold. Too cold.

"Jubilee?" The word was a desperate whisper, torn from the depths of his being. She lay utterly still, her eyes closed, her normally vibrant skin ashen. The emerald dust clung to her hair, her lashes, making her look like a shattered statue crafted from precious stone.

Malakor, now understanding with chilling clarity the extent of what had just transpired, let out a slow, ominous laugh. "Remarkable," he drawled, his voice tinged with grudging admiration. "She severed herself. And you, little brother, you pulled her from the very heart of it. A true bond, for certain. But look at her now. Lifeless. Drained. She emptied herself to defy me. And you... you used whatever meager power you had left to bring her to this state." He took a step forward, a malevolent smile spreading across his face. "Foolish. Now, the Nexus is still exposed, and she is utterly helpless. And you, little brother, are still at my mercy."

Slash didn't respond. He cradled Jubilee's head, pulling her closer, his gaze fixed on her pale face. He could feel a faint, fluttery beat beneath his fingertips, a pulse so weak he almost missed it. Life. She was alive, but barely. And the silence, save for Malakor's mocking laughter, stretched taut, filled with the vast, aching emptiness of spent magic, and a desperate, burgeoning fear.

Malakor moved with a predatory grace, quicker than Slash could have anticipated in his weakened state. One moment, he was taunting, the next, his hands were on Jubilee. A guttural growl ripped from Slash's throat, a sound of pure, unadulterated primal fury, but his efforts to stop Malakor were futile. His body screamed in protest, every nerve ending screaming with pain and exhaustion as he tried to surge forward. He crumpled, his fingers scrabbling uselessly on the stone floor, his eyes wide with helpless horror.

Malakor's grip on Jubilee was surprisingly gentle as he lifted her seemingly lifeless form. Her head lolled against his arm, her limbs limp, her pale hair dusted with emerald, making her look tragically beautiful. Slash's heart hammered against his ribs, a frantic, agonizing rhythm against the silence in the grotto.

"Such a waste of power," Malakor mused, his voice devoid of true sympathy, though tinged with something akin to regret. He ran a skeletal finger along Jubilee's jawline, his gaze chillingly possessive. "All that vibrant magic, spent to defy me. But defiance can be... redirected, can it not?" He met Slash's desperate gaze, a cold, triumphant glint in his red eyes. "You were right, little brother. She is the key. Her connection to the glade, to the Nexus, is absolute.

And now... now I finally understand how to fully exploit it."

He turned, not towards the Nexus as Slash had feared, but towards the grotto's fragmented entrance, the remnants of the Celestial Order and the obliterated High Shades still scattered beyond. "The Watchers are gone, for now," Malakor continued, as if speaking to himself. "And my... original minions... they served their purpose. Now, I have a new, far more potent weapon. A living conduit." He tightened his hold on Jubilee, and a flicker of malevolent shadow magic pulsed around their joined forms.

Slash pushed himself up, trembling violently, his eyes blazing with a dangerous, impossible rage. "Malakor! Don't you dare!" His voice was a raw, strained croak, barely audible, but filled with a depth of threat that defied his physical state.

Malakor merely chuckled, a dry, rustling sound that grated on Slash's frayed nerves. "Don't dare, little brother? You forget your place. You chose this path. You chose weakness, this... balance. I choose power. Absolute. And now, thanks to your... emotional attachment... I have the very instrument I need to bend this glade, and perhaps even wider realms, to my will."

He began to move, carrying Jubilee's unconscious body with disturbing ease. Slash struggled to his feet, every muscle screaming in protest, his vision blurring with weakness. He lunged, a desperate, futile attempt to sever Malakor's hold, but his legs gave out. He fell forward, face first, sending a fresh wave of agony through his body. He clawed at the stone, his nails scraping, leaving shallow furrows as Malakor strode with purpose towards the grotto's opening, the light illuminating his sinister triumph.

"Goodbye, little brother," Malakor called out, his voice echoing in the confined space. "Perhaps next time you choose to interfere, you'll choose wisely. Or perhaps there won't be a next time at all. She will be... irrevocably mine."

And then, he was gone. The cold, crisp air of the deeper glade flowed into the grotto, carrying with it the scent of damp earth and the lingering echoes of battle. Slash lay on the ground, his body shaking uncontrollably, not just from the pain of his wounds, but from a profound, soul-deep despair. The silence that followed Malakor's departure was deafening, amplified by the absence of Jubilee's vibrant presence, the core of light that had illuminated his shadowed existence. He felt her absence like a physical wound, a tearing emptiness in his very being. His furious, helpless roar filled the empty grotto, a desperate cry against an unseen enemy, a silent promise of vengeance upon his brother.

The roar ripped from Slash's throat, a primeval sound of a world shattering. He pushed himself onto his hands and knees, the stone cold against his cheek, the lingering phantom scent of Jubilee's emerald magic a cruel torment. His vision swam, a kaleidoscope of pain and despair, but one image burned through it all: Malakor, carrying Jubilee away. The words echoed in his ears: "She will be... irrevocably mine." No. Never.

With a superhuman effort that tore through already shredded muscles, Slash dragged himself upright. His legs buckled, but he refused to fall. He was a creature of shadow, of endless, terrifying will. He had cheated oblivion before, he would do so again. For Jubilee.

He stumbled out of the grotto, blinking against the muted light of the glade, a glade that felt... wounded. Desolate. The magic that had pulsed with life, that had thrummed with the vibrant energy of his and Jubilee's shared power, now felt flat. Empty. A gaping hole where her light should have been.

Malakor's trail was easy enough to follow, a sickeningly clear path of disrupted earth and lingering, malevolent shadow. It led deeper into the Elderwood, towards the forbidden zones, territories long abandoned by the forest fae, places where shadows clung like old regrets. Despair threatened to drown him, to pin him to the earth like a felled tree, but the thought of Jubilee, pale and vulnerable in Malakor's grasp, ignited a furious, cold flame in his core.

Each step was agony. His ribs screamed, his head throbbed, and the wound from the Elderwood blade, though supposedly healed by Jubilee, now ached with a dull, persistent thrum, a ghostly echo of its draining power. He moved less like an elf and more like a wounded beast, fueled by instinct and an unshakeable need for retribution.

He wasn't sure how long he stumbled, how many trees he leaned against, how many times he nearly succumbed to the blackness licking at the edges of his vision. Time was a blur, measured only by the relentless pursuit, the pounding of his own weakening heart, and the cold dread coiling in his gut.

Finally, he saw it. A rift in the ancient trees, leading into a part of the forest that was always steeped in perpetual twilight, even at midday. It was one of the Black Glades, ancient and corrupted, rumored to be Malakor's ancestral lair. A place where the very shadows shifted and writhed with dark purpose.

Pushing through the dense undergrowth, Slash emerged into a clearing consumed by shadow, even the air feeling heavier, colder. At its center, a grotesque altar of gnarled, obsidian-like roots pulsed with dark energy. And there, suspended above it, her pale form stark against the gloom, was Jubilee. She was still unconscious, ethereal and fragile, but her skin now had an unnatural, almost translucent glow. Tendrils of shadow snaked from the altar, reaching for her, seemingly trying to merge with the emerald dust that still clung to her hair.

Malakor stood before the altar, his back to Slash, his hands raised in some vile ritual. His voice, guttural and resonant, chanted words of an ancient, corrupted tongue, words that spoke of dominance, and the subjugation of light.

A chilling laugh escaped Malakor's lips, echoing in the deathly silent glade. "Ah, little brother. You finally made it. Just in time to witness the commencement of my true reign."

Slash felt a cold fury, so absolute it almost froze the agony he was in. He tried to summon his shadow, to tear through Malakor, to reach Jubilee, but his power felt thin, diluted. A mere flicker compared to its usual roaring inferno. He was a dying ember, and Malakor stood before him, poised to ignite absolute darkness.

"Release her, Malakor," Slash rasped, his voice raw with unspoken threats. "Now."

Malakor turned, his red eyes glowing in the gloom, his face twisted into a sneering mockery of triumph. "Foolish, Slash. You sacrificed everything to rescue her from the Nexus, only to bring her directly to me. She is no longer yours to 'release.' She is the conduit. The key. The instrument. She is mine." A cruel smile stretched his lips. "And you, little brother, are exactly where I want you. Weak. Broken. Powerless. A front-row seat to your own annihilation."

The chilling pronouncement from Malakor, heavy with cold contempt, was a physical blow, a weight settling on Slash's chest. He staggered, the grotto's lingering chill a phantom memory compared to the icy despair that threatened to consume him. "No..." he breathed, his voice a ragged whisper.

Above, Jubilee stirred. Her eyelids fluttered, a soft sigh escaping her lips. The sound, barely audible, snagged on something deep within Slash, a tether that snapped him from the brink of oblivion. His gaze locked onto her, willing her consciousness, willing her strength. The emerald dust on her hair seemed to shimmer, responding to the unseen shift within her.

A faint tremor ran through the gnarled altar, a low hum that vibrated through the very earth. Malakor, still sneering at Slash, paused, his head cocked, a flicker of irritation crossing his face. "What is this?" he muttered, his ritual interrupted.

Jubilee's eyes, a brilliant, unfocused emerald, snapped open, fixing on nothing, seeing everything. A raw sound, half-gasp, half-sob, tore from her throat. A wave of pure, unadulterated emerald light erupted from her, not a focused attack, but a blinding, desperate burst of pure magic, a primal scream of unbound power.

It hit the altar first. The obsidian roots screamed, a sound that was more sensation than noise, a grinding of ancient stone and violated magic. Dark tendrils recoiled, shriveling to ash as the emerald light surged. The very substance of the altar seemed to crack and splinter under the onslaught, shimmering with fractured dark energy.

Malakor cried out, thrown backward by the force. His perfect control shattered, his arrogant smile replaced by a look of bewildered fury. He reeled, fighting to regain his footing, his shadow magic flaring in ragged bursts, trying to push back the unexpected surge.

Slash, though weakened, felt a surge of something akin to electric shock. It was Jubilee's magic, yes, but different. Rawer, more untamed, infused with a power he hadn't witnessed even during their union in the glade. It was the power of the Nexus, untethered and unleashing instinctively. The green light washed over him, momentarily invigorating, sharpening his senses. He saw the genuine shock ripple across Malakor's face, a crack in his seemingly impenetrable facade.

As the emerald burst continued, a chilling realization dawned on Malakor. "She's merging!" he shrieked, no longer gloating, a note of fear entering his voice. "The fool... she's tearing herself apart to channel it all!"

But Jubilee wasn't tearing herself apart. Not yet. She was fighting, fighting the ancient corruption of the altar, fighting the insidious tendrils of shadow magic that had tried to claim her. Her desperate struggle, intensified by Slash's presence, was manifesting not as a controlled flow, but as a violent, unpredictable detonation of pure life force.

Roots, no longer gnarled and dark, burst from the ground around the altar, shimmering with golden light. They snaked and writhed, not in malevolent embrace, but in a chaotic, defensive dance, battering against the crumbling altar, seeking to cleanse its desecrated power. The air crackled with the clash of light and shadow, the glade groaning under the immense, conflicting forces.

Malakor, recovering his balance, advanced, his face contorted with unholy rage. "No!" he roared, summoning a massive wave of shadow. "She is mine! I will control it!"

But the wave of shadow, meant to engulf Jubilee, met the emerald blast head-on. The two forces collided with a concussive shockwave, shaking the very trees, throwing Slash back against a gnarled trunk. The clash was deafening, a symphony of destruction and desperate creation. Jubilee, suspended above the altar, was an emerald beacon, her desperate struggle radiating outward, shaking the very foundations of Malakor's lair.

The ancient, corrupted black glade, long accustomed to stagnant shadow, was now a vortex of conflicting raw magic, and at its heart, a glimmering, terrifying proof that Jubilee was anything but powerless.

57

The concussive shockwave slammed Slash against the rough bark of a twisted tree, rattling teeth in his skull. Pain, a familiar, unwelcome companion, flared through his already ravaged body, threatening to drown him in unconsciousness. But then he saw Malakor's distorted face, twisted in fury, and heard Jubilee's raw, struggling gasp amidst the emerald light. The insidious chill that had threatened to consume him moments ago transmuted into a furious, burning heat. He was weak, yes, but not broken. Not while she fought. Not while she existed.

Malakor, having been thrown back, reeled into a devastating counterattack, his shadows coalescing into jagged spears aimed directly at the shimmering, uncoordinated pillar of light that was Jubilee. "She'll tear herself apart!" Malakor shrieked, a twisted parody of concern in his voice, his true intent a vile hunger for the power she unwittingly unleashed.

Slash's mind, though fogged with pain and depletion, sharpened with a singular, desperate focus. He couldn't match Malakor's raw power, not now. But he knew Malakor. He knew his brother's arrogance, his blind spots, his obsession. And he knew Jubilee, knew the terrifying, beautiful depth of her untamed magic.

Panic, cold and sharp, threatened to grip him. The emerald fury wasn't an attack, not a calculated spell. It was a scream, a shield of pure, instinctual defiance from a being pushed past her breaking point. If she continued to channel the Nexus's corrupted energy without control, Malakor's words would become prophecy. She would be consumed.

"Jubilee!" His voice, raw and strained, was swallowed by the clamor of clashing magic. He pushed off the tree, bones screaming in protest, every nerve in his body alight with searing agony. He was a shadow of his former self, a flicker against Malakor's raging storm, but he had to try.

He wouldn't intercept the shadow spears directly. He couldn't. Instead, he lunged not at Malakor, but towards the swirling vortex of corrupted magic around the altar, a desperate, foolhardy gamble. He needed to get to *her*.

Malakor, caught off guard by Slash's ill-advised charge, hesitated for a split second, a flicker of surprise replacing his rage. He expected resistance, strategic counter-attacks, but not this reckless, suicidal dash. That hesitation was all Slash needed.

Drawing on the deepest, most primordial reserves of shadow, the essence of his very being, Slash willed his form to dissolve. Not to a solid, corporeal shadow, but to a whisper of darkness, a momentary absence in the maelstrom. It was a dangerous, near-fatal maneuver, pushing his already failing body beyond its limits. His vision swam, pinpricks of light exploding behind his eyes. He felt as if his very essence was being torn asunder.

He navigated the tumultuous clash of energy, the emerald forces of Jubilee's uncontrolled burst deflecting Malakor's dark spears. It was agonizingly slow, each dissolve and reappearance a hammer blow to his core. He ghosted past a lashing root, felt the searing heat of an emerald wave graze his arm, but he pushed through, driven by a singular, desperate terror.

His target was the Obsidian Altar, the source of Jubilee's agony, the fulcrum of Malakor's vile ritual. If he could reach it, could disrupt Malakor's connection, even for a moment...

He solidified just inches from the pulsating obsidian, the stone humming with the dark magic that sought to claim Jubilee. The air around it was thick, choked with the oppressive weight of ancient corruption. He grimaced, a bitter taste filling his mouth. This was where Malakor had begun his ritual, binding her to its foul energy.

Before Malakor could react, before his brother could fully comprehend the suicidal defiance of his weakened kin, Slash made his move. With a guttural roar, drawing on a wellspring of protective fury he didn't know he possessed, he slammed his hand, not onto the altar, but onto the pulsing, dark tendril directly connecting Jubilee to its profane surface.

A jolt, blinding and excruciating, tore through him. It was Malakor's unbridled power, the condensed essence of his brother's dark magic, searing through his already brittle form. But it was also Jubilee, a faint, desperate echo of her essence, battling within the tendril's grip.

He wasn't trying to absorb it, not defeat it. He was trying to sever it. To sever the physical link, to break Malakor's insidious hold. He channeled every last, flickering spark of his own shadow into the single point of contact, not as an attack, but as a disruptive pulse, a rogue frequency meant to shatter the fragile, forced connection.

Malakor shrieked, a sound of pure, unadulterated outrage. "You fool! You'll destroy her!"

But Slash held fast, teeth gritted, veins standing out on his neck. His body screamed, his vision tunneling to a single, burning point. The tendril throbbed, resisting, then with a wet, tearing sound, it began to fray, smoke curling around it. A fissure opened in its dark surface, a tiny, emerald crack.

Then, with a blinding flash, every circuit in his body overloading, Slash felt a profound, searing *snap* as the tendril exploded, showering him in jagged fragments of solidified shadow and raw, emerald light. He was thrown backward, colliding with the grotto floor. Darkness consumed him, merciful and absolute. But before it did, he felt it – a release, a surge of free-floating emerald energy, no longer tethered. He had done it. He had freed her.

Malakor's shriek echoed through the Black Glade, a sound of pure, unadulterated outrage that curdled the air. "You imbecile! You've ruined everything!" He stood, shoulders heaving, eyes blazing with a hatred so profound it warped the shadows around him. The remnants of the exploded tendril, shimmering with the last vestiges of its dark magic, disintegrated into dust around him. Slash lay motionless on the grotto floor, a broken discard, his sacrifice seemingly inconsequential in the face of Malakor's escalating fury.

Jubilee, no longer tethered, had fallen, a limp bundle of emerald light amidst the deepening gloom. Her own furious magic, unleashed in that uncontrollable burst, flickered and receded like a dying flame, leaving her vulnerable and exposed.

Malakor's gaze, sweeping from the unconscious Slash to the inert Jubilee, settled on his brother with a chilling intensity. His fists clenched, drawing in the surrounding shadows until they writhed like agitated serpents around him. "You think you've won, brother?" His voice was a low growl, laced with venom. "You think this pathetic defiance frees her? It only ensures her destruction, and yours, by my hand."

He raised his hands, drawing the very essence of the tormented glade into himself. The obsidian altar, scarred but still pulsing, vibrated with renewed, malevolent energy. Dark tendrils, thicker and more numerous than before, erupted from the stone, snaking outwards, searching. But they weren't seeking Jubilee. They were seeking Slash.

"A living sacrifice," Malakor hissed, his eyes glinting with a terrifying madness. "A final, definitive statement. You offer yourself, broken and useless, to fuel my ascension. And she..." A cruel smile twisted his lips. "She will witness it all, before I choose her fate."

The tendrils, fueled by Malakor's rage and the glade's corrupted power, descended upon Slash, binding him. They weren't elegant bindings like before; they were brutal, crushing constrictions, seeking to drain every last drop of life and shadow from his already depleted form. Slash groaned, a faint, ragged sound, as the immense pressure squeezed the air from his lungs. Even unconscious, his body convulsed, fighting the insidious invasion.

Malakor slowly advanced, savoring the moment, basking in the raw power that pulsed around him. "Look, Jubilee," he purred, his voice dripping with condescending triumph. "Behold the futility of his sacrifice. Behold the true measure of my strength."

But Jubilee, even in her unconscious state, was not entirely defeated. A faint, almost imperceptible tremor ran through her body. A single, errant root, untouched by the initial blast, began to glow beside her. It wasn't the vibrant, uncontrolled surge from before, but a slow, pulsating light, like a heartbeat struggling to be heard.

Malakor, too consumed by his vengeance, failed to notice it. He stood over Slash, a dark god ready to claim his due. He lifted a hand, preparing to deliver the final, crushing blow, to rip Slash's essence from his very core and merge it with his own, consolidating his dominance.

Just as Malakor's hand began its descent, a small, yet insistent, emerald light flared from Jubilee. It was a cry for help, a desperate, intuitive lash of magic reaching out, not for defense, but for connection.

A single, vibrant emerald thread, impossibly fine yet undeniably potent, shot from Jubilee's still form. It bypassed Malakor entirely, bypassing the struggling Slash, and instead embedded itself directly into the corrupted obsidian altar.

Malakor paused, his brow furrowed in annoyance. "What is this trickery?" he growled, momentarily distracted.

The emerald thread pulsed. Then, slowly, infinitesimally, the malevolent hum of the altar began to change. A high, discordant vibration began to emanate from its surface, a subtle counterpoint to Malakor's growing dominance.

Malakor's eyes widened, a flicker of genuine fear crossing his face. "No," he whispered, his voice laced with dawning horror. "She's... She's not trying to fight me. She's trying to reclaim it."

The sacred heart of the glade, the Nexus, still resonated within Jubilee. Even unconscious, driven by a primal need for truth and balance, she was reaching out. Reaching to mend what Malakor had twisted, to purify what he had corrupted. And she was doing it through the very instrument of his vile ritual.

Malakor's roar of realization ripped through the air, a visceral expression of his sudden, terrifying comprehension. "No! I won't allow it!" He whirled, his shadowed hand lashing out towards the altar, clawing at the impossibly thin emerald thread that pulsed with defiance. He unleashed a furious blast of shadow magic, raw and untamed, meant to sever the connection, to obliterate the audacious strand and reclaim his monstrous ritual.

But the thread, though delicate, shimmered with an unexpected resilience. Instead of snapping, it absorbed Malakor's attack, drawing his dark energy into the Nexus itself, amplifying the discordant vibrations emanating from the altar. The obsidian surface crackled, not with malevolent power, but with a chaotic, unholy resonance as light and shadow clashed within its core.

Jubilee's body, still limp on the floor, began to twitch. The faint emerald glow at her side pulsed faster, stronger, mirroring the energy now surging from the altar. Her connection to the Nexus, which Malakor had intended to exploit, had instead become a lifeline, a conduit for her restorative magic to challenge his corruption.

"Impossible!" Malakor shrieked, pressing his attack. Tendrils of shadow erupted from his fingertips, slamming against the altar, trying to rend the glowing thread. Each burst of his power, however, seemed to feed the growing chaos within the stone. A high-pitched whine rose from the altar, growing in intensity, vibrating through the Black Glade and setting one's teeth on edge. The very air shimmered, thick with opposing magical energies.

The corrupted tendrils binding Slash convulsed violently, caught in the backlash of the warring powers. Slash, barely conscious, gasped, his body arching under the renewed strain as his own weakened essence was pulled and twisted by the chaotic forces.

"This is your doing, you fool!" Malakor snarled, his eyes darting between the vibrating altar and his struggling brother. He knew, with a chilling certainty, that if Jubilee succeeded in purifying the altar, even partially, his entire ritual would be ruined, his carefully laid plans for dominion shattered.

With a guttural cry, Malakor abandoned subtlety. He plunged both hands directly into the obsidian altar, forcing his shadow magic into its core in a desperate, last-ditch effort to drown out Jubilee's influence. The grotto groaned, responding to the massive surge of conflicting power. Cracks spiderwebbed across the altar's surface, glowing with alternating emerald and shadowy light.

The backlash was instantaneous and brutal. The grotto itself recoiled. Waves of raw, untamed magic, born from the clash of Jubilee's pure essence and Malakor's consuming shadow, erupted outwards like a concussion. The ground shuddered; stalactites splintered and crashed to the floor. The remaining shadows that clung to the grotto walls writhed and tore, unable to withstand the sheer magical force.

Jubilee's body was flung violently to the side, tumbling unconscious. The emerald thread, momentarily overwhelmed by the chaotic energy, snapped. But the impact on the altar had been made. The malevolent hum of the obsidian, though still present, was fractured, tainted by an unfamiliar purity.

Malakor was thrown backwards by the explosion of energy, slamming against the far wall with a grunt of pain. His hands, still smoking from their direct contact with the altar's core, were scorched and shaking. He scrambled to his feet, eyes blazing with furious realization. The altar was damaged. More importantly, it was no longer solely his.

He looked from the unconscious Jubilee to the groaning Slash, then back at the now intermittently glowing altar. A new, terrifying calculation flickered in Malakor's eyes. This wasn't a simple disruption; it was an infection, a contamination of his ultimate weapon. And it had been wrought by an unconscious fae, fueled by a connection he had underestimated. His grand plan, his ascension, now faced an unpredictable, chaotic obstacle. His rage solidified around a terrifying, singular purpose: absolute destruction.

60

The air thrummed with a grotesque hum, no longer solely Malakor's malevolent thrum, but a discordant symphony born from the fractured obsidian altar. It was a dying gasp, a desperate shriek, or perhaps a birth cry - none could tell. What was clear was that the energy unleashed from its core refused to be contained. Instead of dissipating, it radiated outward in erratic, agonizing waves, seeking purchase, seeking targets.

The first to feel its unpredictable touch was Malakor. Scrambling upright, fury a tangible aura around him, he was suddenly engulfed in a blinding flash of emerald light emanating directly from the cracked altar. It wasn't a gentle light; it burned, searing his shadowed flesh, forcing a guttural roar from his throat as he clawed at his eyes. For a terrifying, fleeting moment, his very essence seemed to recoil, his control over his powers shattering around him like brittle glass. Raw pain, a sensation he rarely experienced, ripped through him, leaving him vulnerable, exposed.

Jubilee, still unconscious and flung against the grotto wall, was next. A wave of pure, concentrated shadow energy, twisted and corrupted by the altar's trauma, slammed into her. Rather than draining her, it shocked her system, sending a violent tremor through her fragile form. Her lips parted, a silent scream caught in her throat as her forest magic, though weakened, instinctively battled the intrusion. The ethereal glow that had clung to her faded, replaced by a flickering, unstable darkness that mirrored the glade's suffering. It wasn't a direct attack, but a reverberation, an unintended consequence of the chaos she had unleashed. Her breath hitched, shallow and ragged, her essence teetering on the precipice of oblivion.

But the most profound, unsettling effect of the fractured altar's surge manifested in Slash. Bound by Malakor's draining tendrils, already on the brink of fading, he was hit by a chaotic fusion of emerald and shadow. It was less a wave, more a torrent, a maelstrom of conflicting energies that tore at his essence. Instead of destroying him, it reignited something within. The emerald light, infused with Jubilee's residual life force and the glade's purest magic, sought out his deepest wounds, the lingering effects of the Elderwood blade. It coursed through him like an electric current, jarring every atom. The shadow energy, too, found its mark, but instead of crushing him, it sparked, reacting with the emerald in a violent, unpredictable bloom.

His eyes, previously dull and glazed, snapped open. No longer the familiar violet, they were a swirling vortex of black and vibrant green, an unsettling reflection of the forces warring within him. A guttural growl, deeper and more primal than any Malakor had ever heard from him, ripped from his chest. The tendrils binding him, instead of draining, began to crackle and burn from the inside out, fueled by the volatile power now surging through him.

Malakor, still reeling from the emerald burn, stared in horrified disbelief. "What... what have you done?!" he choked out, seeing the potent, dangerous transmutation happening within his brother. Slash was changing, warping, manifesting something wholly new, something not entirely shadow, not entirely light, but an unholy, potent hybrid of both.

Slash let out another feral cry, the echo reverberating through the grotto, shaking even the bedrock. With a violent, impossible surge, the corrupted tendrils binding him exploded outwards, showering debris across the Black Glade. He stood, swaying, a creature reborn, his body radiating an unpredictable, raw power that sizzled in the air. The emerald and shadow within him clashed, harmonized, then clashed again, promising devastation or miracle. His gaze, an unnerving emerald-black, fixed on Malakor, not with hatred, but with a terrifying, primal emptiness that spoke of untold power. The fractured altar pulsed again, now a violent, unpredictable heart, and the Black Glade braced itself for the storm it had inadvertently awakened.

61

Malakor, caught off guard by the sheer instability of Slash's power, struggled to counter. He unleashed wave after wave of corrosive darkness, but Slash, in his altered state, seemed immune to its draining effects. Instead, the shadow intensified the emerald within him, becoming a furious green flame that crackled around his form.

"You're destroying yourself!" Malakor screamed, desperate as another emerald-laced shadow blast slammed him against the grotto wall, cracking the ancient stone. The fractured altar pulsed violently, mirroring the chaotic surge of power.

Slash closed the distance, his eyes burning with that terrifying, empty power. His hand reached out, not to strike, but to *consume*. Malakor felt a cold dread as Slash's fingers, now tipped with flickering emerald, brushed his temple. It wasn't a physical attack; it was a violation, an attempt to siphon, to unravel his very essence.

Malakor screamed, a sound of pure terror and agony, grappling with the sensation of being drained, not of his life force, but of his very identity. He knew then that this was not merely Slash; it was something else, something born of desperate circumstance and unstable magic, a force that knew no brother, only power. He fought with renewed desperation, knowing that if this lasted, he would be consumed, remade, or perhaps, simply erased. The Black Glade, already scarred, shuddered under the onslaught, threatening to collapse under the sheer, unbridled power of its unexpected master.

62

The black glade throbbed, a living, groaning entity under the relentless assault of Slash's uncontrolled power. What had begun as an attack on Malakor was now a sweeping, indiscriminant rampage, a storm of emerald-laced shadow ripping through the very fabric of the grotto. Roots, already corrupted, withered and then disintegrated under the chaotic energies, leaving behind scorches of raw magic. Ancient stones, once immutable, cracked and dissolved into dust, unable to withstand the sheer, unbridled force.

Malakor, still reeling from the intimate violation of Slash's touch, stumbled back. The drain on his identity, the unsettling sensation of his own shadow essence twisting under the intrusive emerald spark, was an agony far beyond any physical wound. He recognized the pattern, however, a destructive feedback loop of raw power. Slash wasn't aiming; he was simply *unleashing*. Every defensive blast Malakor threw, every surge of his own dark energy, was absorbed and re-emitted by Slash, amplified and poisoned with that virulent green light.

"Stop, you fool! You'll destroy us all!" Malakor bellowed, his voice hoarse, swallowed by the roar of collapsing rock and tearing magic. He darted, ducked, and weaved, no longer attempting to fight back, but merely to survive the terrifying tempest that was his brother. He saw now, with chilling clarity, that this was the result of Jubilee's desperate magic on his own altar, combined with Slash's already unstable power. A fusion gone catastrophically wrong.

Jubilee, still unconscious, was tossed by the magical maelstrom, her form an inert beacon of flickering emerald light amidst the encroaching chaos. Her connection to the Nexus, though fractured, still hummed, acting as a strange magnet for the violent energy. Even as the grotto tore itself apart, a faint, almost imperceptible thread of emerald pulsed from her, feeding, and in turn being consumed by, the very destruction. She lay perilously close to the swirling vortex of power emanating from Slash, untouched by its direct fury, yet dangerously susceptible to its systemic collapse.

Slash, his emerald-black eyes fixed on nothing, was a conduit for raw, unrefined energy. He didn't seem to recognize Malakor, or the sacred space he was tearing apart, or even the unconscious fae he had sworn to protect. He was pure instinct, pure reaction, a whirlwind of destructive creation that threatened not just their lives, but the very existence of the Black Glade. Tendrils of shadow and emerald writhed from his body like an inky, glowing corona, reaching out, touching, and obliterating everything in their path. The air crackled with untold magical pressure, making it difficult to breathe, the scent of ozone and scorched earth thick and acrid.

Malakor, ever the pragmatist, saw his own survival at stake. He tried to erect stronger defensive wards, but they shattered like glass under the unceasing barrage. The very ground beneath their feet began to heave, the obsidian altar at the grotto's center groaning ominously. Cracks, white-hot with contained magic, spiderwebbed across the floor, threatening to swallow them whole.

"I need to sever the connection... cut him off from that... that abomination of power!" Malakor muttered, circling Slash warily, looking for any weakness, any vulnerability in the storm of his brother's rage. He extended a hand, attempting a draining spell, but the chaotic backlash of Slash's energy slammed him against a jagged grotto wall, leaving him gasping for breath, shards of rock embedded in his shoulder.

The Glade, once a bastion of dark magic, was now a tomb, collapsing piece by painful piece. The very air thinned, magic siphoned and expended by Slash's destructive aura. A low, resonant hum began to emanate from the ground, growing in intensity, a sound that spoke of fundamental instability. Malakor's eyes widened in dawning horror. The Nexus. Slash's unchecked power was threatening to utterly destroy the Nexus itself, the very heart of the glade, and in doing so, collapse the entire ancient structure. If it went, everything would be consumed.

Slash, oblivious, let out another guttural roar, a sound that was less voice and more the grinding of tectonic plates. He began to rise, slowly, inexorably, pulling more and more raw energy from the crumbling grotto, from the very air itself. His form pulsed, swelling with terrifying power, threatening to burst. The grotto groaned again, a deep, earth-shaking shudder. This wasn't merely a fight anymore; it was an extinction event. Malakor knew, with a sudden, chilling certainty, that if something didn't intervene, and quickly, the glade, Jubilee, and eventually, himself, would simply cease to exist.

63

Malakor, cornered and desperate, saw a single, terrifying possibility. The Nexus was fracturing, bleeding light and shadow into a maelstrom that would consume everything. Slash, his brother, was no longer Slash, but a walking apocalypse. And Jubilee, the unwitting fuse for this cataclysm, floated precariously at its heart.

"There's only one way," Malakor rasped, pulling himself from the jagged rock, blood streaking his jaw. His eyes, usually cold and calculating, held a flicker of genuine fear, stark in the emerald-black chaos. He had watched the corrupted glade for centuries, harnessing its power, slowly bending it to his will. To see it unravel like this, by his own brother's hand, was an unbearable torment. His gaze darted from the shuddering ceiling to the quivering obsidian altar, then settled on Slash, whose form now pulsed with overwhelming, unstable energy.

The Nexus. It was the key, the source, the power that unified this dark glade. And it was failing. Its raw energy, channeled erratically through Jubilee's brief connection and now funneled into Slash's transformation, was literally tearing their world apart.

Malakor moved. Not to attack, not to defend, but to intercept. He flung himself towards Slash, not with a spell of offense, but with a complex series of hand gestures, weaving threads of pure shadow, not to fight, but to bind. It was a net, finely spun, designed to contain, to channel, not to harm. Slash, lost in his destructive trance, didn't register the attempt until it was too late. The shadow threads wrapped around him, shimmering with dark light, attempting to impose order on the raging storm within.

The effect was instantaneous and violent. Slash roared, a sound of pure agony and protest as the binding constricted him. The emerald-black corona pulsed erratically, threatening to shatter Malakor's carefully constructed bonds. Malakor gritted his teeth, pouring more power, more will, into the restraining magic. This was not a power struggle between brothers, but a desperate attempt to cage a hurricane before it destroyed the very air they breathed.

"Jubilee!" he screamed, his voice strained. "Jubilee, you have to break it! Her connection! Slash, he's... he's pulling power from you!"

His words were barely audible over the groaning of the grotto, but a flicker of emerald light from Jubilee intensified, almost as if she heard him. The thread connecting her to the chaotic energies radiating from Slash and the shattered altar briefly flared.

"You won't defeat me, Malakor!" Slash's voice, distorted and multi-layered, ripped through the grotto, as if a thousand voices spoke through him at once. He thrashed, the shadow-emerald energies around him exploding outward, tearing at Malakor's bindings. Malakor felt the pressure, the sheer, crushing force of his brother's untamed rage. His nose began to bleed, his vision blurred at the edges, but he held fast, fueled by a primal self-preservation.

"He's unstable, you fool! He's going to overload the Nexus!" Malakor yelled, his gaze on the epicenter of the pulsing power. "We share the same source, idiot! If that breaks, we both break!"

Suddenly, Malakor changed tactics. This wasn't working. His bindings were barely holding. There was only one way to drain the overwhelming energy, one desperate gambit. He reached out, not to the bindings, but directly into the heart of Slash's swirling power. He bit down hard on his own wrist, drawing blood, then smeared it across his open palm. A dark, ancient sigil, a symbol of primal containment, glowed on his skin. With a guttural cry, he thrust his bloodied hand into the turbulent energies surrounding Slash, attempting to siphon off the excess power, to shunt it away, anywhere but here.

The reaction was catastrophic. The glade bucked. Slash convulsed, twin explosions of shadow and emerald ripping from him. Malakor screamed, his body arching as the immense, untamed energy surged into him. He was a conduit for a power no one should ever wield, a vessel for pure, destructive chaos. The glade around them began to collapse in on itself, not just tearing, but imploding. Malakor's eyes, wide with a mixture of agony and triumph, met Slash's blank, emerald-black gaze. This was their last chance. His risky gamble would either save them, or condemn them all to oblivion.

64

The catastrophic surge of power that ripped through the glade, a byproduct of Malakor's desperate gambit, did not consume Jubilee. Instead, like a forgotten spark catching flame, it ignited her. Her body, suspended above the fracturing and now imploding glade, shuddered. The thread of emerald light that Malakor had noted earlier, the faint connection to the raw, chaotic energies, flashed. It was no longer a flicker, but a blinding, emerald pulse, radiating outward from her form.

A gasp tore from Jubilee's lips, not of pain, but of profound, searing awareness. Her eyes, still closed, snapped open, revealing pupils that burned with a fierce, untamed emerald light. Consciousness returned to her in a dizzying rush, flooded by the overwhelming resonance of the glade's agony, the Nexus's fracturing lament, and the violent, uncontrolled storm that was Slash. She felt every chaotic pulse, every rending tear in the fabric of their world, intimately, viscerally.

Malakor's guttural scream, a primal sound of agony and triumph as he served as the conduit for Slash's excess power, resonated deep within her. She recognized the desperation, the impossible gamble. And then, she felt it: the essence of Slash, a raw, tormented scream trapped within a swirling vortex of emerald and shadow, trying to rip itself apart. What she had felt within the Nexus, a mere echo of its heart, was now amplified a thousandfold through him, a terrifying, beautiful song of creation and destruction.

Her hands instinctively shot out, not toward Malakor, not even directly to Slash, but to the very air around them, to the swirling chaos itself. A golden-green light emanated from her palms, threads of pure, ancient forest magic, reaching, not to fight, but to contain, to soothe, to channel. This was not the glade's wild, untamed fury, but Jubilee's own innate power, refined by her absorption of the Nexus essence, tempered by her intimate connection to the living, dying heart of the glade.

"No!" she whispered, her voice surprisingly clear amidst the cacophony. It was a plea, a command, a heartbreak. "Not like this. Not him."

The emerald threads from her hands wove themselves into Malakor's blood-sigil-infused siphon, acting not as a counter, but as an amplifier, a rectifier. They took the immense, unruly energy that Malakor struggled to contain and, with a subtle shift, began to feed it back into the glade itself, not in a destructive burst, but in a controlled, restorative flow. Roots, fractured and twisted by Slash's rampage, began to pulsate with a faint green glow. The shuddering walls of the grotto, threatening to collapse, seemed to stabilize, almost imperceptibly.

Slash convulsed violently as the siphoned energy moved not *into* Malakor, but *through* Malakor and *into* the glade. The emerald-black swirl around him began to calm, though his form still pulsated erratically. He was being drained, not by Malakor, but by Jubilee, through Malakor, into a starving glade.

Malakor, overwhelmed by the sudden, unexpected redirection of power, choked. He felt the immense power flow through him, but instead of the destructive agony of before, it was a searing, cleansing heat, pulling not just from Slash, but from Malakor's own reserves, drawing it all into the wounded glade. His eyes, still wide with a mixture of terror and triumph, now turned to Jubilee, burning with a new, horrified awe. He saw not just a powerful fae, but a living conduit, a resonant, conscious heart. He was a mere artery, she was the pulse.

"Jubilee, what... what are you doing?" he gasped, his voice weakening as his own ichor joined the flow of magic.

She didn't answer. Her eyes, still blazing with emerald light, fixed on Slash. She had sensed his pain, his uncontrolled essence, his absolute despair. She had felt the desperation in Malakor's gambit, the twin hungers for power and survival in both brothers. But more than that, she had felt the glade, her sanctuary, groaning its last breath.

A new surge of green energy erupted from Jubilee, enveloping Slash completely. It was a cocoon of pure, restorative power. It was not gentle, but fierce, demanding. She was not just healing the glade, she was reaching for Slash, her lifeline, her destiny. As the glade trembled, no longer on the verge of implosion, but in a profound shift, the true nature of her intervention became clear. She was not merely stopping the destruction; she was rewriting the rules.

65

The golden-green cocoon around Slash pulsed with an alarming intensity, mirroring Jubilee's own struggle. She had called back the runaway magic, channeled it through Malakor, and into the starved glade, but now the sheer volume of power was almost unbearable. Her hands, still outstretched, trembled violently. It was like trying to contain a supernova in the palms of her hands, the raw Nexus energy battling with Slash's explosive, unstable essence for dominance within her grasp.

Malakor, now a withered husk slumped against the grotto wall, watched with wide, disbelieving eyes. The malevolent black ichor that had previously flowed from Slash's wound was now being siphoned, purified, and re-absorbed into the glade, a process that felt both agonizingly slow and breathtakingly fast. He had wanted to control the Nexus, to dominate, but Jubilee was doing something far beyond his comprehension, something elemental and terrifyingly organic.

Within the emerald cocoon, Slash's chaotic pulsations began to lessen, albeit slowly. His form, still distorted by the uncontrolled power, started to coalesce. Jubilee felt every fraction of instability, every surge and ebb within him, as if it were her own heart struggling against an overwhelming tide. Her teeth were gritted, a fine sheen of sweat beading on her brow. This wasn't just healing; it was a fundamental re-ordering, a forcing of shattered pieces back into a new, unfamiliar whole.

Then, with a shudder that vibrated through her very bones, the cocoon began to contract. Emerald lightning arced across its surface, not destructive, but transformative. Slash's form inside snapped into focus, becoming unmistakably him - his strong, lean frame, his dark hair, even the familiar subtle curve of his lips. The terrifying emerald-black swirl in his eyes receded, leaving behind the piercing violet, though now flecked with brilliant emerald sparks that glittered like distant galaxies.

A deep, shuddering breath escaped his lips, and his eyelids fluttered open. His gaze, still hazy from the traumatic influx of power, found Jubilee. A profound sense of wonder, touched with a dizzying disorientation, filled his eyes. He tried to move, to reach for her, but the remaining strands of emerald energy binding him within the cocoon held firm.

"Jubilee..." His voice was rough, barely a whisper, yet it resonated deep within her, a calming anchor in the storm of power she still wrestled with.

"Easy," she gasped, focusing every ounce of her will. "You absorbed too much. You're... re-forming." The words felt inadequate, hollow against the magnitude of what was happening. She was re-knitting his very essence, anchoring his volatile power back into his body, a power that now carried the unmistakable scent of fertile earth and blossoming life alongside its inherent shadow.

The glade around them, though still showing the scars of the earlier battle, began to pulse with a healthy, vibrant glow. Fractured roots were knitting, scarred earth softened, and a fresh, dewy scent filled the air. The Nexus, no longer screaming its pain, hummed with a deep, resonant song, a melody of renewal and astonishing, dangerous growth.

But Jubilee felt the immense drain. This wasn't just a simple healing; it was a monumental act of creation. The very life force of the glade, and of herself, was being poured into stabilizing Slash, into allowing him to contain the terrifying energies he had briefly become. Her glowing hands began to dim, the golden-green light around her flickering.

"The glade... it needs you too," Slash whispered, his voice gaining strength. He felt the profound connection, the agonizing strain she was under. He recognized the desperate sacrifice, the way she was giving of herself to mend his broken essence.

Just as the cocoon shimmered its last, dissipating threads, Jubilee's strength finally gave out. The boundless power she had so fiercely wielded receded, leaving her body weak and trembling. She wavered, teetering on the edge of consciousness, her emerald eyes dimming. The effort was too much, the power too vast.

Before she could fall, Slash, now fully himself, lurched forward, breaking free from the last vestiges of the cocoon. His emerald-flecked violet eyes were ablaze with fierce concern as he caught her, pulling her close against his chest. His touch, typically cool and shadowed, was now warm, vibrant, infused with a newfound, potent vitality. He held her tightly, a primal instinct of protection radiating from him. The grotto, though now strangely serene, held the echo of their shared struggle, and the profound, transformative union that had just taken place.

66

Malakor, a mere shadow of his former malevolent self, watched Slash catch Jubilee, the last threads of the luminous cocoon dissolving. A raw, guttural sound tore from his throat. This wasn't merely healing; it was a transmutation, an integration of light and shadow, and it infuriated him. Slash, the weaker brother, the soft one who sought balance, had somehow transcended his very being. And Jubilee, that irritating forest fae, had been the catalyst.

His eyes, still burning with a vestige of the familiar dark power, fixed on Slash. He was renewed, yes, but also reeling, clearly not at full strength. It was now or never. Malakor had risked everything, revealed depths of his power he never intended, and still, this was the outcome. He would not allow it. He would not allow them to achieve the balance he despised.

With a ragged cry that was more defiance than ferocity, Malakor lunged. His movements were jerky, unrefined, but fueled by a desperate, suicidal rage. He aimed for Slash's throat, intending to claw, to tear, to rip apart the union that mocked his ambition. Dark energy, thin and sputtering, crackled around his fists, a mere ember compared to his former inferno, but enough to burn.

Slash, still cradling the fading Jubilee, felt the faint ripple of malicious intent. Too slow, too late. His new, emerald-flecked eyes narrowed. There was no longer the calculated distance, the sardonic amusement he once held for Malakor. There was only the fierce, primal protectiveness of a creature guarding its mate, its core, its newly found purpose.

Before Malakor could even close the distance, a wave of raw, emerald-infused shadow lashed out from Slash. It wasn't a focused attack, not a precise spell, but a visceral outpouring of his newly integrated essence. It slammed into Malakor, not with destructive force, but with a terrifying, transformative resonance.

Malakor shrieked, a sound of agony and disbelief. The shadowy tendrils rippling around him twisted, recoiled, and began to dissipate, leaving behind a faint, almost translucent green glow. The contact with Slash's new essence was anathema to him, not merely painful, but fundamentally disrupting. It was light where there should be only shadow, growth where there should be only decay.

He stumbled backwards, clutching his chest, his eyes wide with horror as he looked at his own hands. They were trembling, not with effort, but with what looked like... health. A faint, verdant sheen shimmered across his skin, where once only abyssal dark had resided.

The transformation was insidious, agonizingly slow, and utterly anathema to his being.

"No!" Malakor gasped, his voice cracking. "What have you done? You... you taint me!"

Slash, his grip on Jubilee tightening instinctively, regarded his brother with a cold, almost detached new clarity. "You tried to consume, Malakor. You sought to destroy." His voice was deeper now, the underlying rasp of shadow underscored by a resonant harmony, like deep earth mixed with ancient wind. "This is the price of trying to unmake what is destined to be made."

Malakor recoiled further, a primal, visceral scream building within him. The glade, now alive with restored vitality, pulsed around them, mirroring the vibrant energy radiating from Slash. The healing, regenerative magic coursing through the Nexus was washing over Malakor, and to him, it was a slow, agonizing poison.

He turned, desperation etching his face, and began to claw his way towards the grotto entrance, trying to escape the verdant nightmare. But with every strained step, the glade's newfound vibrancy seemed to leech into him, stripping away his familiar comfort of shadow, replacing it with an unbearable, purifying light. His form flickered, less substantial, his power diminishing with every breath of the renewed air.

Slash watched him go, a heavy silence settling between them. There was no triumph in his gaze, only a profound sense of closure, of an old, poisonous chapter finally ending. Malakor, stripped of his power, exiled by the very glade he sought to consume, was no longer a threat. He was merely a ghost, fading into the dawn.

With Malakor gone, Slash's attention flooded back to Jubilee. Her breathing was shallow, her body heavy in his arms. The powerful, terrifying grace she had shown, the sheer will to mend, had come at a cost. He looked down at her pale, still face, a fierce, protective tenderness swelling in his chest. His emerald-flecked violet eyes burned with a silent promise. She had pulled him back from the brink of oblivion, re-forged him. Now, he would return the debt. He would protect her, nurture her power, and guard their fragile, astounding balance.

67

Malakor's spectral form dissolved into the encroaching light, leaving a chilling echo of his agony. Slash hardly noticed. His world had shrunk to the slight weight of Jubilee in his arms, the faint whisper of her breath against his chest. He lowered her gently to the miraculously revitalized moss, her skin a delicate, almost translucent pale, a stark contrast to the vivid emerald life now pulsing all around them. The glade vibrated with newfound power, a testament to her sacrifice, but every beat of its vibrant heart seemed to draw from her dwindling reserves.

Her emerald lights, the very essence of her being, flickered like distant stars on the verge of fading. He could feel the profound emptiness within her, a cavernous space where her abundant magic once resided, now dangerously depleted. The Nexus, which she had so bravely woven into the tapestry of their world, hummed with a fierce, independent life, but Jubilee was merely a thread, fragile and fraying.

"Jubilee," he murmured, his voice thick with a new, unwelcome fear. Panic, cold and sharp, threatened to pierce through his recently restored composure. He had faced down countless foes, stared into the abyss of his own fractured being, but this... this vulnerability in her, born of her fierce loyalty and selflessness, was a terror he was utterly unprepared for.

He instinctively reached out, his new emerald-flecked hands hovering over her. His own re-forged magic, vibrant and thrumming with untold potential, felt foreign, almost too powerful. He tried to send a gentle current of his essence into her, a soft, encouraging push. But his touch, now a devastating blend of light and shadow, was too much. A faint, almost imperceptible tremor ran through her, a shudder of rejection from her exhausted core. He hastily withdrew, a knot of frustration tightening in his gut.

This was not like healing a physical wound, mending a tear in the flesh. This was a profound energetic depletion, a spiritual void that demanded something more than raw power. He needed to understand the mechanics of this intricate network of light she had so gracefully wielded, needed to find a direct vein to its source, not just a haphazard insertion of his own.

He looked around the grotto, now more vibrant than he had ever seen it. Luminescent fungi glowed with a renewed inner fire, water cascaded with a musical clarity, and the very air thrummed with revitalized magic. But the source of this reawakening, the very heart that beat within it, was now threatening to consume its keeper.

He closed his eyes, focusing, reaching out with every tendril of his transformed perception. He sought the

Nexus, the core she had plunged into, the wellspring of the glade's magic. He felt it—a vast, pulsating heart of raw energy deep beneath the grotto floor. It radiated life, power, and a hungry demand for balance.

He drew a breath, the renewed air of the cleansed grotto filling his lungs. It carried the scent of wet earth, burgeoning life, and a faint, sweet, ethereal hum. It was the glade's song, and Jubilee was its voice, now reduced to a whisper.

He remembered her words, her instincts, her innate connection to this place. She had drawn from it, given to it, become intrinsically linked. It was a symbiotic dance, now tragically out of sync. He had to re-harmonize it, restore the flow, or she would simply fade.

His eyes snapped open, a sudden, fierce understanding illuminating their emerald-violet depths. The Nexus pulsed. The grotto thrived. Jubilee diminished. The answer wasn't to force his strength upon her, but to re-establish her connection to the fundamental life force of the glade. She was its rightful conduit, its beating pulse. He had to rekindle that pulse.

A plan, audacious and perilous, began to form in his mind. It would demand everything he had, every ounce of his new, integrated power. It would be a dangerous dance, balancing on the knife's edge between restoration and further depletion. But there was no other way. He would not lose her now, not after she had given him everything.

He knelt beside her, his transformed hands gently tracing the lines of her face, the soft curve of her jaw. Her skin felt cool to the touch, almost fragile. A fierce resolve hardened his gaze. He would dive into the Nexus himself, find the source of its energy, and then, with his own essence as a bridge, pour it back into his exhausted mate. He would become the conduit, the lifeblood, to revive her.

68

Slash pressed a faint kiss to Jubilee's colorless lips, a silent promise, a desperate vow. The audacity of his plan fueled a cold, sharp energy within his transformed core. He wasn't merely going to channel, he was going to merge. To become the eye of the storm, standing within the Nexus itself, a living bridge between raw power and flagging life.

He closed his eyes, extending his consciousness, every fiber of his being reaching for the resonating hum beneath the grotto floor. It pulsed like a second heart, more ancient and potent than any creature's. He didn't seek out its entrance; he simply dissolved, becoming one with the faint emerald-violet mist that rose from his form.

The shift was instantaneous, breathtaking. One moment, his presence was distinct on the mossy ground; the next, he was everywhere, nowhere, swallowed by the immense, vibrant energies of the Nexus. It was utterly disorienting, a symphony of light and raw, untamed power that threatened to atomize his very being. The air was a liquid current of pure magic, vibrating with the collective consciousness of the glade's millennia of existence.

He felt the ancient roots, the unseen rivers of life, the hidden chambers where crystal pulsed with captured starlight. He was immersed in the glade's memories: the gentle caress of elven hands, the fury of ancient storms, the slow, relentless creep of encroaching darkness, and the recent, desperate surge of Jubilee's defiant magic.

It was overwhelming, a cacophony of power and sensation. He had to center himself, find his own core within this boundless immensity. He honed in on the sensation of Jubilee, a precious, fragile beacon in the vastness. Her essence, though faint, pulsed with a familiar connection, a thread of light that drew him.

He reached for it, not with hands, but with an extension of his will, a projection of his own newly integrated light and shadow. The Nexus recognized his duality, the balance within him, and did not resist. Instead, it welcomed him, a tempest acknowledging a kindred storm.

Now, truly a conduit, Slash began the delicate, perilous work. He drew the shimmering, life-giving energy of the Nexus, the very essence that had fueled the glade's revitalization, and began to filter it through his own transformed being. It was like attempting to push a river through a narrow stream. The sheer force threatened to tear him apart, but he held firm, his focus absolute.

He could feel Jubilee's essence, a parched vessel, waiting for this lifeblood. With agonizing control, he began to feed it to her, not a flood, but a gentle, steady trickle, designed to coax her weary magic back to life. He poured his own strength into the flow, becoming the anchor, the mediator, the living pump.

Back in the physical grotto, Jubilee stirred faintly. A soft, emerald luminescence began to emanate from her pale skin, strengthening with each passing second. The moss beneath her vibrated under the escalating flow of magic. Her eyes, still closed, seemed to glimmer beneath her eyelids.

The strain on Slash was immense. He was a creature of shadow, now holding back a sun, distilling its power into a gentle dew. His consciousness began to fray at the edges, the edges of his vision blurring into a blinding, emerald haze. He felt the insidious pull of the Nexus, the urge to simply dissolve entirely, to become one with its eternal hum.

But the image of Jubilee, her fragile beauty, her fierce spirit, anchored him. He felt her response, a weak but undeniable surge of reciprocal energy, like a seed unfurling towards light. It was enough. It was his anchor.

With a final, gargantuan effort, he channeled a wave of concentrated Nexus energy, mingled intimately with his own essence, directly into her core. The pulse that returned was stronger, vibrant, radiating warmth. He had done it.

The instantaneous release was almost as violent as the merging. Slash felt his consciousness snap back, his body solidifying with a jarring jolt. He stumbled, gasping for air, collapsing onto the ground beside Jubilee, utterly depleted, but unbroken.

He looked at her, his vision still swimming with residual Nexus light. The profound paleness was receding, replaced by a delicate flush. Her lips held a faint, natural tint. And then, her eyes, those beautiful, familiar emerald eyes, fluttered open. They were still heavy with exhaustion, but the light within them was undeniable, vibrant, and utterly, wonderfully alive.

69

Jubilee's emerald eyes, still hazy with awakening, met Slash's. A sigh, soft as a forest breeze, escaped her lips, and a fragile smile touched them. "Slash..." she whispered, her voice reedy but present.

But before Slash could respond, before he could drink in the relief of her revival, a guttural groan ripped through the very fabric of the grotto. It wasn't a sound of suffering, but of immense, primal exertion, as if the earth itself was straining under an unbearable weight.

The glade, which moments ago had been bathed in a soft emerald glow, suddenly bucked and writhed. Roots, thick as ancient trees, tore themselves from the earth, reaching blindly into the air like desperate appendages. The air grew thick and heavy, charged with an oppressive energy that felt both familiar and terrifyingly alien.

The new power that coursed through Slash vibrated in discordant rhythm with the glade's violent upheaval. He scrambled to his feet, eyes darting around the collapsing grotto. "What's happening?" he rasped, his voice rough with exhaustion and nascent fear.

The answer came not from the glade, but from within his very being. A searing, agonizing pain tore through his chest, radiating outwards from his sternum. It felt like an invisible hand was squeezing his heart, draining his essence. He staggered, clutching his chest, a low growl tearing from his throat.

Jubilee, now fully awake and sensing his agony, pushed herself up. "Slash!" Her eyes widened in horror as she saw the emerald flecks in his dark eyes begin to dim, his newfound radiance receding, eclipsed by a shadow darker than his original form.

The glade was demanding its toll. Slash's connection to the Nexus, his audacious act of becoming a conduit, had not come without a price. The immense power he had channeled, the life he had brought back, was now being violently reclaimed. His very essence was being siphoned, pulled into the glade as recompense for its forced awakening and rejuvenation.

He fell to one knee, gritting his teeth against the soul-crushing pain. Every spark of emerald light in his vision flickered, threatening to extinguish completely. He felt himself shrinking, the vastness of the Nexus, which had so recently welcomed him, now threatening to swallow him whole.

"It's... the glade," he choked out, struggling for breath. "It's taking it back."

Jubilee reached for him, her touch a faint, emerald warmth against his cooling skin. Her own magic, newly restored, pulsed within her, eager to defend, to protect. But this was different. This wasn't an external threat; it was the glade itself, an ancient entity reacting to an unprecedented intrusion and exchange.

The violent spasms of the earth intensified. Massive cracks spider-webbed across the grotto floor, raw energy seeping from them. Trees groaned and split, their bark peeling away. The delicate moss turned instantly brittle, crumbling to dust. It was as if the glade was simultaneously giving life and violently reabsorbing it, an act of creation and destruction fused into one terrifying process.

Slash's form wavered, shimmering at the edges, hinting at a terrifying dissolution. He was fighting a losing battle, his newly integrated power being ripped from him, piece by agonizing piece. The emerald wisps that had so recently surrounded him now swirled inward, forcefully drawn back into the angry, demanding earth.

"No!" Jubilee cried, her voice regaining strength, filled with desperate ferocity. She threw herself against him, her small hands pressing against his chest, pouring her rekindled magic into him. But her energy merely dissipated, absorbed by the glade's insatiable hunger for the power it was reclaiming from Slash.

His eyes, now almost completely violet again, flickered to her, a desperate plea for understanding, for a way out. He had saved her, only to be consumed himself. He felt the cold, indifferent logic of the glade: balance demanded a price.

The grotto continued its agonizing transformation, twisting and reforming around them. The air grew thin, hard to breathe, suffocating with the immense magical flux. Slash felt his consciousness begin to slip, pulled relentlessly into the heart of the earth, a sacrifice for the life he had dared to resurrect. The glade claimed its ultimate toll, threatening to tear him apart and absorb him into its ancient, unfeeling core.

70

"No!" Jubilee cried, her voice ringing with desperate ferocity. She threw herself against him, her small hands pressing against his chest, pouring her rekindled magic into him. But her energy merely dissipated, absorbed by the glade's insatiable hunger for the power it was reclaiming from Slash.

His eyes, now almost completely violet again, flickered to her, a desperate plea for understanding, for a way out. He had saved her, only to be consumed himself. He felt the cold, indifferent logic of the glade: balance demanded a price.

The grotto continued its agonizing transformation, twisting and reforming around them. The air grew thin, hard to breathe, suffocating with the immense magical flux. Slash felt his consciousness begin to slip, pulled relentlessly into the heart of the earth, a sacrifice for the life he had dared to resurrect. The glade claimed its ultimate toll, threatening to tear him apart and absorb him into its ancient, unfeeling core.

A flash of memory, sharp and vivid, pierced through Jubilee's growing despair. Eldrin. Her friend, her protector, whose light had been extinguished by this very glade, by the very power Slash now wielded. Eldrin had given his life for the glade, and now the glade was demanding another. Not in defiance, but as a cruel, indifferent tax.

A fierce, protective fire ignited in Jubilee's soul, eclipsing her fear. She had already lost too much. She wouldn't lose Slash. Not after everything. The desperation twisted her mind, searching for an answer, a loophole, anything to break this cruel cycle.

Her gaze fixed on the spider-web cracks marring the grotto floor, on the raw energy seeping from them – the very essence of the Nexus, demanding its due. An insane, impossible idea began to form, a desperate, self-sacrificing choice that mirrored Eldrin's ultimate act, but this time, for love.

"It demands a toll," she whispered, her voice resonating not with defeat, but with a terrifying resolve. Slash's dimming eyes met hers, clouded with pain and resignation. "Then it will have one."

Without another word, without a moment for Slash to protest, Jubilee pushed herself away from him. His eyes widened, a flicker of warning in their depths as he sensed her intent. He reached for her, a guttural groan escaping his lips, but he was too weakened, too consumed by the glade's pull.

Jubilee pressed her palms flat against the quaking earth, directly over one of the largest fissures glowing with raw magical energy. She closed her eyes, drawing a deep, shuddering breath, filling her lungs with the oppressive, charged air.

"Not him," she declared, her voice ringing with ancient power, vibrating with the glade's own frantic pulse. "Take me. My essence. My life. My connection to the Nexus."

A profound stillness fell over the glade, a strange, breathless pause in its violent upheaval. The air crackled, thicker, heavier, as if the ancient entity was considering her offer.

Slash, his consciousness momentarily sharpened by the shock of her words, thrashed against the invisible bonds pulling him. "Jubilee! No!" His voice was a raw, broken plea, a shadow of his former power.

But Jubilee was beyond hearing. She focused her will, her entire being, on severing her own intricate connection to the Nexus, to the glade. She imagined her life force, her emerald magic, as a vast, flowing river, and with a wrenching, agonizing act of will, she diverted its entire current. Away from her, away from Slash, and directly into the demanding maw of the glade.

A searing pain, far beyond anything she had ever known, tore through her. It felt as if her very being was being ripped apart, thread by agonizing thread. Her breath hitched, a silent scream building in her throat as her vision blurred, tinged with a blinding emerald light consuming her from within. Her emerald flecks, the core of her being, flared with agonizing intensity, then began to dim, fading, fading...

The glade responded. The violent tremors lessened, the insatiable hunger shifting. The terrifying suction on Slash's essence eased, then vanished entirely. His form solidified, the emerald wisps that had been violently reabsorbed now flowing back, gently, into his skin, his eyes. He watched in horror, helpless, as Jubilee convulsed, her body arching in agony, and the vibrant emerald light that had surrounded her pulsed once, then began to recede, leaving only a faint, ethereal glow.

The transformation of the grotto, moments ago a violent convulsion, softened into a majestic, devastating silence. The ancient roots, once clawing desperately, now settled back into the earth, pulsating with a profound energy. The cracks in the grotto floor shimmered, then slowly began to mend, flowing with a renewed, placid light.

Jubilee's body went limp, collapsing onto the softened moss. The faint emerald glow around her faded to nothingness. The air, re-filled with the rich, earthy scent of ancient magic, seemed to mourn her sacrifice, whispering of a life given freely, a balance restored at an unbearable cost.

71

Slash's breath hitched, a strangled rasp escaping his throat. "Jubilee!" He surged forward, no longer tethered by the glade's predatory pull, but utterly paralyzed by the sight of her. Her form, so vibrant moments ago, lay still, almost translucent against the moss. The ethereal glow was gone, replaced by an unnerving stillness. Her emerald flecks, once so vivid in her eyes, were dull, almost colorless.

He fell to his knees beside her, his transformed hands, now vibrant with emerald-tinged shadow, trembling as he reached for her. He cradled her limp body, her head lolling against his shoulder. Her skin, once warm and vibrant, felt cold, impossibly cool beneath his touch. A primal scream tore from his chest, raw and guttural, echoing through the now-peaceful grotto. It was a sound of agony, of profound loss, a sound he hadn't made since the deepest recesses of his shadowed past.

"No, no, no..." he chanted, his voice broken, desperate. He pressed his face into her hair, inhaling the faint, lingering scent of pine and something uniquely hers that was now fading. Her sacrifice hadn't liberated him; it had imprisoned him in a torment far worse than any the glade could inflict. She had saved him, yes, but at what unbearable cost?

His eyes, now a swirling vortex of violet and emerald, scanned the glade frantically. The cracks in the floor were mending, the pulsing energy radiating with a placid, revitalized glow. The air, rich and earthy, hummed with a renewed power that felt... wrong. It felt full, sated, gorged on Jubilee's essence.

"Give her back!" he roared, unleashing a burst of raw, untamed shadow magic at the mending earth. The glade merely absorbed it, unfazed, almost purring with contentment. His power, still infused with her emerald essence, flowed into its greedy maw, becoming part of its very being, yet failing to restore her.

He tried to pour his new, balanced energy into her, just as she had tried to heal him. He infused her fragile form with the life force he had gained from the Nexus, the power she had just given him. But it was like pouring water into a bottomless well. Her body remained cold, unresponsive. The glade had consumed her connection to the Nexus, to its very lifeblood, and it held her essence captive.

A chilling realization clawed at him: she hadn't just rerouted her magic; she had severed her *connection* to the glade, to the Nexus, to the source of her very life. The glade had taken the ultimate toll, absorbing her life force as recompense. She was gone.

Panic, cold and absolute, seized him. This couldn't be the end. Not after everything. Not after they had just found each other, forged a connection that surpassed ancient animosities, united light and shadow, and dreamt of a new world together. Their world.

He felt the glade's revitalized power pulsing around them, a vast, indifferent ocean. And within that ocean, he felt a faint, heartbreaking echo of Jubilee. Not her life, not her consciousness, but a lingering resonance, like a phantom limb connected to the glade itself. It was the residue of her boundless love, her fierce protectiveness, her very essence woven into the fabric of the re-energized glade.

His enhanced senses strained, searching for a loophole, a thread, anything that could undo this catastrophic sacrifice. He wasn't a healer in the traditional sense, but he was a master of energy, of the very fabric of existence. He had merged with the Nexus, drawn power from it, knew its secrets, its immense, ancient heart. Could he reverse the flow? Could he pull her back from the brink of absorption?

He had to try. He would tear the glade apart, brick by painstaking brick, if that's what it took. He would merge with the Nexus again, delve deeper than any mortal or immortal dared, and retrieve her. He would defy nature, defy destiny, defy the universe if it meant bringing her back.

He laid her gently back onto the moss, her serene face a stark contrast to the storm raging within him. "I won't let you go," he vowed, his voice a raw whisper, his hand closing over hers, intertwining their still-vibrating energies. "You saved me, Jubilee. Now I will save you."

72

His vow hung in the air, a desperate plea to the uncaring glade. Slash knelt beside Jubilee, his head bowed, his emerald-tinged shadows swirling restlessly around him. He focused, pushing his newly integrated power, the very essence of light and shadow, outward. He tried to sense the glade's deepest currents, seeking the 'phantom limb' he'd felt—that fragile echo of Jubilee's formidable essence.

It was there, deep within the heart of the re-energized glade, a whisper of vibrant emerald, almost swallowed by the overwhelming pulse of Nexus power. It was like trying to hear a heartbeat amidst a raging waterfall. But it was *her*.

He closed his eyes, his mind racing, sifting through the vast library of power he'd absorbed from the Nexus. It wasn't merely brute force he needed; it was knowledge, understanding. The Nexus held the memories of the glade, millennia of cycles of life and death, creation and consumption. There had to be a way. There *had* to be.

He plunged his awareness deeper, past the immediate sensory input of the thriving glade, past the hum of revitalized magic, towards the ancient, quiet core of the Nexus itself. Images flickered through his mind: countless seasons, the birth and death of stars, whispers of forgotten rituals, and the deep, abiding wisdom of the earth. He sought anything, any fragment that spoke of such a radical sacrifice, of a life force absorbed and lost.

Suddenly, a thread. Not a clear memory, but a resonance, a faint, almost imperceptible hum that pulled him towards a specific pattern within the glade's energetic web. It was an ancient, almost primordial rhythm, long dormant. He followed it, his consciousness expanding, stretching through the very roots of the grotto.

And there it was. Not a written scroll or an etched tablet, but a crystalline imprint within the Nexus's deepest layers, a pure thought-form of complex magic. A prophecy.

It spoke of a time when the glade, in dire need, would consume a pure essence to survive, and how that essence could be reclaimed. It described an impossible conjunction of cosmic energies, a rare alignment that could open a temporary portal between the living realm and the liminal space where absorbed life forces resided.

"When the Twin Stars align, and the Glade's Heart beats anew, a selfless sacrifice may be undone, but only by a love that defies the Maelstrom and binds the Sun and Shadow as one."

Slash's eyes snapped open. Twin Stars. Their shared power, his shadow and her light, now irrevocably intertwined. The Glade's Heart beating anew—it was happening now, gorged on Jubilee's essence. And a love that defied the Maelstrom... that was them. It had to be.

But the prophecy was not without its cost. It warned that the process was fraught with peril, that the energies unleashed could either restore life or shatter reality, that the "Maelstrom" was a consuming entity, the guardian of lost essences. And the "Sun and Shadow" had to be utterly bound, their wills and powers irrevocably merged.

He looked at Jubilee, her still form hauntingly beautiful in the revitalized glade. A faint shimmer, almost imperceptible, seemed to emanate from her, a ghostly echo of her once vibrant magic. He recognized it for what it was: the very essence the glade had absorbed, the key that could open the gateway to her return.

A surge of desperate hope, cold and sharp, cut through his despair. There was a way. An impossible, dangerous way, but a way nonetheless. He wasn't a healer, but he was a wielder of impossible magic, a master of balance between extremes. And he loved her. More than life, more than power, more than his very existence.

He touched her cold cheek, his emerald-black eyes alight with grim determination. "Jubilee," he whispered, his voice gaining strength, resolve hardening his features. "You're not gone. Not completely. I found it. I found a way." He would brave any Maelstrom, any cosmic alignment, to bring her back. Their journey had just begun.

73

Slash didn't move from Jubilee's side, though his mind was already miles away, sifting through the cryptic lines of the prophecy he'd found. "Sun and Shadow as one." Their current form, his emerald-black eyes, the fused magic he now wielded – it was a start, but the ritual implied a deeper, conscious union, one that would require Jubilee's active participation. And she was gone. For now.

He knew, with chilling certainty, that the glade wouldn't willingly relinquish what it had consumed. The Nexus, in its wisdom, demanded balance, and Jubilee had paid its price. He couldn't force it, not without risking his own essence and destabilizing the very core of their world. He needed external knowledge, a forgotten lore, something that existed beyond the confines of this awakened sanctuary.

His gaze lifted, sweeping over the newly vibrant grotto. The Celestial Order. Malakor. These threats, momentarily pushed back, would undoubtedly return, drawn by the glade's renewed power like moths to a flame. He had no time to waste.

His initial instinct was to tap further into the Nexus, to delve deeper into its ancient memories. But the prophecy itself hinted at limitations. This wasn't a glade-bound secret. This was a cosmic alignment, a conjunction of forces that transcended their personal feud and even the glade's ancient power.

He needed a scholar, an ancient. Someone who dealt with the celestial mechanics, with prophecies and lost arts. His thoughts turned to the oldest beings he knew, the ones who whispered of the void, of the spaces between stars, of the true, raw power that governed the very fabric of existence.

There was only one place to go, one being who might possess such forbidden knowledge. The Keeper of Whispers. A reclusive, millennia-old being from the furthest reaches of the Shadow Realms, rumoured to commune with cosmic forces and store fragmented scrolls of forgotten creation. The Keeper was dangerous, unpredictable, and certainly not an ally. But he was his best, perhaps only, hope.

Carefully, Slash scooped Jubilee into his arms, her body startlingly light. He held her close, feeling the faint, ghost-like shimmer emanating from her – the key, the glade's echo of her life force. He had to keep it contained, safe, until the Twin Stars aligned and he understood the full scope of the ritual.

He moved to the glade's edge, hesitating for a moment. Leaving her, even for this vital quest, felt like tearing a piece from his own soul. He laid her gently beneath the protective canopy of the largest, most vibrant tree, the one closest to the Nexus's core. He pressed his palm against its bark, channeling his newly integrated emerald-black essence into its roots, a silent plea for protection, a binding promise that he would return.

Then, with a deep, shaky breath, he stepped into the surrounding forest, leaving the glade behind. He couldn't risk Malakor finding her, or the Celestial Order. He had to lead them away, draw their attention to himself, while he sought the knowledge that would bring Jubilee back.

The journey to the Keeper of Whispers would be perilous, crossing realms still reeling from the chaos of recent magical surges. He would be vulnerable, his powers still in flux, his heart aching with a hollow void where Jubilee once vibrated. But he held the prophecy like a burning ember in his mind, a beacon in the oppressive darkness of fear and grief.

He vanished into the shadows between the trees, his emerald-black eyes scanning the horizon, not for threats, but for the faint, elusive shimmer of the 'Twin Stars' alignment. He didn't know when it would come, or how long he had. But he would find the Keeper. He would understand the Maelstrom. And he would reclaim his Sun, no matter the cost. His journey, fueled by love and a terrifying new power, had just truly begun.

74

The forest beyond the glade, usually a symphony of rustling leaves and chirping wildlife, now felt hushed, watchful. Every shadow seemed to stretch longer, every whisper of wind carried a hint of ancient secrets. Slash moved with a predatory grace, his emerald-black eyes piercing the deepening gloom, seeking not a path, but a disruption in the very fabric of existence. The Keeper of Whispers wouldn't be found on any map.

He traveled for what felt like an eternity, crossing realms where magic bled into reality, where the air hummed with dormant power. He bypassed shimmering portals that led to forgotten dimensions and avoided territories still scarred by the recent resurgence of shadow. His focus remained singular: Jubilee. Her image, a shimmering emerald ghost, spurred him onward when weariness threatened to claim him.

After days that bled into weeks, guided by the cryptic whispers of the Nexus that echoed faintly within him, Slash found himself at the edge of a place that shouldn't exist. It was a pocket in reality, a tear in the veil between known realms, radiating an aura of profound, almost dizzying, age. Ancient, gnarled trees, whose branches seemed to claw at a sky heavy with silent stars, encircled a vast, unlit cavern entrance. No sound. No movement. Just profound, arcane silence.

This was it. The air here was thick with forgotten spells, with knowledge so old it had turned to dust and then reformed into sentient energy. He stepped across the invisible threshold, and the ancient trees seemed to lean in, their silent scrutiny a physical weight on his shoulders. He felt a deep, resonant hum against his very bones, a sensation akin to standing at the heart of a cosmic engine.

From the deepest recesses of the cavern, a voice, like dry leaves rustling across parchment and the distant echo of a tide turning, rippled through the silence. "The Shadow Seeker returns from the Void... with the Sun's fading light clutched tight."

Slash froze. The Keeper knew. Knew of Jubilee, of her sacrifice, of his desperate quest. A figure began to emerge from the cavern's gloom, not walking, but seeming to uncoil from the very darkness it inhabited. It was not what he expected. Not a wizened fae, not a grotesque demon, but something else entirely.

It was a being woven from starlight and shadow, its form shifting, coalescing, and dissolving with every breath. Two pinpricks of ancient, knowing light pulsed in the space where eyes should be. Its limbs appeared and disappeared, creating an unsettling dance in the air. This was the Keeper.

"You seek knowledge of the cosmic weave," the Keeper's voice continued, a multi-layered murmur that seemed to fill his head without passing through his ears. "Of time's delicate balance, and the thread that binds life to life, even beyond the grave."

Slash's guard, always meticulously maintained, faltered. "You know of the prophecy?" he rasped, his own voice sounding crude in the refined silence.

The Keeper chuckled, a sound like grinding stardust. "Prophecies are whispers of a truth yet to unfold, born from the great Maelstrom itself. You carry a piece of that Maelstrom, young Shadow. Your essence... transformed. Part of the glade's heart beats within you, does it not?"

A cold dread coiled in Slash's stomach. This ancient being saw everything, knew everything. His emerald-black eyes widened slightly. "I need to bring her back. The ritual. The cosmic alignment. The Twin Stars."

The Keeper shimmered, drawing closer, its form briefly solidifying into something vaguely humanoid, though still unsettling. "A heavy price was paid for balance. And a greater one will be asked for its disruption. But come, Shadow of Light. Let us unravel the Maelstrom's cruel intentions, and see if your Sun can indeed rise again."

The air crackled with profound power, and Slash felt a dizzying pull, as if the very atoms of his being were being reordered. This was no simple consultation. This was an invitation into the heart of arcane knowledge, a dive into the very forces that shaped destinies. His journey had truly taken on a cosmic scale, and he feared, for the first time, not for his life, but for the purity of his soul.

75

The cavern deepened, the air growing colder, heavier, as if pressed by the weight of eons. Slash followed the Keeper, his senses overwhelmed by the sheer, unfiltered antiquity of the place. The shifting form of the Keeper solidified just enough to point to a shimmering pool of obsidian-black liquid, swirls of cosmic dust mirroring distant galaxies within its depths.

"The Maelstrom," the Keeper's voice rumbled, its multi-layered tones echoing off invisible walls. "It is not a storm, young Shadow. Not a force of nature as your kind understand it. It is the primal, all-consuming hunger of the Void itself. It laps at the edges of creation, consuming, unmaking, seeking to pull all back into the endless, formless nothingness."

Slash felt a visceral chill, deeper than the grotto's cold. "What does it have to do with Jubilee? With the glade?"

The Keeper swirled, its starlit form briefly revealing a myriad of ancient symbols etched into the cavern walls. "Your glade, your Nexus... it is a rare confluence, a vibrant pulse of creation on the very cusp of the Maelstrom's reach. A beacon. A lure. And your beloved, Jubilee... she is the glade's heart, its purest conduit. Her death... her passage into the Maelstrom's embrace was not mere sacrifice, but a fulfillment of a twisted design."

"A design?" Slash's voice was a low growl, his emerald-black eyes narrowing. "Whose design?"

"Malakor's," the Keeper stated, the name hanging like poison in the air. "He sought to harness the glade's power, yes, but unknowingly, disastrously, he aligned its energies with the Maelstrom's hungry maw. He built a bridge, a conduit, and Jubilee, in her desperation, walked willingly into its maw, thinking to save you, to save her world."

"She's in the Maelstrom?" Slash took an involuntary step back, a fresh wave of terror washing over him. The cold dread returned, this time mingled with fury.

The Keeper rippled, its starlight eyes fixing on Slash. "Not 'in' it, as your corporeal form would understand. Her essence, her soul, is being assimilated. Purified. Prepared. The Maelstrom craves vibrant life, fresh creation. It seeks to consume and then rebirth, not as a creative force, but as a twisted echo of its own emptiness. Imagine... a universe reborn in its image. Bland. Still. Void. Jubilee's essence, the very vibrancy of the 'Sun' needed to ignite its dark heart, is being... refined."

A profound despair settled on Slash. The image of Jubilee, beautiful and vibrant, being stripped of her light, her joy, her very being, was unbearable. "Then she's lost," he whispered, the words tearing from his throat.

"Silence, young Shadow," the Keeper snapped, its voice sharper, like shattering ice. "Lost is a choice, not a fate. While her essence is being drawn, consumed, it is also amplifying the call of the glade's heart, the Nexus's song. It is this dissonance that offers the thread, however thin, however perilous, to pull her back. To save her. To save all."

The Keeper moved, beckoning Slash closer to the obsidian pool. "The prophecy speaks not of reversal, but of intervention. Of a disruption so profound it will tear the Maelstrom's grip. 'Sun and Shadow as one' is not merely a poetic union, but a necessary fusion. You, transformed by the glade's heart, carry its essence, its counter-force to the Void. You are the Shadow of Light. The balance. And the catalyst."

Slash stared into the inky depths of the pool, seeing not cosmic dust, but images, flickering and indistinct, of Jubilee. Her light. Her laughter. The warmth of her touch.

"The Twin Stars alignment," the Keeper continued, "is the window. The moment when the veil between creation and consumption is thinnest. You will use your combined essence, your power, to challenge the Maelstrom on its own terms. You will enter a state of being beyond your understanding, a place where soul and magic are one, and reclaim what is yours."

A new kind of terror seized Slash. This wasn't just about a ritual anymore. This was a battle for Jubilee's very soul, for the essence of creation itself. And he, a shadow fae touched by light, was to be its champion. The price, he realized, would be more than just his life. It would be a confrontation with the very void that birthed his kind, and a choice between embracing it or tearing it apart.

76

A new kind of terror seized Slash. This wasn't just about a ritual anymore. This was a battle for Jubilee's very soul, for the essence of creation itself. And he, a shadow fae touched by light, was to be its champion. The price, he realized, would be more than just his life. It would be a confrontation with the very void that birthed his kind, and a choice between embracing it or tearing it apart.

His gaze was still fixed on the swirling obsidian pool when the Keeper stiffened, its starlit form flickering with alarm. The air, already thick with ancient power, abruptly changed. It didn't grow colder, or heavier, but sharpened, thinned, like the edge of a blade. A distant, metallic hum vibrated through the cavern floor, a sound that quickly escalated into a high-pitched whine.

"Impossible," the Keeper whispered, its multi-layered voice losing its usual resonance, a crack of fear running through it. "They should not be able to find this place. Not yet."

Slash looked up, his emerald-black eyes scanning the impenetrable rock walls. "Who? The Celestial Order? Malakor?"

The Keeper shook its form, a cascade of starlight falling to the cavern floor and instantly dissolving. "Worse. Much worse. A presence... wholly alien. A disruption within the fabric of space itself. They have breached the Veil."

Before Slash could question further, a searing beam of pure white light lanced through the solid rock directly above them, instantly vaporizing a section of the ancient ceiling. The hum intensified, becoming a deafening shriek, and through the gleaming aperture descended a shimmering vessel of impossibly smooth, pearlescent material. It floated silently, emitting no engine noise, only that piercing, mind-numbing whine.

From within its luminous hull, figures began to materialize. They weren't fae, or Grolak, or anything Slash had ever encountered. They were tall, slender, and seemed to be composed of pure, shifting light, encased in crystalline armor that pulsed with an internal glow. No visible faces, just smooth, reflective surfaces where eyes should be. They moved with an unnervingly detached precision, each step utterly silent.

"Interdimensional arbitrators," the Keeper hissed, its starlight form shrinking, pressing itself against the cavern wall as if to become one with the stone. "They monitor the boundaries between realities. Any significant magical surge, any tear in the fabric... they arrive to 'correct' the anomaly. And the Maelstrom... that is the greatest anomaly of all."

One of the luminous figures, seemingly the leader, glided forward, its form radiating an aura of absolute, cold judgment. It raised a hand, and the high-pitched whine coalesced, forming into a single, perfectly resonant tone that pierced Slash's mind, not with pain, but with an overwhelming sense of wrongness, of being out of place, an imperfection to be erased.

A disembodied voice, utterly devoid of emotion, echoed not from the figure's form, but directly within Slash's skull. *"Anomaly detected. Breach of dimensional integrity confirmed. Unsanctioned manipulation of cosmic energies observed. All unauthorized entities are to cease activity and submit for immediate containment and rectification."*

Slash felt a chill colder than even the Maelstrom's purported emptiness. These beings weren't about power or dominion; they were about order, absolute and unyielding. And his quest, his very existence as a fusion of light and shadow, was a colossal disruption.

He instinctively pushed a wave of shadow magic towards the glowing figures, a desperate, futile gesture. His power, which had once seemed so formidable, merely shimmered against their crystalline forms, dissipating like smoke. They remained utterly unaffected, their luminous presence unwavering.

The lead figure raised its hand again, and the resonant tone intensified, causing the ancient cavern itself to tremble. Two more shimmering beams erupted from the ship, not directed at Slash, but at the obsidian pool.

"No!" the Keeper shrieked, finding its voice again, but it was too late. The beams struck the surface of the Maelstrom pool, not with destructive force, but with a chilling, analytical precision. The swirling cosmic dust within the liquid suddenly went still, frozen in place. The energy that had thrummed through the cavern floor, the invisible tether to Jubilee, felt muted, stifled.

The Keeper's starlit form pulsed violently. "They are neutralizing the portal! Containing the Maelstrom's resonance! If the link is severed... she will be lost! Forever!"

Slash's blood ran cold. He had come here to save Jubilee, to confront the void, not to have his last hope systematically disassembled by emotionless arbiters of cosmic law. He glanced at the frozen pool, then at the implacable beings of light. A surge of desperate fury and protective love ignited within him, a fire against the cold, implacable order. He wouldn't let them take her. Not now. Not ever.

77

The Keeper's shriek echoed, raw with desperation, as the resonant beams from the Arbitrators' ship froze the Maelstrom pool. Slash's emerald-black eyes burned with a renewed, ferocious resolve. Lost forever? Not while he drew breath. Not while he had even a flicker of power left. He was a shadow fae entwined with the glade's very essence, and that essence meant Jubilee.

He lunged, not at the Arbitrators, but at the suspended vessel, an impossible, reckless act. His shadow magic, previously useless, surged around him, imbued now with a desperate, all-consuming purpose. He slammed into the pearlescent hull, feeling the cold, unyielding surface, his power splashing against it like water on stone. It was futile, he knew, but he wouldn't stand idly by.

Just as the lead Arbitrator raised its hand again, its resonant tone beginning to build, something shifted. It wasn't physical, not in the grotto, but deep within

Slash, a sudden, blinding flash of emerald. It was faint, barely a flicker at first, then it pulsed, stronger than anything he'd felt since Jubilee had been absorbed. It was *her*.

A wave of pure, untamed Nexus energy, channelled through the faintest thread of their unique bond, erupted from within Slash. It wasn't a coherent attack, not a targeted spell. It was a chaotic, desperate scream of raw power, a flare of the glade's untamed heart reacting to the suffocating order imposed upon it.

The effect was instantaneous and devastating. The high-pitched whine from the Arbitrators' ship sputtered, dying to a choked gargle. The crystalline armor of the luminous figures pulsed erratically, their internal glow flickering like dying embers. The perfect resonance that had pierced Slash's mind shattered into a cacophony of discordant frequencies, each note a painful, jarring dissonance.

The lead Arbitrator recoiled, its smooth, reflective face-plate rippling as if in agony. Its aura of cold judgment fractured, replaced by an unmistakable tremor of something akin to confusion, even alarm. The disembodied voice in Slash's head stammered, *"An-anomalous... counter-resonance... unpredicted... energy signature..."*

The two beams striking the Maelstrom pool wavered, then danced wildly as if controlled by an unseen, riotous force. The frozen cosmic dust within the obsidian liquid burst into frantic, swirling motion, faster, more violently than before. The subtle tether to Jubilee, which had felt muted a moment ago, snapped taut, vibrating with a life so profound it made Slash gasp. She wasn't just flickering; she was fighting.

The Arbitrators, pillars of unyielding order, found themselves enveloped in a storm of exquisite disarray. Their crystalline forms vibrated with unstable energy. One of the lesser Arbitrators stumbled, its silent movement breaking into an awkward, clumsy lurch, an uncharacteristic breach of their perfect precision. Their aura, once cold and implacable, now radiated a frantic, almost desperate scramble for control.

The Keeper, shrinking against the cavern wall, began to pulse with renewed starlight, its multi-layered voice filled with bewildered awe. "Jubilee! The Nexus... she is pushing back! She is refusing neutrality!"

Slash, reeling from the raw power coursing through him, felt a flicker of savage triumph. This wasn't his power; it was hers, a direct defiance of the suppression. It was the glade, the Nexus, rejecting the Arbitrators' cold, sterile order. It was chaos, pure and potent, unleashed from the source of all life.

The lead Arbitrator, regaining some semblance of its composure, raised both hands, its form radiating a painful counter-pulse designed to quell the disruptive energy. But it was too late. The unexpected surge, the raw, untamed fury from the Nexus, had created a vulnerability, a fleeting window of opportunity.

Jubilee, even from within the heart of the Maelstrom, had bought him time. He glanced at the Keeper, who was now fully re-emerging, its starlit gaze fixed on him with a new, urgent intensity. The Keeper knew. This was their chance. This was the opening. He just had to figure out how to exploit it.

78

Slash met the Keeper's shimmering gaze, a silent question passing between them. The chaotic energy thrumming through the grotto, a wild melody of defiance and raw power from Jubilee, was their cue. This wasn't an attack they could plan, but a dance they had to join.

The lead Arbitrator pulsed with a desperate energy, attempting to re-establish its order, but the underlying tremor of instability remained. Its crystalline armor, designed to deflect all but the purest of magic, now shimmered with chaotic internal light.

"The anchors!" the Keeper's voice rippled, a confluence of whispers and astral echoes, yet piercingly clear. "They are bound to the ship! Sever the connection!"

Slash didn't need further instruction. He understood the arbiters drew their crushing power from a central source, likely the ship still hovering above. With an unholy roar, part shadow, part glade-fire, he surged forward. The crystalline bodies of the Arbitrators flickered around him, their movements still fractured by the residual chaos from Jubilee's burst. He weaved through them, no longer striking, but seeking the weakest points in their fragmented energy fields. He channeled the raw, untamed energy still coursing through him from Jubilee, a wild, green-tinged shadow that sparked and burned.

He drove his fist, crackling with borrowed Nexus power, into the back of one of the Arbitrators. The blow wasn't physical; it was a pure magical assault, targeting the fractured resonance within. The crystalline being shrieked, a high-pitched, unheard frequency that vibrated painful dread through the grotto. Its form buckled, then dissolved into shimmering motes of light, instantly drawn back to the mothership.

The Keeper, meanwhile, was not idle. Its starlit form expanded, engulfing itself in the chaos, not trying to quell it, but to amplify it. Spectral tendrils, woven from pure starlight and ancient knowledge, reached for the remaining Arbitrators. These weren't destructive; they were disruptive. The Keeper sought to exacerbate the dissonance within their crystalline structures, to turn their rigid order against them. One Arbitrator's limbs began to move in opposing directions, a horrifying, silent scream of internal conflict. Another's head spun impossibly on its neck, its perfect form twisting into a grotesque contortion.

The remaining Arbitrators, witnessing the rapid disintegration of their comrades, finally broke their composure. Their disembodied voices overlapped, screeching, *"Unstable... Irreconcilable... Abort mission! Retreat!"*

The lead Arbitrator, its own form now flickering erratically, abandoned its attempt to re-establish control over the glade. It lashed out at Slash with a desperate, unfocused beam of energy, more a panicked flail than a precise attack. Slash, his senses honed by the combined energies within him, dodged with impossible grace, the beam striking the cavern wall and turning the stone to shimmering dust.

He didn't pursue. The objective wasn't annihilation; it was disruption. The fleeing Arbitrators were now priority. With a renewed surge of emerald-laced shadow, Slash unleashed a devastating, wide-arc burst of power. It wasn't aimed at killing, but at shattering. The residual chaos from Jubilee's defiant energy, now intertwined with his own, tore through the retreating figures. Their crystalline forms fractured into a thousand splintering shards, collapsing into themselves with faint, internal snaps.

The pearlescent ship overhead, its resonant hum now a desperate, dying whine, started to retract. Its massive maw, which had deployed the Arbitrators, closed with a metallic groan. The two wavering beams that had gripped the Maelstrom pool flickered one last time, then vanished entirely.

Silence descended, though it was a different silence than before. Not the oppressive, terrified silence of Slash's ultimate power, nor the cold, sterile silence of the Arbitrators' dominance. This was the raw, breathless silence of a battle won, a precipice avoided.

Slash's knees buckled. The borrowed Nexus power, the savage surge of Jubilee, had drained him utterly. He collapsed onto the damp grotto floor, his head spinning, his body aching from the sheer exertion. The grotto, though bruised, was still intact. The Maelstrom pool, no longer held rigid by the Arbitrators' foreign magic, churned with renewed energy, a chaotic, vibrant vortex.

The Keeper shimmered, gradually returning to its smaller, more stable form. Its starlit voice, filled with an ancient reverence, spoke, "She opened a path. The Twin Stars... they are aligning."

Slash, gasping for breath, looked at the Maelstrom pool. Within its depths, amidst the swirling cosmic dust, he saw it. A faint, emerald pulse, steady and defiant. Jubilee. She was still in there. And now, she was fighting.

79

The faint emerald pulse in the swirling depths of the Maelstrom pool was an anchor in the storm of Slash's exhaustion. He reached out to it, not with his physical hand, but with the last vestiges of his transformed essence, a desperate, silent plea. His vision blurred, the grotto wavering as he struggled to maintain focus. The Keeper's words echoed in his mind: "She opened a path. The Twin Stars... they are aligning."

Jubilee. She was fighting. He had to reach her.

He pushed away the crushing fatigue, the aching emptiness where the immense power had been. His connection to the Nexus, to the glade itself, felt frayed, but a thin, resilient thread connected him still to that emerald light in the churning void. He closed his eyes, forcing his awareness inward, then outward, toward the vortex of potential.

It was like diving into an ocean of pure sensation. The Maelstrom wasn't truly a void, but a chaotic tapestry of fractured realities, echoes of nascent creation and dying stars. He felt the pull of its hunger, the seductive whisper of ultimate oblivion, but he clung to that emerald light, a lighthouse in the chaos.

He extended his newly integrated emerald-laced shadow essence, a fragile bridge stretching across an infinite chasm. It was terrifying, vulnerable. He was opening himself completely to the Maelstrom, risking his own absorption, but the thought of Jubilee, fighting alone, was a greater terror.

A surge of energy, sharp and familiar, met his outreach. It wasn't the refined power he'd felt when they had connected physically. This was raw, untamed, infused with the Maelstrom yet still undeniably Jubilee. It was furious, defiant, and laced with a profound, aching loneliness.

"Jubilee," his essence whispered, a thought reaching across the conceptual distance. *"I'm here."*

He felt her presence recoil, a flicker of disbelief and then a fierce surge of hope so intense it almost overwhelmed him. He felt the raw emotional landscape of her captivity – the constant pressure of external forces seeking to unravel her, the relentless struggle to maintain her core essence, the despair and the unyielding fight.

Her reply wasn't in words, but in a torrent of images and feelings. He saw glimpses of the Maelstrom through her eyes – not a chaotic soup, but a place where nascent concepts flickered into being, a canvas of creation and destruction. He saw her fighting against the insidious tendrils of the void itself, manipulating them, not with the intention of escape, but survival, of hardening her essence. And then, he felt the pain. The echoing pain of Eldrin's loss, amplified by her unending battle to exist. The fear of being lost, truly lost, in this endless, consuming place.

But beneath it all, he felt the steady hum of the Nexus. Her life force, intricately woven into its fabric, was strengthening, not weakening. She was drawing on it, not being consumed by it. She was becoming something new, tempered by the chaos.

"Don't... let go," her essence resonated, faint but clear, the raw edge of desperation in it.

He braced himself, anchoring his essence deeper, drawing on the memory of their combined power in the glade, the physical connection, the intimacy they had shared. He poured his strength, his love, his unwavering resolve into that tenuous link. He was no longer just the shadow he had been, nor merely the glade's weapon. He was the bridge. Her shadow, now touched by light. Her light, now embraced by shadow.

The emerald pulse brightened, pulsed with renewed vigor. He felt the tendrils of the Maelstrom recoil from the pure, almost painful intensity of their combined, projected will. It was not enough to pull her out, not yet. But it was communion. It was a promise.

He felt the glade respond, a low, resonant thrum beneath the earth, acknowledging the connection. The "Twin Stars" weren't just an alignment in the sky; they were their very essences, meeting, interlocking, even across the impossible divide of the Maelstrom.

He opened his eyes, gasping, sweat beading on his forehead. The Maelstrom pool pulsed, a vibrant hue of emerald-tinged violet. She was still fighting. And now, she knew he was fighting with her. The Keeper gave a slow, knowing nod. The true battle had only just begun.

80

The vibrant, emerald-tinged violet pulsing within the Maelstrom pool was a beacon, a tangible promise. Slash, though utterly spent, felt a renewed surge of purposeful energy. Jubilee knew he was there. That was everything. He looked to the Keeper, whose silent nod confirmed the subtle shift in the cosmic currents.

The reprieve, however, was short-lived.

A cold, metallic tremor rippled through the grotto, echoing not from the Maelstrom, but from the cavern's entrance. It was a familiar, chilling signature – Malakor. The air grew heavy, thick with a malevolent presence, far more potent than his previous assaults. There was a new, focused intent behind it.

"He senses her," the Keeper's low voice cut through the sudden oppressive silence. "He senses the rekindling. He will not allow it."

Malakor didn't appear in a flash of shadow, but manifested slowly, deliberately, as if a deeper darkness was seeping into reality. His eyes, usually pools of simmering malice, now burned with an almost incandescent fury. His form, once sleek and predatory, seemed to ripple with barely contained power, edged with an unsettling, resonant hum.

"So, my foolish brother still clings to the impossible," Malakor's voice scraped, a sound like grinding stone, resonating with a new, dangerous power. "And the little forest sprite... she shows more resilience than I gave her credit for. A pity. It just means the binding must be more... permanent."

With a gesture that seemed to command the very air, Malakor didn't unleash a wave of shadow or summon a creature. Instead, he pulled at the fabric of the grotto itself. The ancient stone walls groaned, not from physical stress, but from some unseen spiritual violation. Then, from the deepest fissures of the grotto, long, obsidian-black tendrils, not of natural rock nor pure shadow, began to emerge.

These were different. They shimmered with an inner light, a malevolent, pulsating energy that seemed to drain the warmth from the air. They were thicker, more resilient than anything Slash had encountered from Malakor before, and they extended with terrifying speed, twining around the Maelstrom pool itself.

"He's infusing it with corrupted Nexus energy," the Keeper whispered, a rare note of alarm in its voice.

"He's creating a barrier. A prison of amplified despair. It will seal her in. Permanent."

The tendrils solidified, forming a dense, impenetrable cage around the Maelstrom pool, each strand pulsating with a sickening violet-black glow. As they locked into place, the pool's vibrant emerald-violet hue dulled, the light within it flickering dangerously, desperately.

Slash felt Jubilee's essence recoil, a sharp pang of terror ripping through their tenuous link. The familiar fight, the defiance he had just reconnected with, was fading, replaced by a wave of raw, mind-numbing despair. The unique energy signature of the new tendrils wasn't just physical; it was soul-crushing, designed to stifle hope itself.

"A cage not just for her energy, but for her spirit," Malakor purred, his voice dripping with satisfaction. "A nullification of her very will. The Maelstrom will consume her then, unimpeded. And then, brother, you will finally understand the true nature of despair. You will be utterly alone in this pathetic little struggle for 'balance'."

Malakor's gaze shifted to Slash, filled with a triumphant malice that promised slow, agonizing torture. He hadn't just erected a barrier; he had severed the connection, plunging Jubilee back into isolation, her desperate glimmer in the Maelstrom fading to nothing more than a faint, sorrowful whisper.

Slash lunged, driven by unadulterated fury and a primal need to reconnect with Jubilee, but Malakor merely extended a hand. A wave of crushing spiritual pressure slammed into Slash, the sheer weight of it pinning him to the cavern floor. It wasn't a physical blow, but a psychic assault designed to incapacitate, to remind him of his current vulnerability.

"Watch, brother," Malakor sneered, savoring Slash's impotence, "as her light is snuffed out forever. This is my true mastery. No heroics, no last-minute rescues. Just... oblivion."

The dark cage around the Maelstrom pulsed again, pulling on the last vestiges of Jubilee's projected light, drawing it inward, consuming it. Slash roared, a beast of desperation, but he was powerless. The silence that followed was even more terrifying than Malakor's taunts, a silence pregnant with the chilling certainty of loss. The emerald pulse—it was gone.

81

The emerald pulse, the very symbol of Jubilee's defiant spirit, had vanished. The Maelstrom pool was now a dark, swirling abyss, reflecting only the malevolent glow of Malakor's newly formed obsidian cage. Slash, pinned to the grotto floor by the overwhelming psychic pressure, choked on a scream that never reached his lips. Despair, cold and absolute, threatened to consume him whole.

"Excellent," Malakor purred, studying the now inert Maelstrom as if admiring a masterpiece. His victory was palpable, radiating from him in sickening waves. "The little sprite has finally understood her place. Now, for the final act."

He turned from the pool, his attention now fixed on the grotto's very fabric. With deliberate, almost theatrical grace, he drew an intricate sigil in the air with one clawed finger, not in shadow, but in a phosphorescent, violet light that hummed with ancient, forbidden power. It was a sigil Slash recognized from the grimoires of old, spoken of only in whispers – the Unmaking Seal, designed to sever the bond between spirit and source.

As Malakor began chanting, his voice deepening into a resonant, guttural drone, the stone walls of the grotto began to weep. Not water, but a thin, dark ichor that pulsed with the same malevolent violet as the sigil. It slithered down the ancient rock, tracing paths towards the obsidian cage, preparing to seep into the Maelstrom and the essence within.

"This ritual will not merely contain her, brother," Malakor explained, his eyes glowing with fanaticism. "It will dissolve her connection to the Nexus, to the glade, to this very dimension. Her essence will be scattered into the deepest, coldest reaches of the void, utterly unrecoverable. A ghost of a memory, quickly forgotten."

Slash thrashed, a furious, desperate animal. His internal landscape was a maelstrom of its own – grief, rage, and a terrifying, soul-deep terror. He poured every last shred of his willpower into resisting Malakor's spiritual assault, but it was like trying to stem a tide with a whisper. He watched in helpless horror as the ichor reached the obsidian cage, beginning its slow, insidious crawl towards the now-darkened pool.

Underneath the overwhelming despair, unnoticed by Malakor, something stirred. Not within the Maelstrom, but *behind* it.

Deep within the grotto's ancient heart, where the Nexus pulsed unseen, a single, delicate root, long dormant, began to glow. It wasn't the vibrant emerald of Jubilee's full power, nor the destructive flash of her fury. It was a soft, persistent luminescence, a faint echo of the life that stubbornly clung to the glade even in its despair. This root, unknowingly touched by Jubilee's final, desperate act of drawing on the Nexus, possessed a sliver of her resonant energy.

As Malakor's chant intensified, the subtle glow from the root pulsed stronger. It was a silent rebellion, a hidden resistance stemming from Jubilee's profound, inherent connection to the glade she had fought so fiercely to protect. The Nexus, though assaulted, remembered. It recognized its keeper. And in a way only ancient magic could, it subtly pushed back.

The ichor on the obsidian cage slowed, almost imperceptibly, as if meeting an unseen, gentle current. Malakor, engrossed in his triumphant ritual, dismissed it as a minor fluctuation, a final dying gasp of resistance. He redoubled his efforts, pushing more power into the chant, his face contorted in a sneer of absolute victory.

"Soon, brother," he rasped, the violet light from the sigil now burning fiercely, illuminating the grotto in an infernal glow. "Soon, she will be nothing. And you will be free to join me, to embrace your true power without this... sentimental burden."

He laughed, a maniacal, triumphant sound that echoed through the grotto. The ichor began to flow once more, quicker this time, determined to reach its target. Malakor saw only the culmination of his plan, the ultimate vanquishing of his brother's hope. He was so consumed by his perceived victory, he failed to detect the almost imperceptible counter-current growing beneath the surface of the pool itself, a glimmer so faint it seemed to be a trick of the light, whispering a silent, undying promise.

82

The maniacal echo of Malakor's laughter died in his throat, replaced by a choked gasp. The ichor, mere inches from coalescing into the Maelstrom pool, suddenly froze. It began to recede, rapidly, as if violently sucked back into the very stone from which it had seeped. The violet light of the Unmaking Seal flickered, then dimmed, flickering more violently with each passing moment.

Malakor's eyes, wide with disbelief, darted from the retreating ichor to the sigil, which now convulsed as if in agony. He snarled, pouring more power into his chant, but instead of strengthening, the vibrant violet light began to glow with an alien, defiant emerald.

Deep within the Nexus, the single glowing root, now joined by countless others, pulsed with furious, verdant light. It was no longer a faint echo but a roaring chorus, a tangible manifestation of Jubilee's inherent connection to the glade. The power, once subtly pushing back against Malakor's ritual, now surged forth, raw and untamed.

The stone walls of the grotto, once weeping ichor, began to thrum with vibrant, emerald energy. Cracks appeared, not of decay, but of fierce, untamed growth, trailing luminous green light down their ancient faces. The obsidian cage surrounding the Maelstrom pool groaned, suffering under an invisible, overwhelming pressure. Thin fissures, glowing with inner emerald, spiderwebbed across its surface.

Malakor shrieked, his voice laced with genuine terror. "Impossible! I severed you! This glade is mine!" He clawed at the air, desperately trying to reassert control, but the influx of emerald light was too strong, too pure. It countered his shadow magic at every turn, burning away his influence.

Slash, though still pinned, felt the psychic pressure ease. He watched, breath held, as the Maelstrom pool, previously a desolate void, began to shimmer. Faint, ethereal green luminescence bloomed within its dark depths, like stars kindling in a midnight sky. It was Jubilee. She wasn't just fighting; she was reclaiming.

With a deafening crack, the obsidian cage shattered. Shards of the unholy rock flew like shrapnel, some embedding themselves in the far grotto walls, others dissolving into wisps of shadow as they met the onslaught of emerald energy. The breaking of the cage released a surge of raw, untamed power from the Maelstrom that slammed into Malakor, lifting him off his feet and hurling him against the grotto wall. He crumpled, stunned, his elegant robes torn, his sinister composure utterly gone.

From within the now open Maelstrom pool, the emerald light pulsed, growing brighter, more defined. It coalesced, not into Jubilee's physical form, but into a swirling vortex of pure, unadulterated forest magic, intertwining with the deep, vast energies of the Nexus. This was Jubilee's will, her essence, reborn and amplified by the very source Malakor had attempted to exploit.

Malakor, recovering, scrambled to his feet, eyes blazing with furious realization. "The Nexus! You found a way to awaken it! You've ruined everything!" He unleashed a desperate, chaotic storm of shadow blades, aiming to obliterate the glowing vortex.

But the emerald light pulsed again, stronger this time. The shadow blades dissolved mid-air, devoured by a cleansing wave of pure growth. Roots, thick as ancient tree trunks, burst from the grotto floor, their surfaces glowing with runic patterns of forest magic. They writhed, coiling around Malakor, binding him, pinning him to the shattering stone wall.

From the heart of the Maelstrom, now a vibrant emerald wellspring, a resonant voice echoed—not spoken, but felt, as if the glade itself was speaking through her. It was Jubilee's voice, amplified, imbued with the raw power of the Nexus, crystalline and unwavering.

"I am the Glade. I am the Nexus. And you, Malakor, will never claim me."

83

Slash watched, his breath catching in his throat, as Jubilee's essence, a swirling vortex of emerald, shimmered within the heart of the Maelstrom pool. Her voice, resonant with the ancient power of the Nexus itself, reverberated through the grotto, a symphony of newfound strength and unwavering defiance. A fierce pride swelled within him, battling with a growing surge of undeniable terror. She was magnificent, terrifyingly powerful, more than he had ever dreamed. But this power... this raw, untamed magic of the glade's very core... could it truly be contained? Could she survive it, or would she be consumed, her light ultimately extinguished by the very source she now commanded?

Malakor, pinned by the luminous roots, thrashed against his bonds, his furious screams echoing the chaotic energy that threatened to tear the grotto apart. But his struggles were a distant hum against the burgeoning roar of the Nexus, the true force now controlling the battle. Slash felt the psychic pressure of Malakor's rage, but it was a fleeting thing, eclipsed by the sheer, overwhelming presence of Jubilee.

He pushed against the last lingering tendrils of Malakor's psychic hold, forcing his weakened body to move. He had to reach her. He had to know if it was truly her, or merely an echo of her spirit amplified by the Nexus. His limbs, still heavy from his transformation and subsequent collapse, protested, but a desperate, driving need propelled him forward.

The grotto floor rippled beneath his feet, the glowing cracks widening, revealing vibrant, pulsing veins of emerald light. The air thrummed, thick with magic, intoxicating and perilous. Slash pushed through it, a dark silhouette against a world ablaze with verdant power. Each step was a battle, not against Malakor, who was now a squirming, insignificant pest, but against the very essence of the Nexus, which radiated with an almost possessive force.

"Jubilee!" he rasped, his voice sounding thin and weak against the booming resonance of the glade. "Jubilee, can you hear me?"

The swirling emerald vortex pulsed, brighter still. It seemed to acknowledge his presence, but the overwhelming power it discharged made reaching it a harrowing experience. Luminous motes of emerald energy, miniature stars of raw Nexus power, spun away from the heart of the Maelstrom, dancing around him, testing his limits. He felt the pull of it, the cold, ancient power of the Nexus calling to him, a siren song promising ultimate power and profound oblivion.

He extended a hand, his own shadow-infused emerald energy reaching out, a desperate line thrown across an impossible chasm. He felt a fragment of her, a fleeting spark of her consciousness deep within the swirling emerald. It was there, intertwined with the glade, but separate, somehow. A part of her was still Jubilee, the woman he loved, the woman who had sacrificed everything for him.

"Jubilee, come back to me," he pleaded, his voice thick with an emotion he rarely allowed himself to show. "Don't get lost in it. Don't let it consume you."

The roots binding Malakor pulsed with renewed force, squeezing the life out of him. The message felt clear: the Nexus, through Jubilee, was asserting its dominance, purging the corruption that had plagued it for so long. But was this an act of the glade, or an act of Jubilee, or an indistinguishable fusion of both?

He reached the edge of the Maelstrom pool, the emerald light blinding him, the raw power humming like a thousand suns. He hesitated for a fleeting moment, aware of the immense danger, the overwhelming possibility of being lost forever within its depths. But thought was secondary to instinct. He had to know. He had to bring her back.

With a silent prayer, a desperate plea for connection, Slash plunged his hand into the swirling emerald abyss. A searing pain erupted, followed by an immediate, profound merging. He felt her. He felt the Nexus. He felt the entire, sprawling consciousness of the glade. It was vast, ancient, and terrifyingly powerful. And at its heart, struggling, shimmering, but undeniably present, was Jubilee. Her spirit, her will, her very essence, entwined with the Nexus, wielding its power yet fighting to maintain her own identity against its overwhelming currents.

He grasped for her, a shadow reaching for starlight, desperate to pull her back from the precipice of absolute power, to remind her of the mundane, beautiful world she left behind. He had found her, but the battle for her soul had only just begun.

84

The instant Slash's hand breached the Maelstrom, a jolt of pure, untamed energy surged through him, threatening to unravel his very being. His emerald-flecked black eyes squeezed shut against the blinding light, and his roar of mingled pain and power ripped through the grotto. He was no longer just experiencing Jubilee; he was immersed in the consciousness of the Nexus itself, a chaotic symphony of ancient growth, decay, and primordial magic.

He felt the overwhelming scale of the glade's suffering – millennia of subtle suppression, of slow, creeping shadows. And then, he felt Jubilee. Not a spark, or an echo, but her entire, vibrant consciousness, burning brighter than ever, yet terrifyingly interwoven with the glade's essence. She was the conductor of this roaring symphony, wielding it with a fierce, untamed grace that both awed and terrified him.

"Jubilee!" he yelled again, a desperate anchor in the turbulent sea of magic. He plunged deeper, his shadow-infused essence stretching, seeking the familiar warmth of her soul amidst the cosmic chill of the Nexus. He found her, a luminous core, shimmering, pulsing, fundamentally *changed*. Her thoughts were no longer singular; they were a confluence of ancient wisdom and raw, untamed instinct. It was like embracing a goddess, a force of nature, rather than the woman he loved.

But amidst the overwhelming awe, he felt her. A flicker of recognition, a primal yearning for connection. She was battling the absorption, fighting to maintain her individuality even as she commanded the glade. She was holding on.

He poured every ounce of his transformed power, every desperate plea, every fragment of their shared history, into their bond. He projected images of their early encounters, the spark of forbidden attraction, the raw passion, the tender moments. He painted mental pictures of Eldrin, of the vibrant glade before Malakor, of dreams yet unfulfilled. He clung to the human, the fae, the woman he had fallen in love with, amidst the burgeoning power of an entity that threatened to consume her.

A faint tug. A subtle shift in the Maelstrom's current. The overwhelming green began to swirl, to coalesce, to draw inward.

Malakor, still pinned by the roots, ceased his struggling, his furious whispers dying as a chilling realization dawned on his face. "Impossible…" he rasped, his eyes wide with a dawning horror.

Slowly, agonizingly, as if pulling herself from the very fabric of reality, Jubilee began to emerge. The emerald vortex spun faster, then tightened, drawing her back into a more cohesive form. Slash felt the momentous shift, the immense mental and magical strain of her returning from the brink of pure energy. It felt like pulling a star from the sky, immensely powerful, yet fragile.

He kept holding, kept pouring his essence into her, a lifeline in a collapsing universe. The glade groaned in symphony with her re-materialization, the roots binding Malakor shimmering, then releasing him with a final, violent shudder that sent him sprawling.

Then, with a gasp that was both human and profoundly ancient, Jubilee broke free.

Her eyes snapped open, blazing with an emerald light that eclipsed even his own transformed gaze. She stood, not as the delicate fae he knew, but as something more. Taller, her movements fluid and utterly primal. Her skin shimmered with a faint verde hue, as if the very chlorophyll of the glade now pulsed beneath her flesh. Her silver-white hair, once soft, now seemed to ripple with subtle currents of forest magic.

She was whole. She was herself. But she was fundamentally, irrevocably changed.

She looked at Slash, her emerald eyes piercing him, seeing not just his physical form, but the merged essence within him. A slow, knowing smile, ancient and fierce, touched her lips. She reached out, her glowing hand brushing his cheek, and he felt the profound, electric hum of the Nexus thrumming through her fingertips, a silent symphony of triumph and undeniable belonging.

"Slash," she whispered, her voice layered with the rustling of leaves, the whisper of ancient winds, the raw power of the glade itself. "My shadow. My light."

85

The touch of Jubilee's hand was pure power, a living current that coursed through Slash, igniting every nerve ending, every atom of his newly forged being. He leaned into it, a silent communion of two souls now exquisitely attuned. The grotto, still scarred from battle, seemed to hum with their combined essence, a harmonious counterpoint to the earlier chaos.

"Jubilee," he breathed, his own voice a rough, primal murmur. Her name felt different on his tongue now, imbued with the ancient magic that flowed through her. He traced the delicate line of her jaw, feeling the subtle pulse of the Nexus beneath his fingertips. Her skin was warm, vibrant, thrumming with life force.

Her smile widened, ancient wisdom and raw, untamed instinct swirling in her emerald eyes. She did not pull away. Instead, she leaned into his touch, her breath mingling with his, tasting of damp earth and fresh rain, and something wilder, something of the very heart of the glade.

His thumb brushed over her lips, still parted from her whispered words. "You... you risked everything," he murmured, the awe in his voice profound. He had seen the Maelstrom, felt its terrifying pull. She hadn't just dipped her toe; she had plunged into its very core and emerged not just whole, but magnified.

"For us," she answered, her voice still carrying the echo of rustling leaves, but now infused with a tender vulnerability that pierced him far deeper than any threat. "For the glade. For our future." Her hand, still resting on his cheek, slid to cup the back of his head, drawing him closer.

He felt the shift in her, the profound connection that transcended mere physical proximity. It was as if their minds, their very essences, had become one, capable of sensing each other's deepest currents. He saw her love for him, fierce and unwavering, a beacon in the storm. He saw the enormity of what she had endured, the battle for her own soul, fought in the depths of primordial magic.

And then, she kissed him.

It was not a kiss of desperate passion, nor of raw hunger, though both were elements of their shared history. This was a kiss of utter certainty, of two universes colliding and finding perfect alignment. Her lips, cool and soft, met his, and a profound, electric hum vibrated through them both. It was a kiss that tasted of restoration, of triumph, of an undeniable, shared destiny.

He felt the glade respond, murmuring around them. The wounded roots stretching across the grotto floor seemed to pulse with renewed energy, a single, verdant tendril reaching out to lightly brush the back of his hand. It was a tangible affirmation of their union, a blessing from the heart of their world.

Slash deepened the kiss, pouring every ounce of his gratitude, his awe, his fierce, possessive love into it. He felt the light within her, not just the soft, gentle magic he had known, but a potent, untamed fire. And she, he knew, felt the shadow within him, not just the darkness, but the protective, loyal core that had braved hell to reach her.

When they finally broke apart, breathless, the air between them shimmered with residual magic. Jubilee's eyes, still glowing with emerald light, gazed into his, brimming with a deep, silent understanding. The chaos of battle, the terror of loss, all faded into the background. There was only this: them, solidified, irrevocably bound.

Malakor, released from the roots, lay a crumpled heap against the grotto wall, stirring weakly. But neither Slash nor Jubilee truly noticed. Their world had narrowed to the space between them, a perfect sphere of shared power and profound intimacy.

"We have work to do," Jubilee finally whispered, tracing the curve of his transformed eye, her thumb brushing over the flecks of emerald within his new, deep irises. "The glade is hurting. And Malakor..."

"Can wait," Slash finished, his voice husky, pulling her tighter against him. He knew the fight wasn't over, but something fundamental had shifted. Eldrin's loss still clawed at him, a raw wound. But Jubilee was here. She was alive, more vibrant than ever, and she was irrevocably, beautifully his. Their hands intertwined, light and shadow, glade and void, a silent promise to face whatever came next, together. Their destiny, once a swirling, unknown current, now felt as solid and ancient as the glade itself.

The fragile peace of their embrace shattered not by intent, but by a raw, guttural scream that tore through the revitalized grotto. Malakor, rousing from his root-bound stupor, clutched at his throat, his eyes blazing with a mixture of pain and unadulterated fury. His earlier disregard melted away, replaced by a visceral rage directed solely at Jubilee.

"You... you dare?!" he shrieked, his voice ragged like torn silk. Dark tendrils, thinner and more brittle than before, but no less malicious, shot from his outstretched hand toward Jubilee. His power was diminished, fractured even, but his intent was lethal.

Slash, his guard still lowered from their shared moment, reacted on instinct. He twisted, pulling Jubilee behind him even as a sliver of darkness grazed his shoulder. The emerald flecks in his eyes flared, reflecting the nascent emerald power that still pulsed through his transformed being. "Malakor!" His voice was a low growl, a warning shot.

But Malakor was past reason. He was a cornered viper, striking blindly. "You tainted it! You tainted everything!" His eyes, usually pools of inky black, flickered with an unsettling, desperate green, a horrific mirror of Jubilee's own essence. The fractured power of the Nexus that Jubilee had channeled and broken through the altar now resonated deeply within him, twisting and searing.

Jubilee, recovering her bearings, stepped out from behind Slash. Her emerald eyes narrowed, her hand instinctively reaching out. Roots, no longer just a defensive barrier, snaked across the grotto floor, vibrant and purposeful. This was not a panicked defense; this was the will of the glade mobilized, directed by its new, fully realized Guardian.

"You've lost, Malakor," Jubilee stated, her voice resonating with an authority that wasn't just her own, but carried the weight of the ancient Nexus itself. "The glade awakened. Not for your dominion, but for balance."

Malakor let out a chilling laugh that devolved into a cough. "Balance? You think this is balance? This... aberration? You will see! You will see the destruction you have wrought!" He mustered every last ounce of his corrupted energy, his body trembling, and unleashed a concentrated blast of pure, oppressive shadow magic. It wasn't the entropic wave of Slash's ultimate power, but a suffocating curtain of darkness, designed to drain and consume.

Slash met it head-on, his own transformed shadows churning. Emerald light threaded through his darkness, bolstering it, lending it an unexpected resilience. But Malakor's desperation gave his attack a raw, visceral force. The impact sent Slash skidding back, scraping his boot on the grotto floor, a grunt of effort escaping him.

Jubilee didn't hesitate. With a surge of newfound power, she thrust both hands forward. From the very air, from the living rock of the grotto, tiny, glowing motes of emerald light erupted. They swirled, coalesced, and then shot forward like a volley of living arrows, striking Malakor, not with force, but with a searing, purifying energy.

Malakor shrieked again, a sound of agony and revulsion. The emerald motes weren't just attacks; they were cleansing agents, burning away the corruption that fueled his power. Tendrils of black smoke rose from his skin, accompanied by the stench of scorched earth.

"This is not destruction, Malakor," Jubilee stated, advancing steadily, her steps imbued with the quiet confidence of the glade. Her power flowed, not in violent bursts, but in a relentless, organic swell. "This is purification."

Malakor scrambled backward, his eyes wide with a terror more profound than any he had shown the Celestial Order or even the Void Beast. This wasn't just a battle of strength; it was a battle for his very essence. He collided with the grotto wall, leaving a scorch mark where his back touched it. His hands scrabbled, desperate for an escape, for a weapon, for anything that could stem the tide of emerald light.

Slash, recovering, stepped to Jubilee's side, his hand finding hers. Their fingers intertwined, a silent renewal of their bond. The fusion of their forms, of their essences, now felt like a natural state, a symbiotic dance of destructive and restorative power. They were two halves of an undeniable whole, facing their fractured past, and an uncertain future, together. Malakor, a symbol of their past, writhed under their combined light, his desperate screams echoing through their hard-won sanctuary.

Malakor's screams reverberated through the grotto, less a sound of pain and more a howl of pure, unadulterated spiritual agony as Jubilee's purifying emerald motes continued their relentless assault. He clawed at the grotto wall, desperate, his dark essence visibly eroding, a stench of burning ozone filling the air. Slash, his hand entwined with Jubilee's, felt the ebb and flow of her immense, newly refined power. He watched Malakor, a flicker of something unreadable in his emerald-flecked violet eyes - not pity, but a cold, final calculation.

"It won't hold him," Slash murmured, his voice a low thrum against the backdrop of Malakor's suffering. "Not permanently."

Jubilee understood. Her purification would burn away his corruption, but it wouldn't extinguish the spark of Malakor himself, nor the insidious dark arts he commanded. He would regenerate, given time, and return more vengeful than ever.

A flicker of a new strategy ignited within Slash. The chaotic fusion that had transformed him had granted him more than raw power; it had awakened latent abilities, a deeper understanding of the glade's intricate fabric. He felt a resonance with the very essence of imprisonment, a concept both ancient and absolute.

"Jubilee, stop the purification," Slash commanded, his grip tightening on her hand. His voice held an unfamiliar authority, a stark edge that cut through the turmoil.

Jubilee, still immersed in the flow of her energy, blinked, startled. "But he's still burning, Slash! This is working!"

"It's not enough," he countered, his gaze fixed on Malakor, whose screams were beginning to diminish into ragged gasps as his essence was cleansed. "Trust me."

Reluctantly, Jubilee pulled back her emerald motes. Malakor, gasping, slumped against the wall, a raw, exposed wound of darkness, his skin still smoking. He stared at Jubilee with incandescent hatred, but the terror in his eyes had solidified into a chilling resolve. He would escape. He would find a way.

Slash stepped forward, separating himself from Jubilee, though their bond still hummed under his skin. He raised both hands, his eyes, now a swirling vortex of emerald and night, fixated on Malakor. He didn't draw on the glade's power, nor his raw shadow. Instead, he reached deeper, into the essence of the grotto itself, where ancient ley lines intersected, where the very concept of eternal containment was etched.

86

The grotto began to hum, a deep, resonant vibration that pulsed through the earth. The air grew heavy, crackling with an unseen energy. Malakor, instinctively sensing a new, more profound threat, began to thrash, attempting to summon what little shadow he had left. But it was too late.

From the very stone of the grotto, from the ancient, unmoving roots that laced its foundation, thin, shimmering lines of pure, untainted emerald light began to emerge. They were not Jubilee's raw, vibrant energy, but something older, colder, infused with the glade's ancient, unwavering will. They snaked towards Malakor, not with aggression, but with an unnerving purpose.

They solidified into intricate, glowing sigils on the grotto wall, radiating a faint, almost imperceptible pulsation. Then, like threads from an unseen loom, they began to weave themselves around Malakor, binding him, not physically, but metaphysically. It was an enchantment of absolute nullification, designed to sever him from all magical influence.

Malakor shrieked again, a high-pitched wail of utter disbelief and mounting panic. He tried to draw on his shadow, but the glowing threads absorbed it, unraveling his very essence. His eyes, fixed on Slash, widened in dawning horror.

"No! What is this?!" he rasped, his voice weaker, fading.

Slash's voice, colder than the deepest void, answered him. "This, Malakor, is the glade's oldest secret. The very first enchantment placed upon its heart. Not for destruction, but for containment. Eternal containment, of that which threatens the balance."

The glowing threads tightened, not squeezing, but dissolving. Malakor's form began to flicker, to pixelate, like a drawing being erased one line at a time. His screams became silent, his body coalescing into an increasingly smaller, darker point of light.

"You won't return," Slash stated, his words a final, unwavering decree. "Not here. Not ever."

With a final, infinitesimal pop, Malakor winked out of existence, leaving behind only the faint, glowing sigils on the grotto wall, humming with residual power. The silence that followed was profound, absolute, devoid of even the haunting echo of his tormented screams. slashed had revealed a new depth to his power, a control that went beyond brute force, securing their sanctuary in a way Jubilee hadn't imagined possible.

The lingering hum of the containment sigils faded, leaving an ethereal quiet in their wake. Slash stood amidst the stillness, his chest heaving, the emerald-black swirling in his eyes slowly receding, replaced by the familiar haunting violet, now flecked with vestiges of green. He looked spent, the exertion of wielding such ancient, absolute magic visible in the subtle tremor of his hands, the faint sheen of sweat on his brow. The sheer power he had just commanded was staggering, far beyond merely deflecting or destroying. He had erased.

Jubilee, still processing the absolute finality of Malakor's disappearance, rushed to him. Her hands cupped his face, her gaze searching his, a mix of awe and concern warring in her emerald depths. "Slash... what was that? Are you alright?"

He leaned into her touch, a sigh escaping him, deep and weary. "A power I barely understood, even when it manifested. Malakor forced my hand, revealed a depth... a purpose to this new core." His thumb stroked her cheek, a soft, intimate gesture. "I felt the glade's will, its ancient need for true, unwavering stillness. For what it felt... Malakor was an infection."

She shuddered, the brutal efficiency of his act both terrifying and undeniably attractive. His control, his fierce protective instinct, had saved them all. "He's truly... gone?"

"From here, yes. Erased from this plane. His essence is bound, nullified, unable to manifest. It's not death as you understand it, but a permanent unmaking, a disjunction from all that nourishes his kind." He closed his eyes for a moment, then opened them, a profound weariness settling over him. "It cost... much. My connection to the Nexus is... unstable. And the glade demands balance for such an act."

Jubilee's heart constricted. She knew the cost of power, had felt it in her own near-sacrifice. "What do you mean, balance?"

He gestured around the grotto, now strangely peaceful, almost pristine. "The glade is restoring itself, purer than before. But it will crave stillness, true equilibrium. Our purpose here is not just to defend, but to nurture. To maintain the balance its heart desires."

She looked at the glowing sigils, now fading to faint phosphorescence on the grotto walls. "So, our fight is over?"

A wry, almost tender smile touched Slash's lips. "For now. The Celestial Order will return, eventually. Old wounds fester. But for this moment... this glade, our sanctuary... is truly safe. And it accepts us both." His gaze deepened, drawing her in. "Perhaps because our light and shadow, intertwined, have finally brought it the perfect stillness it craves."

He pulled her closer, his arms circling her waist, cradling her against his body. The lingering hum in the grotto seemed to resonate with their intertwined heartbeats. Jubilee leaned into him, feeling the solid comfort of his presence, the unique blend of his warmth and chill that had become her constant.

"We did it," she whispered, her voice thick with emotion. The relief was a wave, washing over her, leaving her utterly drained but profoundly content. All the fear, the desperation, the overwhelming chaos of the past days—it receded now, replaced by an intoxicating sense of peace.

Slash buried his face in her hair, inhaling her earthy, forest scent. "We did. And the glade remembers. It knows its protectors." His voice was a low rumble against her ear. "It knows its healers. Its destroyers. Its lovers."

The word hung in the air, charged with unspoken truths, with shared passion and sacrifices. She felt a blush creep up her neck, but she didn't pull away. It was true. Amidst the chaos, amidst the profound and terrifying journey, their connection had deepened, irrevocably. They were bound, not just by desire or destiny, but by blood, by magic, by the very heart of this glade.

"What now?" she asked, her voice barely a whisper, a question about their future, about the untold chapters stretching before them.

He pulled back, his violet eyes, now clear and steady, meeting hers. A sliver of his old challenging glint returned, tempered by a newfound tenderness. "Now,

Jubilee, we rest. And then… we explore. Our power. Our connection. This glade that is now irrevocably ours. Together." He kissed her then, a slow, deep kiss that tasted of quiet victory, of hard-won peace, and of an infinite, breathtaking promise. It was a kiss that sealed their intertwining destinies, a new dawn rising in the heart of their sacred glade.

The hum of the grotto settled into a gentle pulse, a lullaby after the storm. Slash's kiss lingered, a warm brand on Jubilee's lips, a silent promise of the peace they had earned. For a long moment, they simply held each other, the weight of their shared battles slowly lifting, replaced by the profound lightness of survival.

"Rest," Slash murmured against her temple, his voice a balm. He gently guided her to a patch of moss where the transformed glade now bloomed with an extraordinary vibrancy. The air itself felt sweeter, purer, as if the destruction had purged something anciently wrong.

Jubilee sank onto the soft bed, her limbs heavy with exhaustion, yet her spirit soaring. She watched as Slash moved, his movements no longer burdened by the frantic energy of combat. He knelt, his hand brushing the earth, and a ripple of emerald light pulsed through the grotto. Roots stirred, vines unfurled, and the very air shimmered with a benevolent magic. He was tending it, healing it, just as she had. A warmth bloomed in her chest, a quiet joy at this shared purpose.

87

The coming days were a soft tapestry woven with quiet moments. They worked together, not with the urgency of battle, but with the steady rhythm of nurturing. Slash, no longer solely a force of destruction, revealed a surprising connection to the glade's growth. His shadow magic, now infused with iridescent emerald, coaxed life from the soil, clearing lingering scars with a touch. Jubilee found herself learning from him, her gentle forest magic evolving, gaining a subtle strength, a deep anchoring from their entwined essences.

They discovered new sections of the grotto, untouched by the recent chaos, where ancient roots formed natural alcoves, perfect for quiet meals and stargazing. The night sky, viewed from within the heart of the glade, seemed closer, brighter, constellations a glittering map above their sanctuary.

The challenge wasn't in fighting, but in the stillness. The adrenaline, the constant threat, had been a driving force. Now, they had to learn to simply *be*. For Jubilee, the echoes of Eldrin's loss still resonated, a phantom ache that sometimes surfaced in the quietest hours. She spoke of him to Slash, of his loyalty, his unwavering belief in the old ways. Slash listened, his presence a steady anchor, his dark eyes surprisingly empathetic. He didn't offer platitudes, but a quiet understanding, a shared acknowledgment of sacrifice.

"He was very important to you," Slash observed one evening, tracing the delicate curve of a newly bloomed flower.

"He was," Jubilee confirmed, her voice soft. "He deserved more than to be a stepping stone."

Slash nodded, his gaze distant. "Malakor believed all things were merely means to an end. A belief I once shared, in part. True stillness, true balance... it requires respect for all life." He looked at her, his expression deep with newfound wisdom. "Even those who oppose you."

He was changing, evolving beyond the dangerous renegade she had first met. And so was she. The wild, untamed power that had erupted from her in those desperate moments now flowed with a calmer, deeper current. She felt the glade's heartbeat within her own, a constant resonance that told her when a root needed nurturing, a bloom needed coaxing.

Their nights were a continuation of their days, a slow exploration of the intimacy born from shared peril.

There was no rush, no desperate craving, but a tender unfolding. They slept entwined, the unique chill of his skin against her warmth, a comforting paradox. Kisses were deep and unhurried, hands explored with a reverence for newfound peace. Every touch was a reaffirmation of their bond, a silent conversation between light and shadow.

One morning, Jubilee awoke to find Slash sitting cross-legged, absorbed in a trance-like state. Emerald sparks danced around his fingers as he channeled something deep beneath the earth. He looked up as she stirred, a faint smile on his lips. "The glade hums a new song, Jubilee. A song of stillness and growth. And it's... beautiful."

She moved to him, resting her head on his shoulder. Their connection, forged in fire and deepened in peace, was now an inherent part of them. The challenges would come, she knew, but for now, in the heart of their sacred, renewed glade, they had found their own quiet, profound sanctuary.

The newfound stillness, the tender peace, held them captive for weeks. But eventually, the vastness of the glade, beautiful and beloved as it was, began to subtly chafe. The whispers of the world beyond, long muffled by their desperate struggle, grew louder. Slash, ever practical, was the first to voice it, one twilight evening as they watched the twin moons rise above the ancient oak.

"This sanctuary," he began, his voice a low rumble, "is a precious thing. But it is not the only thing."

Jubilee, nestled against his side, traced patterns on his arm. "You mean the Celestial Order? Or Malakor? Even banished, he is a shadow."

He shook his head, his gaze far-off. "More than that. The glade is revitalized, yes. But it is changed. And so are we. Our magic... it reverberates beyond these roots. The Nexus hums with a new song, as you said. A song others will hear. Those who seek knowledge, those who seek power, those who would once again try to control what they do not understand."

A familiar prickle of apprehension traced its way down Jubilee's spine. The peace had been so profound, so earned. To shatter it, even for a necessary truth, felt like a betrayal. "What do you propose?"

"Knowledge," he stated simply, turning to meet her gaze, his emerald-flecked violet eyes burning with a quiet intensity. "We need to understand this new age. We need to learn what the Nexus is truly capable of, beyond healing, beyond what Malakor sought to twist it into. And we need to prepare. The glade is our home, our heart, but it cannot be our cage."

He then revealed his plan, a daring proposal that sent a shiver of both fear and excitement through her. "There are those who guard ancient lore, deeper even than the Keeper of Whispers. Hidden libraries, forgotten scholars. And there is a particular sect of Elderwood mages rumored to possess a grimoire of nexus-attuned magic, long thought lost. If anyone can truly explain what we are, what the glade has become, it is them."

Jubilee's mind raced. The very thought of venturing beyond their renewed sanctuary, of facing the unknown, was daunting. Yet, Slash was right. Their power, their bond, the glade itself – they were no longer isolated. They were now a beacon in a world hungry for magic, a world that would inevitably seek them out. It was better to seek, to learn, to grow, than to wait to be found.

"And alliances?" she asked, remembering his fleeting mention of the Celestial Order, and the deeper threat that had been implied before Malakor's dramatic entrance.

Slash's jaw tightened. "A delicate dance. Some may be allies, some may be threats disguised as such. We move with caution, not simply seeking power, but understanding. Understanding strengthens more than any blade."

The decision, though weighty, settled in her heart with a surprising clarity. She looked around their grotto, serene and vibrant. It felt whole, complete. But for them, the true journey was only just beginning.

"The glade is ready to stand on its own for a time," Jubilee murmured, a deep connection telling her this truth. "It has been reborn, strengthened by the Nexus. It can sustain itself." Then she looked at Slash, a smile growing on her face, a mischievous glint back in her eyes. "But what about Eldrin? He would have a fit."

Slash chuckled, a low, resonant sound that vibrated through her. "He'd scowl, then he'd grudgingly admit it was probably for the best. And then he'd follow us, of course. For protective purposes." He squeezed her hand. "Are you ready?"

She took a deep breath, the scent of fresh earth and life filling her lungs. "Ready. But we take a piece of the glade with us. Always."

As dawn approached, painting the grotto in hues of rose and gold, their preparations began. It was not a flight, but a purposeful journey. A journey into the world, armed with their profound love, their terrifying new power, and an unshakeable bond, ready to face whatever lay beyond their sacred, silent glade.

About the Author

Kimberly Kogut is an accomplished author, and a school bus driver, known for their insightful and engaging writing style. With a passion for exploring the complexities of human relationships and the resilience of the human spirit.

Born in Connecticut, Kimberly developed an early fascination with the interplay of love, betrayal, and forgiveness, themes which she herself has gone though and is able to bring into her work.

When not writing, she enjoys cooking, crafting and creating art anyway possible, and is often found when not at work, at her desk writing, designing some new diy craft or reading a new adventure.

A life long reader and lover or the written word, she dreamt of becoming an author for thirty years before publishing her debut in 2025.

Her first novel, Hearts In Shadows, is one of the things you should probably read.

Kimberly currently resides in Connecticut with partner and Mini Dew (cat)

Connect with Kimberly

https://www.kimberlykogut.com

www.ingramcontent.com/pod-product-compliance
Lightning Source LLC
LaVergne TN
LVHW100509110826
845146LV00002B/569

* 9 7 9 8 2 1 8 7 6 5 5 8 3 *